PENGUIN BOO

HAPPILY EVER

Jenny Diski was born in 1947 in London, where she lives and works. Her other novels are *Rainforest*, also published by Penguin, *Nothing Natural*, which received universal acclaim, *Like Mother* and *Then Again*.

JENNY DISKI
———————

HAPPILY EVER AFTER

PENGUIN BOOKS

PENGUIN BOOKS

Published by the Penguin Group
Penguin Books Ltd, 27 Wrights Lane, London W8 5TZ, England
Penguin Books USA Inc., 375 Hudson Street, New York, New York 10014, USA
Penguin Books Australia Ltd, Ringwood, Victoria, Australia
Penguin Books Canada Ltd, 10 Alcorn Avenue, Toronto, Ontario, Canada M4V 3B2
Penguin Books (NZ) Ltd, 182–190 Wairau Road, Auckland 10, New Zealand

Penguin Books Ltd, Registered Offices: Harmondsworth, Middlesex, England

First published by Hamish Hamilton Ltd 1991
Published in Penguin Books 1992
1 3 5 7 9 10 8 6 4 2

Printed in England by Clays Ltd, St Ives plc

For Trombley

Contents

What happens happens.
You could say that everything turned out for the best.
You might call it a comedy.
Or a tragedy.
Or just call it a story.
There is a certain inevitability, but that doesn't prove anything
one way or the other.

What happens happens.
If it's recorded, it's just a story anyway.
If that's not the truth, I'll eat my hat.

What happens happens.
Look at it like that.

PART ONE

1

Liam Broods

Houses don't cry. Anyone could tell you that. People cry, sometimes; the most houses do is absorb the sound so it doesn't leak out into the streets to disturb the passers-by.

A being – an investigative angel, let us say – sent to study the workings of a disparate group of people, might focus on a particular house and its inhabitants, but she would not, if she were rigorous – and what investigative angel would not be? – confuse the inert fabric of the building with the life and emotions of those who live in it. Obviously.

To our scientific angel, the confining exterior walls and interior segments would be as test-tubes and flasks are to a human experimenter: mere containers of the real substance under scrutiny. Of course, it would be necessary for her to describe the house, as any experimental set-up must be described. But she would not, rigorous as she is, allow sentiment to creep in and link notions that do not properly belong together. Such as *house* and *home*, for example, where the first term describes a material environment, and is therefore a *what*, and the second a subjective emotion, which is more of a *why*, and quite a different matter altogether. Confusions of *what* and *why* account for a great deal that is untenable in human thought, but our theoretical angel would have no problem with knowing what was what, and not why.

She would know that houses don't cry, and if anyone suggested otherwise, she would, quite properly, dismiss the idea, not only as impossible within the constraints of the planet she was studying, but also as too fanciful to be allowed into the objective data she had been sent to collect.

*

3

The house was fourth along in an Edwardian terrace of three-storey houses. It was a side street in a kind of neither here-nor-there, rather dowdy part of London that is described variously as Paddington or North Kensington, depending on whether you want to emphasize its convenience for transport or its proximity to somewhere smarter.

On account of the nearby main rail station, and its failure to be the better part of Kensington, many of the houses in the area had been let off as rooms to single people who had just arrived in London from other places, or who had not achieved the success in life that would have enabled them to live somewhere more desirable.

The fourth house along in this particular Edwardian terrace had, for many years, been just such a rooming house, but an astonishing rise in property values in the early 1980s had turned it, like many others of its kind, into a highly saleable commodity, ripe for development. The tenants were the sort that came and went with some frequency, so it was easy for the landlord not to replace those who left, and to offer a more or less decent sum of money to those who remained, to make the property vacant. Or almost vacant. An elderly woman who lived in the attic proved too stubborn for the landlord. She had rights as a tenant, of course, and offers of cash combined with mild threats did nothing to move her. For some reason she was determined to stay, and the landlord, who wished to cash in on the property boom but who was not a monster and therefore unwilling to exert the necessary pressure, was obliged to take a lower price on the house than he had hoped, having, as it did, a sitting tenant in the attic.

It was fortunate for the buyer, who got a decent enough old house for well under the market price, especially as his income was almost non-existent, and his prospects even worse.

Liam did not, however, feel very fortunate as he sat glumly in his study on the middle floor of the house he had purchased two years before. He listened, in an alcoholic torpor, from the depths of his armchair, to the sounds of the house, some of which would have alarmed a more concerned householder. The central heating boiler growled dangerously about its age, while a not very powerful wind rattled the window frames like bones being shaken in a box. From time to time, there was a creaking sound, more like a tree being felled than a ghost walking the floorboards, but Liam was concerned neither about the boiler blowing up, nor about the back addition separating from the rest of the house; he was listening for the sound of the door slamming and footsteps coming up the stairs. All the other noises could go hang, for all he cared. He was interested only in Grace coming home, and not at all in the condition of the house, which was not bad, considering its age and use, but which none the less could have done with some attention.

Liam had no feelings about the place, other than that it was a necessary shell in which to live out his current existence. He had had a house once that he had cared for, but that was gone, finished, and he couldn't regret it. He had what he wanted now. It was hell, perhaps, but he wanted it.

Next to his study on the middle floor was the bedroom, with a kitchen and bathroom on the same level in the back addition. This floor was where he lived, and it was the only part of the house that he had attended to, and then only with a perfunctory single coat of white paint and a carpet in the bathroom because Grace had insisted. The rest of the house was untouched.

There were two uninhabited rooms with basic furnishings, and a bathroom, on the ground floor; and there was an attic, a large space with a kitchenette on the landing outside, where the sitting tenant lived. Liam had no interest in what was below him or above him, he wished only to be left (though not in peace) to live the life he had to lead.

He would, indeed, have preferred not to have the house at all. Buying it, cheap though it was, had taken all his severance pay and much of his savings. He loathed the idea of owning a property. He had long ago thrown over his obligations and had no desire to take on any new ones, but Grace had been adamant. Liam supposed that she had been advised by her parents to insist on buying a house when they returned to London, as security, in case things did not work out well. As if there was the slightest chance that they would. Liam could not have cared less, but he bought the house because he had no desire to engage in a debate about the division of marital property, or anything at all.

So he sat in it, a dank, unloved, empty-smelling thing (except where

Grace had titivated in the bedroom and bathroom), brooding and waiting for the return of his love from wherever she might currently be.

In the last few years, Liam had taken to alcohol in much the same way as, once, he had taken to meditation in the mountains of the Hindu Kush. Neither addiction had functioned in the way it was supposed to – that is, they did not make him serene, nor give him the impression, however erroneous, that his life was happy.

Meditation had failed, and he had given it up. Alcohol had failed, too, but he had not, as yet, given that up. It served another purpose: it gave him blank spaces in his life and a good reason for behaving badly – as well as the additional blessing of passing out every night. Aside from these benefits, he also suspected that his body might now seize up without a minimum daily input of alcohol in his bloodstream. He wasn't prepared to take that risk, and the risk which he was taking was obscured from him most of the time by the light haze in which he drifted around for the greater part of every day.

All in all, life went on for Liam, and he was fairly sure that it was as good as it was likely to be. Which was to say that it was very far from good, but lived up entirely to his expectations.

If alcohol was his addiction, love was Liam's problem. He needed to be in it, just as he needed alcohol to be in him. Disappointment shading into despair was the tenor of his life, and love was his chosen method of sustaining it.

Of course, *love* was a funny concept, Liam reminded himself, and veered away from self-analysis to something that better matched the vagueness of his alcoholic haze.

'I'll write a book about it,' he muttered. 'That'll fix it.'

This notion pleased him. He was able to think of his emotional distress as research, which was a kind of comfort.

If anything needed a definitive volume, Liam thought, love did. Not that enough words – more than enough – hadn't been spilled on the topic. All the outpourings of fiction, poetry, drama, opera, biography, autobiography, philosophy, sociology, psychology (Liam loved to make lists) had focused on the subject. He was hard put to think what wasn't about love. Handbooks on the rearing of dormice as exotic foodstuffs, maybe. But he doubted it. There the word still lay – *love* –

limp with use, like the broken spine of a library book abused by the desperate and unfulfilled curiosity of readers in search of answers. A paraplegic word that would never get up and make its own way in the world. However much language was spent in expounding on love, it was never enough. It was a word without meaning; or with any and all meaning. There was no question that the world would be a better place if someone would just finally nail the thing down for once and for all, so that everyone could get on with more important things.

'I'll write a book about it. That'll fix it,' Liam muttered again and, having satisfied himself that his intentions were intellectually valid and likely to benefit humanity, he allowed his mind to revert to the contemplation of his wife's breasts, and the hand that was not his, that was, in all probability, caressing them at this very moment.

If alcohol was his addiction, and love his problem, then sex was Liam's pain. He had given up everything for sex: wife, children, home, job and the respect of anyone who knew him, including, most import-antly, his own. He didn't mind. There was great gratification to be had in the loss of everything for what he knew amounted to nothing serious at all. Liam was an old hand at absurdity, relishing his own above anyone's. He did not rate sexual desire high in the scheme of things, and he liked very much the paradox that he had given all for that for which he had no respect. It was pure and clean. It served him right. And the notion that something served him right, and resulted in him getting what he deserved, was very pleasing. It put him in his place, he felt, and thereby gave him a place in the world. He thought of this place of his as a metaphysical gutter; a combination of Harry Lime's rat-infested sewers and Dante's flaming inferno; but, in fact, he hadn't got there yet. Not to the final depth and degradation of the physical world, not to the exquisite agonies of eternal spiritual punishment. His current existence was no more than a way station, both metaphysically and materially. But he didn't know that. He was always giving himself airs. Each time he took his spiritual pulse it seemed to him that nothing stirred, and so, each time, he pronounced himself finally dead to the world. He drank deep of the satisfaction of his dissatisfaction. Here he was, nowhere, in a house that was no more than a shell, with a love that was nothing more than a husk, and all entirely of his own doing. He was not a man to underestimate the blessings of purgatory.

While Liam sat slumped in his armchair, properly situated in the nether regions of the great scheme, he also drank deep from the glass of whisky clamped inside his interlaced fingers. He dipped his head to allow his lips to reach the rim of the glass, in a gesture that could have been mistaken for supplication by a short-sighted observer who entered the room without knocking. The effect would have been heightened by a certain dampness that appeared in his eyes when he raised his head again and swallowed. The short-sighted observer would have concluded that whatever Liam was praying for was not forthcoming.

She would have been wrong. Liam's most fervent prayers were perpetually answered. The whisky slipped down his throat and provided proof that there was, indeed, certainty in the world. Alcohol had the intended effect and Liam's mind floated a little lighter than it had before.

One prayer answered.

Liam's floating mind retrieved the image of Grace's breasts being fondled by an alien hand, and he let the vision grow strong and active, as intimate and detailed as a pornographic movie that had him as both producer and director.

Another prayer answered.

All Liam wanted was to be forever more or less drunk, and forever enmeshed in sexual daydreams. He needed to be alert only as much as it took to listen for the key in the lock of the front door and footsteps on the stairs. So Liam's prayers were not difficult to answer, even for a God whose existence was as doubtful as the chances of Liam's book on love ever seeing the light of day.

The only necessary and sufficient condition for the answering of Liam's prayers was, by definition, fulfilled; he was no more and no less than a member of the human species, which meant that he possessed a full-sized working copy of a brain that required endorphin production to keep it happy, and had the right balance of hormones – plenty of testosterone, just enough oestrogen – pumping around his system.

Dark daydreams were Liam's current vocation.

2

Daphne's Hat

The intruder was, in fact, long-sighted and wearing a black velvet hat. She could see into the distance with a clinical accuracy, but whatever was close to looked decidedly foggy. When Daphne entered the room without knocking she saw instantly that Liam was sipping a large Scotch and taking much pleasure in its journey down his oesophagus. It was also clear, from the shifty look in his eyes, that he was thinking about sex. Daphne wasn't one to confuse lust with prayer.

'Liam,' Daphne declared, in her usual practical tone, 'I love you. And I've decided that I'm going to write a book about it.'

Liam had lifted his head at her entrance but, seeing that it was her, returned his gaze to the whisky and did not bother to look up again from his glass when she spoke.

'Piss off, I'm busy,' he said.

Daphne knew he was annoyed at having his fantasy interrupted and that he was trying to retrieve it, but she continued, quite undaunted.

'I love you, Liam. I want to celebrate our love in prose.'

Liam had come to believe that she was the devil, or his most trusted emissary, sent especially to taunt him. Her tone of voice rang with a terrible mocking irony in his ears. She seemed to announce his faults and failures, whatever the content of her speech, with all the clarity that long-sightedness could bring.

Daphne could not help these things. This was the way she was. But she loved Liam, none the less, with a passion that was indulged by the fuzziness of close-up. He was hardly a matinée idol. His face was as creased and crumpled as his clothes. His rust-coloured hair and beard were almost wild for lack of trimming, and he was, not to put too fine a point on it, portly, though some might give him the benefit of the doubt and call it cuddly. Daphne knew Liam to be a tiresome, pathetic, self-pitying and melodramatic old fool, but she had a soft spot for him and there it was. He was, after all, a fully human human being, which accounted for all his faults which were nothing if not human. And she was a dried-up, 68-year-old ex-lady novelist living in his attic, which, she conceded, might account for some of hers.

Daphne had conceived a passion for Liam when he bought the house. She would have him for her own. She intended to take his human foolishness, his softness, and suck it into her own well-aged, desiccated system. She wanted to absorb him and have him run through her; lubricating her dry, old veins. The devil was supposed to take a man's soul, but that was a cold, eternal thing, Daphne thought. She wanted Liam's heart and all his warm, squashy bits. If she was a devil, she was a devil in search of sentiment and offal. That was the nature of her demonic desire. She was perfectly sure that Liam would fill her craving nicely. And if that wasn't love, then she was damned if she knew what was.

So far as writing a book about her love for him was concerned, it was just something she'd thought of on the spur of the moment to strike terror into the heart of her beloved — she had no desire for his comfort or well-being — but, well, why not, she thought. Liam might fondly imagine writing a book that finally nailed love (she had been listening outside the door while the poor fool muttered to himself). But a book about Liam and Daphne finding love together might offer a truly definitive description of the human race. It was so much more useful to describe than define, she knew. And apart from being useful to students of human nature, it would be a task to fill a small part of eternity. Perhaps she really would write it. Oh, dear, yes, perhaps she would.

'Forget Grace, my darling,' Daphne instructed Liam, and started to pour herself a substantial slug of Scotch. She did no more than shrug when Liam leapt out of his chair to snatch the bottle and glass from her hands. 'I know she's broken your heart and ruined your life, but I can make you just as unhappy, if you'll only give me the chance, dear.'

Liam returned to his chair clutching the bottle in the crook of his arm and muttering oriental curses at her. Daphne crouched down beside him, causing Liam to jerk his head away from her, leaving it at a very unusual and somewhat painful angle. She went on, speaking into his left ear, half answering his abuse and half continuing with her train of thought.

'All right, so my body isn't exactly fresh, and my titties don't jiggle and joggle around under my sweater as if God's attached elastic to the nipples and bounces them in time to some celestial boogie. But you could get over that. There's more to sexual attraction than firm flesh, my dear. Liam, darling, you're not trying to see things my way . . .'

She had said all this, or something very like it, before, and she really didn't expect to have any more success this time than usual. But Daphne knew that you had to keep chipping away at things you want and other people think they don't. You have to keep presenting new and unthought-of possibilities. Who was to say that one day her chosen love might not get curious, at least? Daphne had dedication, too.

Liam had stopped murmuring and now turned his face towards her, baring his teeth and staring at her with his usual mixture of fury and disgust. Daphne didn't mind. She was thick-skinned. That was one of the benefits of a well-aged body.

'Get away from me. Get out of my room and leave me alone,' Liam finally hissed. 'I don't know why you're still in this house. This is my house. How many times have I told you I want you out?'

'More often than even I could remember, Liam dear, though I hang on your every word.' She smiled sweetly at him and stood up, her knees creaking slightly. 'But don't worry, I won't leave you. I'll always stay close, so that the moment you come to your senses I'll be within reach. You only have to stretch out your hand, dearest, and some hungry part of my anatomy will be vibrating under it.'

'Go . . . !' Liam thundered.

Daphne sensed that she had outstayed her welcome, and she knew that it was important not to overwhelm people, especially people by whom one wishes to be loved. She moved to the door and blew Liam a gay kiss across the distance between them.

'Well, I'll be off now, my sweet. Think of me, above your head, thinking of you. You have no idea what dirty thoughts old women in love can have. And what's the point, Liam, my love, of having dirty thoughts separately when we could have them together? All right . . .

11

I'm off . . .' she added before Liam's open mouth could bellow at her again.

She left Liam to his private thoughts, making sure to slam the door hard, and returned to her attic room and her mute, ever-patient, waiting typewriter.

Daphne had not refused to leave her attic only because of her desire for Liam, or sheer cussedness, though both played a part in her decision. She had other reasons for staying put.

She sat now at her table in front of the big office Underwood typewriter whose bulk had always been as good an excuse as any for not moving from her attic. Liam's attempts to get her out and her love for her reluctant landlord had given her further incentives for staying where she was. Now the rightness of remaining in her attic had come full circle, back to the Underwood. She was going to write her new book, and it was certainly not time to pack up and move house.

The attic had been her home, and the Underwood's, for thirteen years. She had moved into it with a small suitcase in one hand, containing her clothes, a handful of old photographs and three hardback books; and the bulky Underwood typewriter clutched under the other arm. She had promised herself that day, as she stopped on the pen-ultimate landing to rest some of the weight of the typewriter on the window-sill, that this would be her final move. Nothing would induce her to carry the machine another inch: downstairs, upstairs or hori-zontally. Not ever. The attic would be its – and therefore her – final resting place.

But apart from the difficulty of moving the machine and her refusal to release Liam from his so far unacknowledged obligations to her, there was a completeness about ending her sedentary days in the attic of this particular house. She had, after all, begun her days on its ground floor.

The two rooms and little kitchen that was now a bathroom, at the bottom of the house, had been her childhood home, where she had lived with her mother until she was fifteen. In two years she would have completed another fifteen at the top of the house. A cycle would have been finished. She would have done her stint. She could move on to what was next, satisfied that the requirements of pattern had been fulfilled.

It had been decidedly odd, her moving in to the house for the second time. So many years had passed, so much had happened, so much had had to be blanked out that, at first, arriving at the house, she had no idea of where she was. She hadn't recognized the address. The name of the street was vaguely familiar, but, at the age of fifty-five, her life was so filled with terrible familiarities as she went about her business – things half remembered and best forgotten – that she rarely demanded recollection of her poor, tired brain. By then she could be almost certain that she wouldn't want to know why there was something about this face, or that street, that nudged her memory. But she had been given this address as a place with a room to rent, and had focused only on the chance of somewhere to live when she counted the house numbers. It wasn't until she was halfway up the front steps of the house that she became aware of where she was.

There were eight steps up to the front door, and even though her brain had tried to keep the information to itself, her body knew it. It remembered how many bumps of the back wheels of the pram there had to be before the ground levelled off. Later, when she began to walk, her feet had taken up the count, as they paused together on each step up or down to steady her for the next. Her ears had received confirmation from the voice of the adult who held her hand – the sing-song sound that marked each level her feet achieved; the words had no meaning at first, but the sound of counting was always the same, in the same sequence, whether she had begun at the bottom or the top.

Her 55-year-old feet, forty years away from the last time they had descended the steps, still knew, would always know, how many there were, and how many there were to go. The passing years made no difference to them. But it wasn't until Daphne was on the fourth step that she realized she had been counting them in her mind: one, two, three, *four*. The rhythm of the counting, and the emphasis on *four*, told her that her mind was as certain as her feet that there were four more to go.

She had stopped on that fourth step, annoyed by the persistence of her memory and those parts of her that gloried in repetition. Mindless repetition, she had thought, crossly. But not entirely mindless, because somewhere, connecting her feet to that bit of her brain that thought without permission, was a sensation that oscillated between relief and fear, comfort and anger, when faced with the increasing proximity of the front door; and that part of her, too, which felt those conflicting things, had full knowledge of the one-two-three-*four*-five-six-seven-eight sequence. A feeling, a thought of sorts, generated by the memory of the counting that ended with eight and a blue front door.

Daphne had not wanted to tread the remaining four steps, but logic told her that if she didn't, she would have to go down four, and that would make up the sequence anyway. And besides, she needed somewhere to live, and it seemed to be beyond the once blue but now black front door at the top of the steps. So she had shaken off the numbers and the memories they threatened to summon with a flick of her head, and averted her eyes when the landlord opened the door and led her up the staircase, so that she would not see the two closed doors on the ground floor which had once been her home.

She could have rejected the attic and tried the next house on the list, but by the time she was at the top of the stairs, she had become intrigued by the pattern-making obsession of life. She'd show it, she had decided, she wouldn't allow herself to be driven away by the past. She took the room, and moved into it that afternoon — still avoiding those doors on the ground floor — with her small suitcase and large typewriter.

She had unpacked her few clothes and put them in the wardrobe; the photographs she put in a drawer without looking at them; the three pristine hardback books she placed in a small pile next to the Underwood, on the table that was going to serve as her desk. Then she sat down and picked up the top book, turning it over in her hands. Long ago she had taken off the dust jackets, displeased by the photograph of the young author on the inside flap. The orange boards were blank, except for the spine, printed in gold lettering: *The Clouds of Morning ... Daphne Drummond*. It was her first novel, the one that was published in 1942, when she was just twenty.

Now, at sixty-eight, thirteen years after moving in, Daphne glanced at the bookshelf she had put up, on which the three books, among others, rested. She hadn't opened them that day when she had moved in, nor since. She hadn't opened them, since she stopped writing. My life has been a closed book since 1955, she thought. She chuckled and pulled the Underwood towards her. On a blank sheet that she found in the desk drawer she typed:

Her life had been a closed book since 1955.

Then she rolled the paper back to the top of the sheet, and in the top left-hand corner typed:

–1–

A start had been made and, better than that, it began at page one, if not the beginning. It was enough writing for the day. It wouldn't do to rush things.

She stared at the short sentence she had achieved, the new beginning, and absent-mindedly scratching an itch on the inside of her thigh, found herself thinking back to the child and young woman who had inhabited the pages of her previous books, and who surely bore no relationship to the elderly but spritely woman that Daphne now was. Daphne could make no connection with her youthful self. No matter, Daphne had her story on paper. Three books were filled with a young woman and her story, and the world had certainly connected them with Daphne, even if she now found it difficult. Autobiographical novels, they had been called, which for a while Daphne, along with the rest of the world, had taken to mean the same thing as *true*.

It was an understandable mistake, Daphne acknowledged: the three novels she wrote in her youth – the only novels she had so far written – *were*, as everyone suspected, based almost entirely on the events of her life. *The Clouds of Morning*, her novel about childhood, was an exact description of her own upbringing by her schizophrenic mother. Or so she was later diagnosed. It was the truth that when her mother, dark, deserted, demented creature, was in the grip of her madness, she would lock Daphne in a cupboard in the hallway under the stairs. Whether it was to keep her daughter safe from the demons that chased her, or whether it was to keep herself safe from the demon she thought her daughter was, Daphne never found out. And her mother, Daphne supposed, never really knew herself.

But however much Daphne fought and screamed, her mother always had strength enough to drag her into the cupboard and turn the key in the lock. There had been no light except for a chink that showed under the door. Black, bloody black it was in there, Daphne remembered with a shudder, fingering, as if for comfort, the velvety brim of the hat she wore. She never could be sure that her mother would come to her senses before she died of suffocation. How long she stayed in the locked cupboard depended entirely on how long the madness took to pass. Sometimes it was enough hours for a day or night to go by. No one came to their house; the neighbours and the other tenants kept away from the beautiful, crazy woman and her pale, etiolated daughter.

Daphne had written the book when she was nineteen. A precocious talent, everyone said. A great future was predicted for her, and Daphne was taken up by the London literary set who thought her remarkably touching and original; so young, and hardly educated, but with a raw talent for fiction.

Then, five years later, at twenty-four, she wrote her next book, *The Blazing Moon*, another astonishing *tour de force*, most said. It dealt with a young uneducated girl, taken up by society, neurotic and out of her depth, who sleeps her way around the smart set with increasing desperation and hysteria while bombs fall all around her, until she finally comes upon a titled Englishman who loves her, makes her pregnant and deserts her. She is left swollen with child, and alone in a blitzed city, having been dropped and turned away by all her former friends.

It was hailed as brave, this book, although one or two reviews in the more obscure little magazines suggested there was a strain of unrelenting self-pity, and perhaps the novel would have been better for a touch of humour. At the time, Daphne did not see what humour could have to do with it, nor did she really comprehend the signs of favour falling away. She had not been immediately excluded from the literary and social circles. She was still invited here and there in spite of the embarrassment she had caused by her scandalous pregnancy, and the social awkwardness of the child dying of scarlet fever when it was six months old. Bad enough to have borne it, but quite unacceptable to give her acquaintances the distasteful task of dealing with her bereavement. She made the mistake of turning up on people's doorsteps, weeping and helpless, asking for assistance. No one said go

16

away; most gave Daphne a cup of tea and a five-pound note, but somehow within a few months she was quite alone in the world, with nothing but her memories of a cupboard under the stairs from which all light was excluded, and a small dead creature lying limp in her arms. Her name was Felicity. Daphne did not notice at the time how the end of the book, made up — perhaps the first genuinely fictional passage she had written — immediately after the death of her child, predicted by a few months the end of her acceptability in London circles.

The final book, written when she was thirty-three, told the story of a wretched and drunken woman, no longer with youth and freshness on her side, spiralling down from high society to the lowest dives that London in the early fifties had to offer. It was unforgiving and stark with what was to become typical fifties social realism. The kitchen sinks in *Curtain Across the Sun* were not just there, but filled with vomit and the remains of self-induced abortions. Drugged jazz musicians and vicious East End gangsters walked across the broken landscape of the alcoholic, drug-addicted heroine, who died, diseased and overdosed, in a bleak back room with a broken window, and a torn and filthy curtain flapping hopelessly in the icy wind of winter.

It was definitely downbeat. But this time she knew enough to pay attention to the endings of her books. When *Curtain Across the Sun* came out it was to rave reviews. Changing the face of English literature, they said. A bold and devastating book. But the author had disappeared off the face of the earth. The cry went up: 'Where is Daphne Drummond?' closely followed by 'Who is Daphne Drummond?' and finally 'Is there a Daphne Drummond?' Daphne knew better than to answer. She spent the last ten pounds of her advance on a bender that was certain either to kill her or get her hospitalized. She didn't care in the slightest which it turned out to be, but, as it happened, she ended up unconscious on a pavement, and the NHS spent God knows how much time and effort in keeping her alive.

She was severely emaciated, her liver was sclerotic, her blood awash with dexedrine and barbiturates. Why they fought so hard for her and took such care had taxed her imagination, and she remained perplexed until she finally came to understand so many years later. It turned out to be nothing very remarkable at all; just that in the ordinary way, life had a value, and, in their ordinary way, people generally tried to hold on to it in themselves and others. It was simply that there was a feeling abroad that living things should stay that way for no other reason than that they were living. There were people who felt this way, Daphne discovered, but she discovered it very slowly, and understood it not at all in her mid-thirties. It wasn't how she saw things then.

She felt rather foolish to have taken so long to have come to this unastonishing thought. She had imagined the truth would have to be something very deep and complex. And, most of all, startling. The truth she had learned about why people tried to keep other people alive was far from startling. Banal, she would have said in her thirties. It was banal now, Daphne reflected; but then, what had she expected? Something that no one had ever thought of before? Idiotic to imagine that if there were any great truth to be found, it would not have been found already, revealed long ago, long since. What is there to know but what we *can* know, you silly woman, she chided herself. And if we can know it, you can be sure that someone would have mentioned it already. Always looking for something else, something unthought of, weren't we? Yet it had taken her almost seventy years to come up with a minor understanding of the world which any six-year-old could have told her, but wouldn't have unless she'd asked, because any six-year-old would assume *everyone* knew it.

Well, however it might be, in spite of all the autobiographical detail in Daphne's novels she came to realize, as she recuperated and tried her hand at a fourth novel, that they spoke not one word of truth. She was gripped by the knowledge that truth was something she knew nothing about. Not in her novels, not in her life. And this was true, too, of everyone – or everyone she had ever met. Only recently she had come across a statement of Wittgenstein's, which she suppose she should have known, but there it was, she was poorly read. *If lions could speak we would not understand them.* Or something close. It was precisely what she had understood about truth. If there was any, beyond the obvious, we poor humans wouldn't be able to make head nor tail of the stuff. We'd mistake it for dogshit on the pavement, or the unconsidered angle of a knife beside a loaf of bread, or the weight of a dead child, or something. Recognize it? We wouldn't even stoop to pick it up and examine it.

Daphne lived aimlessly after her recovery, unable to understand what she was doing on the planet. She couldn't kill herself since she felt it would be ungrateful to all those nice doctors and nurses who had worked so hard to keep her alive. The renewed life they gave her became her burden, and she carried herself about the world like a sleepwalker with a great weight attached to her ankles. She lived in a series of rented rooms, moving every few years for no particular reason. One day she would pack up her few possessions, her books, photographs, the typewriter, and find herself another room which was, in essence, no different from the last. When the royalty cheques for her novels petered out she got work as she could find it, as a shop assistant or a filing clerk, whatever was nearby and available. For thirty years she dragged around, being nowhere in particular, doing nothing in particular, just hanging on to the life some strangers had saved for her. It was the only reason she could think of for continuing to live in it.

For the first decade she had a series of lovers, people who worked with her, or whom she met by chance. There was never much passion in most of the affairs, and then, as she entered her mid-forties, they petered out just as her royalty cheques had done. The past slipped away and finally became disconnected from the present. She stopped thinking of herself as a writer, or even an ex-writer, and she stopped thinking of herself as a sexual being. Only the old sense of desolation kept her in touch with her past, and that had, like her occasional inexplicable voluntary visits to the cupboard as a child, become almost a comfort.

Looking back, it seemed incredible that her life had come to a stop for three decades, but when she thought about it, it seemed to her that the long period of deadness balanced the earlier thirty-year period of non-stop melodrama. She supposed that she was exhausted and needed a long rest. Well, she'd had one, and now things were going to be different, she thought with something very like glee. She would not be driven, as she had been in her youth, by an addiction to disaster, nor would she be dormant, terrified of experiencing anything. Now she would be herself. At last, and about bloody time, she thought, as she pushed back the typewriter, rolled up her sleeves and took herself off to the kitchenette on the landing to get to grips with the dirty dishes waiting in the sink.

Part One

Daphne continued to wear her hat while she washed up. In fact, since she had bought it the week before from a fancy shop in the West End, she hadn't taken it off. It cost a week's pension, but she couldn't be worrying about that. The hat was made of the blackest velvet, with a soft brim that flopped in what should have been an elegant fashion down over the brow. It was not unlike a hat her mother had worn, but Daphne's had a rather high crown, and there were some diddly bits of decoration appliquéd around it, just above the brim, which, being made of black velvet also, were somewhat camouflaged. Very subtle, Daphne thought.

Daphne wore her hat all the time now. Round the house, up and down the high road to do her bits of shopping, even in the bath. Especially in the bath. Daphne's idea was that it should age nicely, and she was sure damp and heat would help to do the trick. Then there was the dust when she emptied the vacuum cleaner and, best of all, spits and spots of grease from frying eggs and bacon for her breakfast. Even if she had cared a hoot about cholesterol, she would still have maintained her egg and bacon habit for the sake of the hat.

It was her belief that continuous wear under normal domestic circumstances would produce the patina of age that she required. She would have preferred to have the real thing, her mother's old hat, passed on (like her poor mother) and gently aged over decades. As she herself had, Daphne would have added. But the fact was that she had aged suddenly, in fits and starts, putting on ten years in a night, and then having to catch up on herself. So a new hat was quite appropriate. In any case, life had not proceeded in such a way that she had access to her – well, not her patrimony since she had no recollection of her father, so she supposed it would be her matrimony – and she had to settle for finding what she needed for herself and getting it prepared. Not unlike her plans for Liam, now she came to think of it.

The black velvet hat was for her very old age (as indeed, it occurred to her, was Liam), which she proposed to begin when she reached seventy. It was then she planned to free herself from the shackles of a settled life and go a-wandering. She started to hum a little song they used to play all the time on the radio, years before, about going a-wandering along the mountain track and loving to sing with a knapsack on her back. 'Val der reeee, val der ahhhh, val de reeee, val de ah-ha-

ha-ha-ha-ha . . .' she trilled into the washing-up water. She was going to become a baglady; and, knowing that a hat was an essential part of any baglady's equipment, she had bought hers and set about making it ready for its future with her as a baglady's hat. And none too soon. She had only two years to get it just right.

Of course, as far as Liam was concerned she was already an old lady – well, no lady, a frightful old cow and a mad one to boot. But she didn't consider herself either of these things. It was very difficult to think of herself as old, and it may have been that she was a little backward in that respect. She didn't think mad was a very good description, either. It was a laziness on Liam's part (and how young and sane was *he*, she'd like to know) that allowed the description 'mad' to suffice. She supposed that since he wished her out of the way, he was not prepared to put too much effort into rethinking his prejudices about her. She regarded it as her task to put him right on these things, and more.

The fact was that she had been gripped a year ago with a *joie de vivre* that hitherto had been completely missing from her life. Her new-found energy and enthusiasm could be mistaken, by a glum bugger like Liam, for madness, but only if you expected people of sixty-eight to sit around tapping their feet waiting for death to knock on the door and carry them away. This view made death a kind of refuse collector, scooping up decaying material and disposing of it. What would we do without it, she wondered. Watch old apples wrinkle, and good red meat turn grey, that's what. Well, she may be wrinkled and she was certainly grey, but she was not ready to be thrown out yet, thank you very much. On the contrary.

Liam had given up, she knew, on the idea that she would move out voluntarily; he was pinning his hopes on her insanity – which he delicately called 'confusion', hinting at the possibility of Alzheimer's disease when he phoned up the social services and told them to take her away.

She had never been less confused in her whole life. For example, she did *not* forget to turn off the tap at the sink in which she was currently elbow deep. She *remembered* not to turn it off. This was because the sink was directly over Liam's desk in his study (though if study was what he did in it, then there ought to be a PhD available in dirty

21

thoughts), and it was her intention to remind him of her continued and devoted existence. In fact, a mark of her sanity was that she always managed to pretend to the charming social worker who arrived at Liam's request that she *did* forget to turn off the tap, that she *was* just a little absent-minded, but none the less quite capable of looking after herself. Nice, pink-cheeked Alison was beginning to get the idea that Liam was a typical bourgeois pig of a landlord whose motives were not to be trusted. They got on jolly well, she and Alison, and Alison didn't believe for a moment Liam's tales about Daphne making sexual advances. She knew Daphne to be a sweet old dear with an interesting past, and she was going to make sure that Daphne wasn't exploited by capitalist self-interest. How was that for sanity?

Daphne *had* had an interesting past, as it happened, but it was her plan to have a much more interesting future, with Liam at the centre of it. Eventually, he would see the sense of this, for himself as well as Daphne, and would no longer fight the inevitable. Fate and Liam's sexual incontinence had thrown them together, and Daphne was a great believer in giving fate and incontinence a helping hand. Liam would come round to her view and, funnily enough, she could wait.

It seemed the older you got, the longer you could wait for things. This was something of a paradox; one would have thought it to be the other way round, but there it was. Perhaps youth strove so urgently for what it wanted because it wasn't sure of getting it. That had certainly been Daphne's experience of youth. Now, she had no doubt that she would get what she wanted, and so there was no hurry. And here was a piece of everyday magic if ever there was one: the very fact of knowing that what is wanted will be got makes the achievement inevitable. It was like a spider waiting in its web not doubting that, once it has made the initial effort to spin the trap, prey will come its way. Did it put up flashing neon signs: FLIES ALIGHT HERE? Did it offer irresistible incentives: THREE FREE FLY SWATTERS FOR EVERY LANDING? Did it set up a soap box and harangue assembled flies with its theory that flies were invented so that they might land on spiders' webs and would they now take a vote and thereafter act appropriately? No, my dears, Daphne thought happily, it did not. It just created the right conditions and dinner arrived, as night followed day. And so it was with Daphne. Liam would be hers, whether he knew it now or not. There was nothing to be done about it.

And from whence came this positive and optimistic view of the workings of the world, and at such a late stage in life, too? It certainly couldn't be put down to a loving and secure childhood and youth.

Daphne's childhood had been baleful. But it was such a long time ago that she couldn't see what it had to do with anything any longer. Oh, all right, she conceded tetchily to herself, it had *something* to do with the fact that her teens, twenties, thirties, forties and – well, yes – her fifties, too, were almost entirely miserable. But, now look, here she was, sixty-eight, full of hope for her future, and happy as a schoolgirl in love. Not that she had been happy as a schoolgirl in love – it was careless similes like that that had been one of the reasons why she put down her pen at the age of thirty-six to have a good hard think, and hadn't managed to pick it up again since. It had struck her, like a bolt from the blue, in the middle of her fourth book, which happily never saw the light of day, that every word she had written previously was essentially untrue, though she wasn't quite sure why; and then, having thought that, she couldn't think of any words that *were* true. And that had been that as far as her blossoming career as a writer blossomed.

Until now. Now she had her late-flowering love to write about, her geriatric courtship; her whirlwind autumnal romance. And she had no doubt that truth would just slip off her pen like the stuff that exudes from the tip of a schlong, all ready and waiting to get on with the job. At any rate it would (though not from a pen, because she preferred a typewriter), once she got going. And hadn't she already written the first sentence? Truth, she was certain, wasn't going to be a problem any more.

She had decided, when she committed herself, a year ago, to future happiness, that the childhood business was not going to be a problem any more, either. Why should she listen to the echo of an opinionated old man from a European backwater? Austria, indeed. And nineteenth-century Austria, at that. And look what happened to Austria, thank you very much. She could choose, surely. She could say, in her sixty-ninth year: Thank you, Professor Freud, and goodbye. She would be what she decided to be and consign her childhood, and his theories, to the dustbin of history, where they both belonged. Why should she continue to play the dismal game of consequences? She would have been better off without it. So what if everyone agreed that the pompous old moralist had changed the face of the twentieth century? It didn't mean that they were any more right than he was. And what, she'd like to know, had been so wonderful about the twentieth century that we should be grateful to the old buffer for changing it? All Daphne could say was that she hoped someone would change it back again, and the sooner the better as far as the well-being of the world was concerned.

In fact, it now occurred to Daphne, unthinking the twentieth century ought to be the major task of the twenty-first. If it had any sense, which she frankly doubted that it would. It ought to be: goodbye it-goes-without-saying Freud; goodbye it-goes-without-saying fitted kitchens; goodbye it-goes-without-saying Marx; goodbye it-goes-without-saying one-man buses; goodbye it-goes-without-saying Post-Modernism; goodbye it-goes-without-saying environment-friendly underarm deodorant; goodbye it-goes-without-saying Elizabeth David; goodbye it-goes-without-saying mid-life crisis; goodbye it-goes-without-saying shrink wrap; goodbye it-goes-without-saying no fucking for the over-sixties.

But it probably wouldn't be, and if it was, by the end of the twenty-first century there'd be another set to be done away with. It was enough to make a bright-eyed, sex-crazed old dear take to the bottle. But then, she was still partial to a bit of a drink – another reason why she and Liam would fit together like matching duvet and pillowcase. And duvets were another thing that the twenty-first century might like to consider.

Daphne finished the washing-up, and tucked a stray lock of hair that had fallen over her face back under the brim of her hat. She wiped her damp and still soapy fingers on the crown to dry them, and to give the hat a helping hand on its journey to bagladydomness.

The sink was full of dirty, foaming water, in which floated a suspension of the results of three days of cups of tea and Marmite toast. A thin stream of water still ran into it from the cold tap which she hadn't turned off. Well, she was a woman of very limited means. She smiled at the prospect of an advance for the new book and promised herself that she would celebrate the arrival of the cheque by leaving the *hot* tap running into the overflowing sink. Just once.

Daphne returned to the attic room she had inhabited like a lair for thirteen years to see if it contained any evidence of her new energy for life. It was not promising, very little changed from when she had moved in. In the room there was the same walnut wardrobe, mahogany chest of drawers, single divan bed, threadbare patterned carpet, rosewood table that she ate on, the Underwood pushed back against the wall. She had added the small pine bookshelf and an old silk shawl that served as a bedspread. Nothing more. Outside, on the landing, her little kitchen: a small electric cooker, and the butler's sink with the floorboards around it stained and always damp from the tap that was so often, as now, not quite turned off.

And that was it, she decided with a hoot of triumph, she had found it. The proof of the new her. The damp floorboards that were the other side of the stained and saturated ceiling of the room below. The dripping connection between her attic and Liam's study. Between Daphne and Liam. Water seeping through, rotting the fabric of the house, making a line of communication between her and the future. Drip, drip, drip. A new energy, Daphne's new life: the two of them. Destiny, if she had anything to do with it. This was today's truth. Daphne's truth. And there was no more to be said about it.

3

Grace's Breasts

Liam suffered from a facial tic, an excessive blink that, at its worst, seemed to close down his face as well as shut his eyes. Now, he allowed himself his most luxuriant version of it, clamping his eyelids together so tightly that every feature was distorted. His whole face seemed to be crushed, as if his head were imploding. He sincerely wished death of a most unpleasant variety on the mad old cow in the attic.

After a moment his whiskered face went back to normal, but he postponed his return to Grace's breasts and the invasive fingers, while he fumed and fretted about his lodger. He knew she would never leave, and spent some pleasurable moments in thinking of ways of disposing of her; all of them painful, some of them downright disgusting. He should have been ashamed of himself, but it was entirely her fault. She was his devil, all right, tormenting and teasing him, laughing at his desires, when only he had the right to do that. She taunted his lust with her own.

An old woman, for God's sake. A burned-out writer, whose flame, Liam guessed, had never done more than flicker anyway. Liam had found her few (entirely predictable) titles when he looked her up in the catalogue of the British Library. Of course, they were all out of print. Daphne Drummond, a 68-year-old has-been lady novelist who refused to move out of his attic, was driving him mad; distracting him from, and depriving him of, his great project, which was to drive *himself* mad with all the intensity, passion and despair of the self pitted against the self.

Liam had offered her as much as he could manage to induce her to leave, because he wanted an empty house inhabited only by himself and Grace, which was as near as he could get to an empty world inhabited only by the two of them. But the Drummond woman was determined to stay and persecute him. She was, undoubtedly, a witch, a harpy, a filth-minded old baggage with a foul mouth, who used words like *desire* and *love* to taunt him with his own anguish.

But he was able to console himself with the thought that she was surely an aspect of his punishment. She had come into his life in the way that just deserts do — quite naturally. Daphne in the attic was what he deserved; part of the package that God dealt out to those who throw everything good away for nothing — for a mess of sexual excitement. For a lot of sexual excitement, and a glorious mess, Liam muttered, correcting God. For a lifetime's worth of the stuff. And misery to match. The crone upstairs was undoubtedly God's jocular voice in Liam's ear. He listened to the creaking floorboard above his head where Daphne stood doing the washing-up, and considered, with relish, the process of punishment that had been meted out to him for failing to . . . well, for failing.

After Liam left Sophie and the children for his student bride, and before they had gone into self-exile in Zambia, things had gone from bad to worse in a way that Liam could only describe as highly satisfactory. Sophie had refused to see him and would not let him visit the children. Her anger was righteous and unforgiving. Quite properly. And nothing he had said to her, all of it true but utterly absurd, could possibly have helped. He told Sophie when he left her that he loved her totally, still loved her absolutely, that his feelings for her were in no way changed. He explained, again with complete sincerity, that the children meant everything to him and that without all of them his life meant nothing, his existence would be a blank. They, Sophie and the three children, were his entire world, but unhappily, indeed tragically, he explained in a sombre voice, he was, nevertheless, leaving them to go and live with Grace, who had none of the qualities he valued in Sophie — her intelligence, her wit, her beauty, her elegance, her capacity for love and humour.

Sophie listened to what he had to say in silence. After a moment, Liam, who naturally was on his knees, looked up at her, pleading for her insight into his nightmare.

'Do you understand?'

It was never clear whether she understood – understood his sincerity, his love for her – because she got up and left the room without saying a word. Liam wasn't sure on the journey back to the small flat where Grace waited for him, if he was relieved or disappointed by her reaction. He had expected Sophie to be more engaged in his dilemma. Surely, it was nothing if not interesting to have given up a woman who had exactly what he wanted in a partner, for an unfinished girl who had . . .

Grace had breasts. Full, young, bursting with life, breasts. And that was it, more or less. It was true that after a while, during their illicit love-making in his office at the university, he had discovered other sectors of her body – the curve of her hips, a line that ran from neck into shoulder, the backs of her knees, the swell of her belly – which caught his passing attention. But her breasts were the centre of it all. By the time he had moved in with her, Grace's body had become an ordnance survey map, whose routes for Liam began and ended always at her breasts, as a Londoner might conceive of all routes on a map of England as being to and from London. On the way there were stopping-off points – towns to be visited leisurely during the journey to the capital, their particular architectural features and individual ambience appreciated before passing on, heading always in the direction of his final destination. Grace had become the capital of his life.

Sophie was disgusted by Liam's limited but obsessive desire, and Grace, at least in the early days, protested from a vaguely feminist point of view that he did not love her for her mind. But all the women in Christendom might march day and night with banners outside his door for all he cared. Nothing, no disapproval or rejection, could be more punishing than his own fanatical and fractured lust. His shame was monumental, and had nothing to do with the world's opinion of him.

Liam took his tawdry love, in both its metaphysical and fleshy manifestations, to a far-away country, where a university post awaited him, and no one but Grace and himself knew of its unseemly nature and origins. He had married her before they left, because she was a conventional girl who thought that a legal contract could legitimize a fatally flawed union. Then he took the lectureship in Zambia that fortuitously had been offered to him the previous academic year. He hoped to bury the pair of them in darkest Africa where the white man had so often sought refuge in, and from, his most primitive urges.

The irony of this was not lost on Liam. His heart might be a soggy and unsightly mass, but his intellect at this point remained its old watchful and amused self. He was after all an anthropologist by profession, and a modern enough one to reject, like the rest of his colleagues, the imposition of the *exotic* on other cultures that had so marred the work of his predecessors. But when shame and disgrace suffused his life, and he needed to hide from the world that knew him, Africa had sounded in his head like a gong. His intellect raised an amused eyebrow at the sloppiness of his heart. It was too wise to imagine that it could reason with what would never be reasonable. Well, well, it said, its metaphorical lips quivering with the effort of not laughing out loud, we'll have to see what happens, won't we? And knowing that it wouldn't be needed for some time to come, if indeed ever, it settled back comfortably, waiting for the amusing times that were certainly ahead.

There had not been much call for intellect over the next two years. Liam had lectured in anthropology to undergraduates for more than a decade, and much of what he had to impart was by now automatic. Zambia had offered him a job because he had done his fieldwork there a decade before, studying the interface between tribalism and industrialization in a modernizing African society. Published fieldwork has a long half-life, and if he had thought of publishing something new, he rejected the notion now. To be a participant observer in the best tradition of ethnography would mean going to live in his chosen area, alongside the people with whom he would be updating his study. He could not consider leaving Grace alone for even a single night, let alone for months at a time. He contented himself with occasional articles in journals, rehashing his own work or writing critiques of studies by those who had been more recently in the field.

If intellect was not much required for his work, it was positively dysfunctional when it came to what he chose to think of as his real life. His task was Grace. The real work of each day occurred between coming home to Grace in the evening and leaving her for the university building the next morning to lecture or conduct tutorials. And, like any dedicated professional, he took his work with him even during what he thought of as his hours of rest. The difference with Liam was that it was all reversed. Grace hovered beneath, and broke through, his thoughts when he should have been relaxing at the relatively easy business of teaching and writing. She was Liam's ever-present anxiety. He was like an ambitious executive who was unable not to worry about his standing with the boss, even during Sunday afternoon walks in the park.

There was no place for intellect when it came to Grace. Liam's mind, or at least the part of it responsible for serious thought, and, more importantly, humour snoozed. Momentarily, it would grunt, half wake and snuffle, before realizing that the alarm had not gone off and it could turn over and sleep again. The other part of his mind, all fevered imagination, was in a condition of perpetual insomnia. Crazed by its own productions and lack of rest, it went into overdrive, building image upon image, fantasy on fantasy, at the exponential rate at which cancer cells divide and carelessly – suicidally, it would seem – destroy the life of their host.

Liam had no peace; but since he had turned his back on peace when he walked, trancelike, away from Sophie and the children, and towards Grace, he had come to suppose that a lack of peace was what he chiefly wanted. Best, then, not to think about it too much. Better let his thought processes sleep on.

Over quite a short period of time, Liam lost all his ability to laugh at himself. It had been the part of him in which his humanity resided. The place that had recognized his long-time despairing ache for something greater than himself (for belief, or God, or . . .) but that also recognized the comedy of the very small longing for the immense, and laughed, not without affection, at the joke of it all. Now Liam had transferred his longing to the confined space of Grace's body, and the joke was over. In losing his laughter, he had lost the better part of himself. He had narrowed down to a small obsession, unable to live with the greater. Yet, settling for the possible had not worked well for him.

Grace had become impatient with Liam's lust even before they left for Lusaka. The novelty of having an older man (who was, moreover, her teacher) hopelessly besotted with her had faded quickly. She found herself isolated from the student group to which she naturally belonged, and had to watch from a distance the sexual dance that her contemporaries performed. Alliances were made and split with great rapidity. At one moment the scales fell from young female eyes and revealed that the young man who had sat across the table at tutorials for an entire term was, in fact, utterly gorgeous and exciting. It was impossible that she hadn't noticed before. Then another moment, and her eyes dulled over at the sight of him, but sparked against another familiar but, until that moment, utterly unknown pair of eyes just to the previous beloved's left. Girls stopped eating, boys drank too much lager, when their current love went off with someone else. Shoulders were wept on and turned out, often, to belong to the next beloved. No one quite knew how they managed to get a single essay finished given the frantic busyness of their emotional lives.

Grace was excluded from all this carry-on, and could only watch the parade of pain and joy with the gnawing envy of one who had relinquished her right to it. Her daily visits to Liam's office had to be kept a secret, so she was deprived even of the pleasures of sharing confidences. And by the time Liam had left his wife and they had moved into a flat together, Grace had given up her course entirely. It was obviously not practical to remain a student under such circumstances. Although Grace did not very much miss the academic work, she was finally severed from her age group. And by that time, too, she had begun to find Liam's slobbering, wet-eyed lust more than a little disgusting.

As she gradually withdrew from the almost mutual passion they had acted out on the carpet tiles of the department, Liam's desire increased. It seemed that her indifference fired him, although she couldn't understand how that could be. The more he had to cajole, indeed, sometimes beg, often on his knees, the greater was his passion. He was never so happy as when Grace, fed up with him going on and on, and embarrassed by his kneeling position in front of her, peremptorily pulled off her sweater and her tights and, hiking up her skirt, stood over him with an expression that clearly said: Well, get on with it, then. What are you waiting for? Let's get this over with, because there's something on the telly I want to watch.

She would have been utterly perplexed, not to say terminally disgusted, had she known that at those moments Liam felt an extra *frisson*, which even he was surprised to discover was the fervent hope that she might complete his happiness by urinating all over him.

Liam flushed with excitement and terror on these occasions – and by the time they were living together, there *were* only these occasions. The thrill of her matter-of-fact, distasteful presentation of her body for his animal lust was almost too much to bear, but the fear of her curtailing his explorations with a 'Hurry up, can't you? I'm starving' made him fear for his sanity.

'Why don't you get on with it? You're a pervert. Do you know that?'

If she only knew, Liam thought. He supposed she had been reading up on the subject during her empty days at home.

'You're supposed to put that thing in me. You're going to do it in the end, so why can't you just do it now instead of making me stand around all this time while you *fiddle* with me? Please hurry *up*, Liam.'

But this was only in her most generous frame of mind. Sometimes she simply pulled away from his exploring hands and devouring mouth, announcing that she had better things to do than stand in front of him for hours while he did disgusting things to her. She would dress herself and snap on the television with the finality of an impatient parent snatching a bag of half-eaten sweets from her child's hand and putting it firmly on the topmost, unreachable shelf of the kitchen cupboard.

'Oh, Grace!' Liam now moaned aloud into his whisky glass, from the depths of the armchair.

In Lusaka Grace had discovered the pleasures of sex. Sex with others, that is. During the first couple of months Liam had become alarmed. Grace seemed to be pining. She watched the undergraduates and the younger members of staff with the gaze of a pale princess locked away from the world by her fiendish guardian. She seemed, his buxom love, to lose substance. To Liam's horror, her breast beneath his upstretched palm seemed smaller, lighter, the nipple drooping, less forthright. He looked at her carefully, in spite of the impatient clicking of her tongue. Was there something scrawny about the flesh of her hips and thighs, which had been so lush and full? But then his extra-concentrated stare had brought her loveliness back, making him double up with the pain of wanting her. It was only his imagination, he thought, but based on something; fed by a look in her eyes, a set of her lips, the sound of her sighs.

Then, one day she was bursting with well-being, glowing and succulent like a ripe fig, and Liam knew immediately what had happened.

He said nothing and kept the pain to himself. Cherished it, actually, and allowed it to feed his hunger. Now he had to beg all the harder for the privilege of kneeling before her naked body, and his secret knowledge told him why. The pain of knowing she had a lover acted as a catalyst on his desire, and he quivered in a kind of ecstasy in front of her, coming close to losing consciousness on several occasions. Grace noticed that something was wrong, and stared down at him wide-eyed, wondering if he had gone mad — and almost panicked herself. What would she do, all alone in a foreign country, with a mad husband more than twice her age? But Liam always seemed to regain control eventually, and she remembered her new lover, one of Liam's most promising students, and that made her feel better.

Having a lover made her feel better altogether. She put up, albeit tetchily, with Liam's devotions by thinking of what she and Daniel had done together that afternoon. Sometimes Liam was surprised to find her usually reluctantly dry vagina positively damp and ready for the climax of his slow adoration. For a second there was a flash of pleasure at her excitement, but only for an instant before he realized what had excited her, and then he shivered with the different pleasure that new agony afforded.

Grace was not promiscuous, but she had a great deal of time to fill. Once she had given up her studies she found her interest in reading seemed to dissipate, apart from the odd popular novel. She had no hobbies or outside interests. That, really, was what being at university had been supposed to provide her with — time to find out what she liked to do. She had had no great ambitions, so three years' studying for a degree was essentially about *finding herself*, as her understanding headmistress had explained to her parents. But Liam put a stop to all that, and Grace found herself alone with a middle-aged sex fiend in a country she would have difficulty pointing to on a map. All that was easily available, apart from books, were young men, and her youthful instincts told her forcefully that they were an excellent form of outside interest for someone of her age.

Eventually, it became necessary for Liam to resign his post and return with bad Grace to England. She didn't see herself as bad, but her affairs had become legendary. Grace's idea of discretion — for she had no particular desire to taunt Liam or get him into any difficulties — was to keep her extramarital relationships intramural, that is, within the anthropology department, students and staff, as if this were somehow more ethical. She had a definite feeling that it wouldn't be *right* to sleep with someone from another faculty. It was like keeping it in the family, and therefore less dangerous, or hurtful, or something than . . . anything else.

Liam was finally unable to take seminars, or attend faculty meetings, knowing that half the male members in the room (was he being over-optimistic?) had had carnal knowledge of his bride, very probably that morning. He suffered from noticeable losses of concentration as he wondered, glowering at waist level around the assembled group, which of them had underpants sticky with his love's love. He began to mark essays erratically, according to which writer he considered to be seeing his wife more often. He would vote against any motion, no matter how productive or imaginative, that came from a fellow member of staff he suspected of having knowledge of Grace's breasts, which were his own, his dearest, possessions. Finally, he was found, by someone whose knock had not been heard, in a corner of his office crouching on the carpet, weeping, like a wounded puppy.

His head of department suggested that he wasn't well, but Liam took this to mean that he wanted him out of the way, incarcerated, so he could have his way with his wife. Liam stood and, though no more than average height, towered over his now seriously alarmed head of department, and hissed into his face, 'Oh, no. No, no, no. You're not going to get rid of me that easily. You'll have to queue up along with everyone else, I'm afraid, old thing. There are no favourites in this department when it comes to the favours of my lovely, lovely, lovely wife.'

The head of department cowered, wondering if Liam was dangerous, and if he ought to call the police, but he didn't want Liam yelling to the entire campus that he was being carried off because the head of faculty was having it off with his wife, because he *was* and he certainly didn't want it to get back to his own wife.

Liam understood for himself that he had to leave when he found himself cornering her latest lover — the son of an ex-chieftan turned minister of finance, who was in his first year in the department — and discussing with the terrified young man the finer points of Grace's anatomy. He wanted to compare notes, he explained, because now when he touched Grace and made love to her, he found that he became his own rival, split away from himself on his knees like ghostly plasma, and watched, insanely jealous, as the hands that were no longer his caressed and explored his most precious possession.

Clearly, things were out of hand. He resigned, informed Grace, who did not mind at all, that they were returning to London, and added bitterly that he was now unemployed as a result of his passion for her, and that he had no idea how they would survive. Grace could not imagine not surviving, so she wasn't worried, and the prospect of going home cheered her up so much that she stopped seeing anyone but Liam for their last few weeks in Africa. But Liam wasn't fooled into thinking that anything had fundamentally changed. He didn't really want it to; he just wanted things to go on going on, spiralling down to hell, in a place that was more familiar than darkest Africa.

Liam got up unsteadily from his armchair and poured himself another Scotch. He considered the possibility that he had been the victim of misfortune. That passion had fallen on him like a tree picked up and dropped by a hurricane. An act of God. Ho ho, he thought, as he sat down heavily into the armchair. Extraordinary that an act of God should be synonymous with accident, although perfectly proper that insurance companies refused to pay out. Perhaps Lloyds ought to take over the running of the Church. They knew retribution when they saw it, and doubled the punishment by withholding the cash. Quite right. *Of course* it was your fault if the ground opened up and swallowed you, and of course it was Liam's fault that Grace had taken off her jacket to reveal her divine, bra-less, diaphanously covered breasts at the same moment as Liam had requested the light turned on in the seminar room a lifetime ago.

He was now more than moderately drunk, and while half of him — his ears and what remained of his consciousness — strained towards the front door, listening for Grace's key in the lock, the rest of him meandered around in his past, like a child in a muddy stream, trying to find in which direction the current of his life went.

He remembered Mo, his friend at the university before Grace had happened, who had gone off to the rainforest in Borneo and tried to tidy it up. Her terrible need for order had done for her. He had written to Mo asking her to leave something out there in the forest unnamed and unmeasured for the likes of him, but a far-away disorder hadn't satisfied him. He had wanted it close. And his terrible need for disorder had done for him.

But it all stemmed, he knew, dragging himself further back into the past, from disappointment; from a great unquenchable sadness at the realization that he would never be anything more than clever, and that he would never do anything better than good work. Once . . . when? . . . long ago . . . he had known himself to be remarkable, special, destined for an exceptional existence. During his adolescence in the early fifties, it was as if he had walked arm in arm with God. He *knew* what he was, even if he hadn't seen yet what it was that he would do. His high Anglican, Anglo-Irish family had given him a taste for glory and a sense of the articulation between past and present. He studied history at Oxford, and then, thinking it his own special destiny, took off, unaware of the hordes in front of and behind him, on the great sixties trek to discover the geographical and metaphysical East.

But if he turned out to be not brilliant enough for his own expectations, he was too clever to deceive himself that acid and mantras and begging from the already woefully underprivileged would take him closer to the source of wisdom. He was too clever and too essentially conservative not to realize that wisdom, if it is there to be found, lives close to home, not half a world away in a culture and religion designed for those to whom it belongs. And yet, he could not imagine wisdom living in the cold stone churches and the droning prelates of his childhood. And history, while interesting, was not enlightening. He was lost. God vanished like a cheap conjuring trick before his very eyes. In the East he'd seen enough gurus pluck Rolex watches from the air for the benefit of miracle-hungry Americans who would have been disappointed had they only manifested a flower. He'd heard enough dull sermons in damp Ireland about duty and sacrifice, and love of a higher but apparently indefinable sort. His eyes were opened, he saw only what was there, no shadows in the nooks or crannies pointing to paths of truth. He had gained atheism and lost the light.

He turned from history to anthropology, thinking that he might replace his lost sense of awe with a passion for mankind. To no avail. Academia gave him a career, but did nothing for his suspended soul. And so Liam discovered disappointment, and became a high priest of a certain kind of sentimental cynicism that is bred among those who would know God but who find themselves left off God's invitation list.

He married Sophie, who knew him for what he was, and became a morose joker, a despondent clown in the anthropology department. He was all set to live happily ever after, with the occasional jest about suicide, when Grace came along. But while Grace's breasts had struck him as perfectly contoured to fit the vacant space inside him, the real truth was, and he knew it, that he needed to fling himself face down into the mud. He longed for ruin, which was, at least, the reverse of glory, and despised himself for his capacity to be contented with the love of Sophie and to delight in his children. Without ruin, without absurdity, there was no possibility of redemption. He wanted to be reunited with that old trickster, God. He went for broke. He ran off with Grace, allowing his obsession full rein, in the hope that he was running either towards destruction or to the light.

In fact, he had run to seed. Neither God nor Nemesis had taken pity on him. He was, he explained to the bottom of the whisky glass, a disappointed drunk, trapped inside a ludicrous passion of his own invention.

Liam had not noticed the darkening of the already well-stained patch on the ceiling above his desk. As yet Daphne's washing-up water hadn't seeped through the attic floorboards to run its accustomed route along the crack in the plaster. His eyes were lowered, staring gloomily into his refilled whisky glass, seeing into the past. But now he'd had enough of old misery. He wanted the present kind, and brought himself back. One more gulp of Scotch and his mind was altogether elsewhere.

Not else*where*, exactly, because he didn't know who owned the hand that presently caressed his wife, and so couldn't know where the event was taking place. This annoyed him; it was important to have the details right. Imagination depended on particular information if it was to take wing. Not knowing who or where deprived him of the full potential of his fantasy. Places and faces were essential; generalities just would not do for Liam. He wanted to see clearly the hand on the flesh that he knew so well. The *rêve* wouldn't come fully alive unless he knew whether the nails were well manicured; if the fingers sported a ring; how gnarled or smooth was the skin on the back of the hand. It mattered because the clarity of his vision of Grace's silken breast was marred if he could not know the texture of the flesh that played upon it. Contrast or similarity made all the difference to the flavour of his daydream. Both were terrible – and, of course, delicious – but he had to know if it was one or the other to continue satisfyingly. Or both, he wondered for a moment. Two hands, one of each sort, perhaps. But, no, he doubted that Grace would permit that sort of thing. And his daymares demanded reality. The pain of two separate hands on his Grace would have been exquisite, but only permissible if it were true. He admitted to himself that he was horribly hampered by his tendency to social realism.

He gazed blankly at the opposite wall, trying to make Grace and her lover as real as he possibly could, given his lack of information, but all the time he was distracted by the business of detail. *She was sitting naked to the waist in a chair* . . . but what kind of chair? He tried a few: Queen Anne reproduction, contrast piping Conran, stickback wooden kitchen. But each demanded a décor to go with it – bedroom, living room, kitchen – and each décor needed a decorator, and the vision foundered as his attention was drawn once again to the hand that ended at a wrist, that wouldn't connect to an arm, shoulder, neck, *face*. He started again, once he had replenished his glass. *Grace completely naked on a bed, her arms extended* . . . but to whom? It was no good without her lover clearly in the picture. He tried to superimpose old lovers on to his screen, but it wasn't any use. His imagination knew he was cheating. Old lovers had no more reality than faceless ones. He couldn't fake it. He had to know the facts of who and where.

Liam was well past retribution. He had no desire to confront or punish Grace's latest lover. He was further down the spiral than that. He had come to accept what was known and had learned how to mingle desire with pain. He could join in by becoming the secret conductor of the real events occurring *at this very moment*. And more than that, although jealousy could not be overcome, X – all the Xs – could be, all unwittingly, deprived of his Grace if Liam controlled their thrashings in his mind. *They* did not have her, though at the moment they were with her, while Liam positioned them thus and so on her body, and made them whisper his words into her ear. She was still his, and they were no more than toys, dangling puppets that he allowed to move. But still, it only worked when he knew who was at it with his Grace.

No one, it seemed, at that precise moment. The front door slammed shut and footsteps in the hall below moved towards the stairs. Grace was home.

Grace stood in the open doorway of the study and looked at her husband who had, with difficulty, got out of his chair and was extending his glass of whisky towards her. She could see he had been drinking all afternoon. His eyes bulged, as if surprised to find themselves open. But Grace knew by now that the bulging and surprised look were only the effect of the reddened rims that stood out so starkly against his sandy lashes. He swayed a little as he pushed the glass towards her.

'Here, have a drink, my dear. It's cocktail time in all the best homes.'

'You know I don't like whisky,' Grace said, making a face and tossing her hair out of her face. 'Have you eaten anything?'

Liam knocked back the contents of the glass in a single swallow and then refilled it.

'I forgot, you're a child. And children don't like the taste of Scotch. Well, what will you have, my darling? A tinkling thimbleful of Tia Maria, perhaps? Or one of those pineapple milk shake things – what are they called? A Penis Collector?' Liam chuckled to himself, pleased with that one.

'You're so disgusting.'

Grace glared at him, and Liam's face fell. He knew that in moments he would be on his knees in front of her. Perhaps he should write his little joke down, he thought, before it got trampled by his remorse and longing. But it was too late. She had turned to go.

'Grace . . .'

It was more sigh than articulation. The word whispered through the air like a plume of smoke until it reached Grace's retreating body and curled itself around her, trying gently to hold her there and make her turn towards the whisperer. She stopped and turned, rolling her eyes in exasperation. She knew what the sound of that particular *Grace* meant. Pleading, apology and demand, all rolled into one. To her it had the tone of the hissing of a snake, and there *was* something hypnotic about it. She did stop. She did turn. But she did not move back towards Liam.

'No,' she said, but with resignation in her voice. 'I don't want to.'

'Grace,' Liam sighed again.

The maudlin ritual was inevitable, whatever Grace thought about it. It was payment in kind. They both knew that she would allow him to do what he wanted. To maul her sadly, to love her hopelessly, to track the scent of her lover across her flesh until Liam arrived, on his knees, to the dark centre where he could – such joy, such pain – smell and taste the evidence that he and Grace were not alone in their dismal universe.

She closed the door with a sigh of her own, and stood sullenly in front of him like a smuggler waiting to be frisked. They were locked into this, the two of them, into the ceremony of guilt and detection. Without analysing it, Grace had learned to play her part. She no longer washed her afternoons of illicit sex away before she went home. She kept the dried-up sweat, the stains, the sharp scent, for Liam; a gift of pain, like her evident disgust at his drunken touch, a kindness she did for him that she didn't begin to understand.

Liam undid the buttons on her dark pinafore dress, and then, opening her blouse, buried his damp whiskers in her neck, making small moaning sounds.

'You're pathetic,' she hissed.

'Thank you,' Liam breathed into her skin. 'Sometimes I want to travel round the country lighting candles in every cathedral I come to, in thanks . . .' he murmured, running a necklace of kisses to her other shoulder.

'For what?' she asked crossly.

'For the fact that you weren't called Beatrice,' he said, still muffled by his journey down her body.

'What?'

'It happens to be a name I deplore, my dear. I must remember to thank your parents next time I see them.'

He wanted to distract her with conversation, as a doctor would a child having an injection. He hoped that she would not notice that his face was between her breasts, sniffing at them like a rabbit, sifting the scents he caught. He dismissed the wafts of the cheap-smelling deodorant and perfume she liked, as mere distraction, but found another ersatz smell mingling with them, tangier than the sweet, childlike stuff she wore, and he followed it like a thread towards the freshly shaven cheeks that had deposited it on her breasts. Beardless, then. But this one was not an inexperienced, over-hasty boy. He was thoughtful enough to shave in the middle of the day so as not to scratch his lover's tender flesh as he pressed his mouth against it. And careful enough not to leave irritated marks for his lover's insanely jealous husband to find. But he wasn't perfect, his wife's boyfriend, he had his faults. He was too vain, too narcissistic to leave off the aftershave that gave away his presence on Grace's naked body. He liked to look at himself in the mirror, this one, patting designer cologne on his cheeks, imagining where his well-tended face would be, not so very long from now.

'Oh, my darling,' Liam moaned, dizzy with excitement at this initial breakthrough. He pulled off her tights and knickers, and followed the piquant trail down Grace's torso, where at the swell of her belly he picked up the real scent of his prey, the smell of sweat and sex that were not Grace's alone. He enjoyed her smells in passing, but only briefly, turning his concentration to the foreign smells that led inexorably down, a pathway to despair.

Grace stood with her legs apart, her arms folded across her ribcage. Liam was on his knees, nuzzling and sniffing at her. She looked down at his rusty, dishevelled, too long hair and wished it darker and properly cut. As Liam pressed his face against her pubic bone, she thought of her lover whose hair was well cared for and styled to her liking.

41

Reaching home, Liam lifted his head for a second and looked up at Grace like a soldier about to sacrifice himself for Queen and Country. He hoped, perhaps, for a wave, a salute to his resolution and bravery. Grace's arms remained crossed, her face showed irritation.

'Must you? Must you?'

Liam smiled gently.

'Yes, I'm afraid I must, my dear.'

The taste of the other man on his tongue brought Liam close to losing consciousness. His terrible lust exploded in his head, making rainbows of jealousy, love and dread, arching together, pressing upwards on his skull until he thought it would shatter from the intolerable pressure. This was everything and nothing. All there was and absolute absence. He looked back up at Grace, his eyes damp with excitement.

'Tell me his name,' he whispered.

'Shut up.' She tried to pull away from him, but he held her firmly to him around her thighs.

'Tell me. His name,' Liam insisted.

'For Christ's sake, Liam!'

'I know what he smells like. I know what he tastes like. I want to know his name. Please.'

'I don't know what you're talking about. Do you want to make love to me or don't you?'

She turned her head to one side to avoid his insistent eyes, and stared down at the paper-strewn surface of Liam's desk. A small pool of inky water lay on the top sheet, spreading slowly over the page of handwriting. A drop splashed into the pool from the ceiling, and a moment later another; then two together, and they began to come faster, spreading the puddle beyond the edges of the top sheet. Only a few lines of handwriting at the bottom of the paper were still more or less intact.

Grace raised her eyes to the ceiling.

'Look, Liam! Look, there's water coming in.'

4

Sylvie's Sofabeds

Sylvie hadn't lived anywhere, nowhere settled, nowhere that was hers, since leaving her parents, and that had been a long time ago. Nothing had ever been sustained enough to cause her to strike roots – not places, not work, not relationships. And the idea of *home* had dwindled in her mind so that it was a notion that had nothing to do with her.

There were probably reasons why Sylvie had wandered aimlessly around the world, never finally settling as her contemporaries had done, but the reasons weren't clear. She had known no more unhappiness during her ordinary enough suburban childhood than anyone else, and less than some. But it was as if the everyday business of living inhabited a part of the brain which, in Sylvie, was damaged. She simply could not manage things and seemed never to have learned how. If she had been carefree, a joyful traveller through life, a free spirit, it wouldn't have mattered; but Sylvie was anything but a free spirit.

Nobody doesn't live *any*where of course. Sylvie lived everywhere and wherever, so long as it was reasonably comfortable and for as long as she was put up with. Sylvie was an eternal visitor. A near-to-tears, shoulders-drooping, backpack-toting arriver on other people's doorsteps.

If you are an eternal visitor, certain things follow. For example, you don't receive bills: electricity and gas are as nebulous as they are in nature, never pinned down to quantity, never filtered through a meter that has your name on it. You simply use their airy substance, enjoying the heat for which someone else would be billed; eating the food, most of which would have been cooked anyway, causing therms to accumulate; having urgent chats at a distance that don't feel like the sum of units each costing so many pence and part of a penny. Sheets need to be laundered, extra potatoes purchased, lightbulbs replaced more frequently after working overtime to keep the urgent three-in-the-morning conversations about what was to be done with one's life illuminated. None of these minor, extra costs are presented in the form of a bill to the visitor. They are absorbed into everyday expenses. Written off to friendship.

But there is an accumulation, of course. The calculations are made silently, unnoticed in a barely ticking adding machine at the back of the householder's mind, until a certain point is reached when the overall cost — financial and emotional — reaches a level that causes something in the atmosphere to change.

The practised visitor notices this before the householder has become conscious of a tightening of his or her lips, because sensitivity to these minute clues are essential if friendships, and therefore future visits, are to continue. Nothing is said, but almost instantly it turns out that the visitor has to go, for reasons that have nothing apparently to do with not being welcome any longer. The householder is genuinely sorry that the visitor has to leave; even, obscurely, a little guilty, and, of course, will look after a box of books, a bag of unseasonal clothes, or even a cat, until the departing visitor gets properly settled.

This had been the pattern of Sylvie's life from the time she left home. At twenty-nine, she had never lived anywhere for longer than it took the lips to tighten. She inhabited spare rooms, or, where there weren't any, unfolded sofabeds that had been bought just in case. She was always about to get herself somewhere permanent, but things fell through, or emergencies came up that made sorting out housing irrelevant for the time being. Every couple of years, Sylvie would leave the country — the circle of friends having been completed, the full set of sofabeds unfolded — to give everyone time to welcome her back and let her stay again when she returned while she 'sorted herself out'.

Sylvie had never been on a voters' register, or received junk mail offering her financial security in her old age for just a small monthly outlay. The Inland Revenue didn't try to find her because they didn't know she existed. She was exempt from making a moral or financial stand on the issue of poll tax. She never had to make a decision about the character of the man who came to the door and offered to clean the windows. 'I'm sorry, I don't live here. I'm just a visitor' was all that was ever required.

Sylvie's friends felt they were the more responsible for having to take decisions about window-cleaners, and having their names and addresses computerized so they might be offered the opportunity to refuse to buy the *Encyclopaedia Britannica* in monthly instalments. If, from time to time, they felt burdened by the responsibilities and annoyances of running a home, they did not, on balance, envy Sylvie her freedom from these things because she did not seem to them to be free in any enviable sense. They put her up, and put up with her, because they felt vaguely sorry that she lacked their ability to take on responsibility; and somewhat guilty, faced with her recurring panics and desperation. They did not feel that her life was more exciting because they, for the most part, had had excitement when they were supposed to, and now quite liked being in charge of things, and even having to pay bills.

Sylvie was someone whose impossibility and incorrigibility her friends laughed or fumed about on the telephone to each other; the subject of concerned or infuriated conversations. But even their anger contained the small satisfaction she brought them by confirming that their chosen lives were essentially right. The cast of friends varied somewhat over time as those who could not take any more dropped out, or Sylvie found occasional new members to add to the pool. But there was a hard core of old friends, people she had known at school or college, who remained and who continually asked each other why it was they put up with her. Someone had to, they would eventually shrug, though no one could say why that was the case, either. Very little was expected of Sylvie, other than to have the good sense to move on when the goodwill had reached a low point.

Sometimes Sylvie lived in two places at once. This was when she got involved with a man. She would invariably move in with him – or if he was married they would move in to somewhere together – but before long she would turn up late at night at an old friend's door, distraught, begging asylum, a couple of bottles of wine and a sympathetic ear. Her affairs were brief melodramas that couldn't include domesticity for long. She would bounce back and forth from lover to asylum until the pattern was broken by the man finding someone who was prepared to stay put, or returning to his wife. Sylvie always felt betrayed. He had never really loved her. When the friend providing asylum pointed out mildly that most people preferred quiet comfort to continual tempests, Sylvie looked confused and repeated that it was clear he hadn't ever *really* loved her.

Apart from boxes, bags and the occasional cat that Sylvie had dotted about the world in other people's care, there was a six-year-old child called Divya. Divya, whose name was a Hindu word meaning Divine Love, was the outcome of a relationship during a brief orange-clad period in Sylvie's life. For a year or so she had been Ma Savita, and hung around the Rajneeshee communes of Chalk Farm. She had, she told her friends, at last found herself, and they, though they looked dubiously at the picture of Bhagwan that hung heavily between her breasts over diaphanous orange muslin, felt some relief and wanted to believe that what she said was true. She had become, she told them, spiritually and sexually free, her chakras were activated, and she had been assured by her lover, who was very close to Bhagwan himself, that she was approaching enlightenment at an astonishing rate. Ma Savita's old friends were pleased for her, and relieved that their spare rooms would no longer be needed, since one could assume that a spiritually enlightened person could find a place of their own to live. And what was even better news was that she was going very soon to Oregon to have an audience with the Master himself and live in the community of love.

But enlightenment was not to be. Just before she gave birth to Divya, her lover returned to Oregon at his Master's urgent command and had never been heard of again. Later, it was suspected that he was a victim of Rajneesh's sinister deputy, Ma Sheela, who had been trying to silence growing opposition to her by means of drugs and rat poison. Ma Savita's lover was not the only one who disappeared, and eventually even the most devoted or most paranoid disciples around the world had to acknowledge that there was something rotten in the state of Oregon. The Rajneeshee communities, including the one in Chalk Farm, dissolved in confusion. Ma Savita reverted to being Sylvie, the perennial visitor, but with the added and inappropriate burden of a tiny baby. No one among her friends was prepared to take care of a child indefinitely while she 'got herself sorted out', and after a short and sorry spell in a mother and baby hostel, Divya was taken into care.

Sylvie returned to do the rounds of her friends and wept additional tears for Divya, but assured everybody that it would only be a temporary thing because she was sorting out somewhere permanent to live and she could have the baby back as soon as she moved in, which would be any day now.

Six years later, Divya was still in care, and Sylvie still homeless, though, whenever possible, when she wasn't out of the country or away from London, she visited her daughter and took her out every other weekend. Whenever Sylvie got into a new relationship she explained to social services that she was now settled, and Divya moved in with her mother for as long as it took for the relationship to founder. After a while, Divya's social worker vetoed any further sudden moves, and insisted that Sylvie had to prove herself genuinely settled before they would think of returning the child to her care. So far it was unprovable.

It was 2.30 in the morning. Lights burned in the living room and kitchen, two empty bottles of wine stood next to a third that was half full and two pairs of weary ears had listened sympathetically for as long as they could. Sylvie gulped wine from her glass, her legs curled under her bottom in a corner of the sofa. She wore a huge hand-knitted sweater of pink and taupe stripes that almost covered her substantial thighs, which were encased in tight black leggings. She seemed to have a cold. At any rate she sniffed a lot between gulps of wine.

Sophie was slumped in the armchair opposite the sofa, her legs spread wide, straight out in front of her, and a look of exhaustion in her eyes, which kept losing focus so that she was obliged to blink hard to get them back to seeing straight.

David sprawled elegantly on the *chaise longue*, his ankles neatly crossed, his wine glass balanced on his chest and a look of exquisite control on his face.

'If we let the silence go on any longer, we will be obliged to repeat the conversation that we've just repeated four times already. Four times will do. I've thought of a new definition of hell, tonight; it's the fifth repetition. Thank you, Sylvie. Without you, I'd never have come up with it.'

'Shut up,' Sophie said, dully.

'Excuse me,' David said with great politeness, and closed his eyes as if in pain.

'I'm sorry to be so much trouble. I just don't know what to do,' Sylvie said with a whine in her voice.

'Please God, help me. Don't let it start again,' David groaned with his eyes closed.

'Shut up,' Sophie said, with even less energy than before.

'Sophie. Darling. Why don't you explain to her that being offered a place to live is not generally regarded as a life-threatening tragedy. Most people, on the contrary, would think it quite a nice thing to happen. Especially if they had nowhere to live. Tell her that she should break the habit of a lifetime and go and live in it, and then we can go to bed. And if, one day, God forbid, it so happens that someone else wants to spend the night here, they won't be able to because first thing tomorrow I'm going to take the sofabed into the garden and make a bonfire out of it.'

Sophie dropped her head into her hand.

'Take no notice of him,' she said to Sylvie, who had sniffed heavily several times during David's speech. Then she turned to David. 'David, it isn't as easy as that, and you know it. It's only an idea. We'd have to check.'

'Don't worry, she won't take any notice of me,' David assured Sophie, and answered her other point. 'It *is* as easy as that. You pick up the phone tomorrow and make the arrangements. He'll be delighted to get the rent and she ought to be delighted to have her eternal housing problem finally solved.' He opened one eye and looked appealingly at Sophie. 'There, I've made it easy. Can I go to bed now?'

Sylvie swallowed the rest of her wine, sniffed and threw a vicious look at David, whose one open eye had travelled hopefully in her direction.

'David, you're a shit.'

'Yes,' he agreed. 'But at least I'm a shit who's got a bed to call his own. Sophie,' he begged, 'please, can I go and lie on it now?'

'Let's all go to bed,' Sophie sighed. 'We can talk about it in the morning, Sylvie.'

'After I've gone to work,' David muttered, rousing himself and staggering towards the door. 'Which I do at 8.30. Thank God I don't have long to wait. I hate to waste time sleeping.'

Upstairs, David gave as much vent to his fury as tiredness would allow. Sylvie had slept on his sofabed for three weeks, eaten his food, wallowed like a sea elephant in his bath. Now, Sophie had come up with a brilliant solution that looked set to make everyone happy again. Wasn't that as much as anyone, even someone as hopeless and neurotic as Sylvie, could expect? Was he supposed to do her shopping for her, too?

'That's a point,' Sophie said, and wondered aloud if Sylvie was capable of going round a supermarket and coming out at the other end with anything to eat. But David had finished with the topic of Sylvie; he was asleep before Sophie got to the end of her question.

Sylvie was neurotic, Sophie knew. She was also a manipulator with a mysterious quality that you couldn't quite put your finger on, but which kept people who were perfectly aware that she was a scrounger, offering her what she asked for. Guilt was obviously one reason; people with houses feel bad when confronted by people without them. But it didn't take too many of Sylvie's extended visits before the guilt vanished beneath the stress and disturbance she caused in people's lives. Perhaps, thought Sophie, people still took her in just because she stood at the door and asked. Surely that was too simple? Would she, Sophie, get everything she wanted if she asked for it? But then, she, like most people, didn't know exactly what it was she did want. Perhaps Sylvie's quality — it certainly wasn't charm — was knowing what she wanted. You say what you want, and people give it to you. But Sylvie never seemed to have what she wanted in spite of people apparently giving her everything she asked for. So, presumably, what Sylvie really wanted was not what people gave her. She had an inkling of what that might be, but decided not to pursue the thought. Tomorrow morning, early, three small children would wake and need to be dressed and given breakfast. Sophie decided that David was right; sleep, rather than thoughts about Sylvie, was the priority.

The following morning, David left for work after delivering a message through teeth clenched with tiredness and rage.

'You have got to do something about your friend. Today. I love you and I need you. I also love and enjoy your three children. Every morning I welcome you all into my life, and give thanks that I have been welcomed into your lives. *But I don't want Sylvie here any more.* Please' – his eyes screwed up with pleading – 'make her go away'.

Sylvie emerged at nine o'clock from the living room, where she slept, cross at having been woken by the sounds of breakfast. She had a bad head, and sat sniffing miserably at the table in the kitchen, while Sophie made coffee and gave young Katie pieces of banana. Sylvie's dark curly hair fell in wiry tangles on to her shoulders; her face was puffy with sleep. She wore a nightdress which she must have had since childhood; a cotton, floral printed thing that had thinned with the years as she had grown, so that her body was clearly visible through it and her breasts pressed against the stretched material. There was something of the slattern about her. She looked overblown and faintly grubby, and the continual sniffing didn't help. Sophie wondered if she had post-nasal drip, and then decided it was not her problem.

'So what about moving into the house? There are two rooms on the ground floor with a small kitchen in the front room. You don't have to stay for ever if you don't like it, but it'll give you time to sort yourself out. And it'll be your own place.'

'But I have to have somewhere permanent. They won't let me have Divya back until I'm living somewhere permanent.'

There was a resistant whine in her voice. Sophie wondered what possible responsibility she could have for this grown-up disaster area, but gave up the thought as too stressful.

'But you *can* stay there.'

'But I haven't got a job. How can I pay rent?'

Sophie gritted her teeth.

'You *get* a job. Get a part-time job, and social security will pay the rent if you're not earning enough, and you can have Divya back. Come on, Sylvie, it's not impossible. It's not even very difficult.'

'You don't know how difficult it is,' she said sullenly. 'What am I going to do? Work in a shop or an office, or something? And how will

I manage with Divya? I'm not used to looking after children. She'll have to go to school, and she'll have to be fed all the time, and all the clothes will have to be washed . . . and . . .'

Sophie shook her head in despair.

'Sylvie, *everyone* does that. You'll manage because you have to. It'll be all right once you're doing it. You'll have a home of your own and a home for Divya.'

'You don't do that stuff. You don't work.'

Sophie just barely controlled herself. Katie yelled a protest as the last piece of banana was crushed in her mother's hand.

'I've got three children under seven. I'm also doing research for David,' she said in a voice that anyone but Sylvie would have recognized as dangerously quiet.

'Yes, but you don't go *out* to work. And David's always having holidays. Sometimes he makes dinner . . . Who's going to help me?'

'Well, you can't have David. Look, there's a house,' Sophie said, hanging on to the last remnants of her patience. 'There are empty rooms. We can phone Liam now and ask him about renting them. You can't stay here any more. David won't have it.'

'You live here, too. Why don't you tell him you want me to stay?'

'Because I don't!' Sophie yelled, making Sylvie jump and spill her coffee on the table. Katie jumped, too, and began to cry. 'David and I have got enough problems working out the relationship between ourselves and three children who aren't his. With you here, it's becoming impossible.'

'Well, don't blame me for your relationship with David,' Sylvie said, lifting herself straight and speaking in a knowing tone she had picked up during her time with the Rajneeshees. Then her shoulders slumped again, unable to carry the weight of her head. 'I *can't* live on my own.' She perked up suddenly. 'I've got an idea. You and David need a break from each other. Why doesn't he go and stay in the house, and I'll stay here with you? Just till I've sorted myself out. I need your support, Sophie.'

'Well, you haven't got it,' Sophie said quietly as she turned her back on Sylvie, hoisted Katie on to her hip and left the kitchen.

5

God Denies Everything

Shortly after ten that morning, Liam settled into the armchair in his study with his first whisky of the day. Grace was already out. Seeing about a job, she had said, going for an interview. After his first long draught, Liam was ready for the day's pain and pleasure to begin, but the phone rang before he had even decided on the venue of his wife's current adultery.

It was Sophie. She did no more than speak his name, and his heart convulsed. It was jolted initially and immediately by the sound of her voice: his love leapt from a quiet place in him and almost choked him. But, almost simultaneously, his heart thumped with terror. Obviously, something was wrong with one of the children. One of them was ill – one of them had died – all of them were dead. He saw a picture of the catastrophe – an impossible accident – a car out of control – a bus – and all their broken bodies.

'What? What is it? What's happened?' His voice strangled with the horror of what she had yet to tell him. But as he spoke he realized that Sophie's voice had no hint of tragedy about it. Rather, it was remote, polite and clipped. The call was perhaps no more than a rearrangement of the weekend plans for him to visit the children. For a curious moment, he wondered if he was disappointed. Of course he didn't wish his children hurt or dead, but perhaps he imagined a drama would bring Sophie and him ... Nonsense, of course, his exile was total. There could be no going back after what he had done. He should be grateful that Sophie had relented enough to allow him to have the children on Saturdays, but he knew the new man, the interloper, her new lover, had been responsible for that. It was unbearable that Sophie so accepted the situation she could open the door to him once a week. Her distant smile was a knife to his heart. She was happy enough with her life to smile at him as if he were nothing more than an ex-husband. God wouldn't save him and now nor would Sophie. Everyone seemed to get on perfectly well without him.

'Nothing's happened,' Sophie reassured him. 'I've got Sylvie staying with me. Remember her?'

Remember her? Of course he remembered her; he used to be Sophie's husband, he knew everything about her life and her friends and her plans. Sophie continued, assuming from the silence that he did remember Sylvie.

'She needs somewhere to live, where she can have Divya. Something permanent. I thought of you. You've got a couple of empty rooms, and I imagine you could use the rent money. Or have you found a job?'

Sophie's disgust at her ex-husband had made her want nothing from him. She had kept their house but refused to take maintenance, even for the children. She wanted as few ties as possible. This had been horribly hurtful to Liam, who, when he was in Zambia, had sent a monthly cheque anyway. Now, of course, he had no money to send.

'Since when did Sylvie pay rent to anyone?' he asked.

'She wants to get properly settled. She'll get a job of some kind. And social security will pay her rent. What do you think?'

He thought he'd rather have a nest of scorpions renting his empty rooms than sniffling Sylvie, to say nothing of her wretched child who would probably whine as much as Sylvie sniffed. But Sophie was right, the rent would come in handy – he had little hope of Grace finding a job that actually paid money, and he wasn't getting more than the occasional article and didn't seem to get round to writing those that were commissioned. And Sophie was asking him for something.

'All right, my dear. If you think it's a good idea. How are you?'

'We're fine. I'll send her round.'

'David well, too?' Perhaps David had left and the Sylvie thing was just a way for Sophie to make contact.

'All of us, we're fine. Will you pick up the children as usual on Saturday?'

'Will David be there?'

'Of course, he lives here.'

'Then I won't come in. It gives me such pain . . .'

'Fine, suit yourself. I'll see you Saturday, then.'

Liam returned to his armchair and his whisky. Sophie would never forgive him. She would never want him again. She had been his life, his home. She had forgotten him. And quite rightly, too, he told himself. But his mind was already half on the man, whoever he was, who was interviewing Grace. He was, however, given no chance to immerse himself in misery this morning. Just as he had Grace opening the office door, stark naked, to be interviewed, he heard the tap, tap, tap which meant, he knew only too well, that his desk was, once again, getting a soaking.

This was it. This was enough now. For the second time in two days his ceiling had dripped water on to the papers on his desk. Now, in addition there was the business of Sylvie moving in. He couldn't have said no to Sophie, but he didn't like it one bit. He wanted the house to himself. For him and Grace. How could he concentrate on anything that mattered with a crazy old woman upstairs, persecuting him? And now there would be two lunatics in the house — if he didn't count himself, which he didn't for the purposes of stoking his rage — or three, if you included the child who would certainly be as neurotic as they come at six or seven or whatever she was. Now, as if the very house had a life of its own, refusing to be a mere shell and insisting on intruding on his solitude, the water was seeping through the ceiling again. It was time, finally, to deal with the mad woman in the attic.

Liam hadn't set foot in Daphne's attic since the day he bought the house. They had communicated, when essential, on the staircase or by the front door — apart, of course, from the times when Daphne wandered into his study without knocking.

Liam stamped up the stairs to the door of the attic, the line of his mouth set beneath his whiskers as he banged his fist on her door.

Daphne was delighted to see him.

'Liam! You've come for a visit? You're tired of sitting downstairs all alone, thinking your impoverished thoughts, aren't you? You want a little chat. A little human intercourse. Well, dear, Daphne's here, for any kind of intercourse you fancy. Don't be shy. Don't be a stranger. You just pop upstairs any time you like . . .'

'Look!' Liam bellowed on the landing, pointing behind him at the butler's sink with its tap running and the water gently spilling, like a fluid curtain, over the edge on to the floorboards.

'Liam! The water's overflowing! Why on earth don't you turn the tap off? It'll go through to your study, if you're not careful. Here, let me.'

Daphne brushed past him and made a dive for the sink.

'Your reactions are awfully slow. Too much booze and not enough affection, dear, that'll slow you up every time,' she smiled at him, wiping her washing-up-water-wet hand on her hat.

Liam stared at her from his newly reversed position. He was now standing in her doorway; Daphne was beaming at him from the top of the stairs. The idiot woman wore what would have been an amusing hat on a 25-year-old out for lunch, designed as it was to parody the sultry, mysterious creatures of the thirties. On Daphne it was more a case of out *to* lunch; to say nothing of it being disgustingly filthy, and spotted with he hated to think what. Below it, a thick crinkled mass of grey hair stuck out at an angle, down to her shoulders, as a scarecrow's would if an old hat had been pulled over a bundle of straw to do service frightening the birds. There was something distasteful, to Liam's mind, about old women with long grey hair. Something faintly disquieting, as if they were exposing their private parts, whose existence he had no desire even to contemplate.

She wore a dress in which, he supposed, she had once been a young woman. Long ago. Its frill around the low-cut, heart-shaped neckline, tight waist, close, elbow-length sleeves and to-the-knees wavy hemline emphasized the youthful body Daphne no longer had. Her exposed neck, upper chest and – heaven help him – cleavage offered their slack, dead-poultry-coloured skin for his inspection, promising breasts, clearly not brassièred, that he profoundly wished he were unable to imagine. Above her camel-coloured carpet slippers, her legs were naked, which Liam regretted: stockings might have hidden the wrinkled, varicosed flesh from his sight. This indiscreet, tasteless old baggage had torn him from the contemplation of his lovely Grace, and, what was worse, mocked her with every inch of her aged body. Everything Daphne was, Grace was not. He deeply resented Daphne flaunting Grace's impermanence at him.

Daphne smiled serenely under Liam's gaze and straightened herself provocatively.

'Yes, it's all yours, for the taking, dearest,' she pouted at him.

Liam's voice rasped with distress.

'Why are you doing this to me?' And then, realizing he was in danger of being sucked into her sexual discourse, clarified his question for the benefit of them both. 'Why do you keep leaving the tap on? This makes twice in two days.'

'But last night you only yelled up at me from the bottom of the stairs. Now look, see how we've progressed? Here you are at my very door. This is a kind of breakthrough, my dear, what you might call a watershed.' She waited for him to appreciate the joke. He didn't, so she carried on. 'Already we're closer to each other, aren't we? Come inside, I've got your favourite tipple on my shelf, waiting for you. It hasn't even been opened. I prefer a nice drop of sherry myself, to tell you the truth.'

Liam began to quiver with rage.

'Not the DTs I hope, dearest?' Daphne said, concerned.

'You are driving me mad. If that social worker of yours doesn't come and cart you off, I'll . . .'

Daphne giggled.

'Don't be silly, Liam, no one's going to cart me off. I'm in full possession of my faculties, if not my facilities. Why, I've even started work again. Young Alison will be delighted with me. My novel about you, darling. My book of love.'

'Your book of . . . ? How did you — you've been creeping about listening at doors, haven't you?'

'Well, I wasn't so much listening as paying attention. It's sad when people are so alone they have to talk to themselves. I was just being neighbourly, and making sure your thoughts didn't fall on deaf ears. Which, incidentally, mine are not. The old senses are in tip-top condition, you know. Touch is the sharpest of all. Just touch me, Liam, and you'll see how instantly I respond.'

Liam stared murderously at Daphne, or tried to before his facial tic overcame him and he had a blink that lasted almost a full ten seconds.

Daphne made a sympathetic noise with her tongue on the roof of her mouth.

'Stress, my dear. You don't relax enough.'

'I'm warning you,' he said, edging cautiously round her to get to the stairs. 'Leave me alone. If that sink overflows once more, I'll disconnect it from the mains.'

'Oh, no – and leave me without running water? Alison wouldn't like that at all. She'd probably report it to someone. Still, I'd have to do my washing-up in your kitchen, I suppose. That might inconvenience you a bit, but then, if you had a double sink put in we could do the washing-up side by side. That would be nice, don't you think?'

'Daphne,' Liam said with unnatural calm. He had managed to get her back where she belonged, in her doorway. 'Listen to me. There would be lots of company in an old people's home . . .'

'Alison tells me they're called sheltered accommodation these days. That's funny, isn't it? As if everybody else lived in places without walls and a roof. But the thing about old people's homes is that they're full of old people, dear. It doesn't appeal to me at all. Anyway, I only want to be with you, Liam. Don't worry, things will work out . . . we'll be together . . . Liam? Liam?' she called as Liam thundered back down the stairs.

'Well,' Daphne said, patiently. 'That *was* a short visit. Perhaps you'll come up and have a drink and another chat tomorrow.'

Daphne decided to make herself a cup of tea – a nice cup of tea, she always told herself, because it sounded even better. Warmth, comfort and niceness – all that in something she could promise herself and then deliver. There was nothing wrong with that. Comfort was so easy to find if you called things by the right name and were careful to make them the way you wanted them. Daphne liked a good, strong cup of tea, and it had to be just right. The idea had to be followed up with reality.

She put two Assam tea bags, which were pricier than your everyday tea, but necessary, into a small brown teapot. She didn't bother with warming the pot – she was no ritualist, no fanatic, she just wanted a cup of tea that tasted the way she wanted it to. The trick was to let it stand a good long time, six or eight minutes, and then pour one teaspoonful – no more, no less, and the right size teaspoon – of milk on top of it in the cup. If there was something a bit finickity about measuring the amount of milk, she didn't care, years of contented tea consuming proved it worked, and that was what mattered. Then it needed three teaspoons – rounded, but not too rounded – of sugar, and there was the nice cup of tea; dark, bitter, sweet and always just right. Satisfaction easily come by with just a little attention to detail.

While she waited for the tea to brew – at least eight minutes, if not ten – she had a little chat with her Maker.

Daphne and the Lord were on fairly intimate terms. They had been conversing with each other for the last decade, since her early days in the attic.

In her fifty-ninth year the Lord spake unto Daphne, saying, 'Daphne, Daphne, why won't they forsake Me?'

Daphne had looked around the empty attic for a moment, and then said, 'Pardon?'

'Why won't they forsake Me? *I said*, why won't they forsake Me?' the Lord repeated, a little snappishly.

Daphne wasn't altogether surprised to hear a voice coming from nowhere, but she wanted to get things straight.

'Why won't who forsake Whom?'

'Why won't *they* forsake Me, the Lord their God?'

'Well, why are You asking me? You're the Lord their God, You're supposed to know everything.'

'A calumny. It simply isn't true, and, moreover, it's a quite unreasonable expectation. Just because a Higher Being makes something, it doesn't mean They know everything about it for ever more, or want to. Isn't it enough that they've been made? Why don't they leave Me alone? I can't be held responsible for everything.'

Daphne thought for a moment before replying.

'But what else have You got to do?'

'Brood,' God replied broodily. 'Brood darkly over the face of the waters.'

'Oh,' said Daphne.

God explained to Daphne that the Creation had never been intended to be a major project. He was just diddling about in an idle moment (well, week as it turned out). Now, He was constantly being disturbed by exhortations and exaltations and praise and prayers; sung to, implored, adored, abhorred, revered and reviled – well, everything, and all of it noisy and demanding, when all He wanted to do was to be left alone to get on with a bit of brooding, which was what He liked best. Why, He wanted to know of Daphne, couldn't they get on with it and leave Him be?

'Well, *I* don't know,' Daphne had replied, a little impatiently. It wasn't really her problem, she thought. Her life may have been a bit of a mess, but she'd never brought God into it. She'd left Him alone, and she'd expected the same to apply to God in relation to her. She said as much to the Lord her God.

'Well, exactly,' God replied. That was precisely why He had taken the matter up with her. The whole thing was a misunderstanding. All right, so He'd made the firmament and divided the waters, and caused it to rain, and formed man of the dust of the earth. But that was as far as it went. After that, He'd left well alone. He'd rested on the seventh day from His labours and then got back, with considerable relief, to His brooding. Creating just didn't grab Him. Whatever happened after that was nothing to do with Him.

'What nothing? What about the Fall? Adam and Eve and the Garden of Eden and all that stuff?' Daphne asked, a little taken aback.

'Nothing to do with Me,' God said.

'What about the Tower of Babel?'

'Nothing to do with Me,' God said.

And nor was the parting of the Red Sea, the Ten Commandments, the dietary laws ('If I were man, there's nothing I'd like better than a chunk of crispy crackling. Someone was having you lot on,' God said), or the torments of Job.

'Good Christ!' Daphne breathed, astonished.

'Nothing to do with Me,' God said.

Since then, Daphne had taken it upon herself to explain the ways of man to God, and God was grateful, though a bit perplexed. But then so was Daphne, who thought that He probably ought to be getting His information from a more educated source, and suggested a few universities that might be able to help Him better. God thought that, on the whole, Daphne did fine.

They'd got to the point now where they had occasional chats about this and that, though Daphne was careful not to ask for advice or miracles or anything. It was just nice to have Someone to talk to when she was alone and needed to think things through. God was happy to oblige when He wasn't deeply brooding, because Daphne didn't make demands.

Now, as she waited for her tea, she told God about Liam's temporary resistance to their inevitable affair.

'What makes you think it's inevitable?' He boomed down from on high.

'Well, of course it is. It's fate. We're fated, Liam and I, to love each other.'

'Oh. Do you believe in that stuff, then?'

'What stuff?'

'You know, fate. Destiny. That sort of thing.'

'Well, Dear, as a matter of fact, I do. Some things are meant, don't You think?'

'I don't know,' God replied, tentatively. 'It sounds a bit like magical thinking to Me. You lot have so many different things to believe in, it gets Me quite confused. If it's meant, who meant it?'

'Well, You, I suppose,' Daphne said a bit doubtfully.

'Not Me, Dear. I don't mean anything. I'm very liberal about what goes on down there. Actually, I couldn't care less.'

'I'm not suggesting that because something's meant, one shouldn't *do* anything about it. Like leaving taps on, and that sort of thing.'

'Sounds like a good idea to Me. Hedge your bets, I should say, because I can tell you, organization is not My strong suit. I'm afraid I quite burned Myself out toying with that creation business. All I can say is, I hope things turn out nicely for you.'

'Thank you, God.'

'Don't *you* start. I'm sick to death of all the thanks I get. I just *wish* they'd get it into their heads that I haven't done anything. Actually, I was in the middle of rather a good brood, I wonder if you'd mind . . .'

'No, please, don't let me keep You, Dear,' Daphne said, pleasantly. 'My tea's ready to pour now, anyway.'

'Well, keep Me posted,' God said in a half-hearted way, and returned to doing what He did best.

PART TWO

6

Sylvie's Day

It was ten o'clock the next morning and Sylvie was still asleep. Liam's footsteps in the hall outside her room, as he picked up the paper from the mat, did no more than cause a slight quiver of the tips of the fingers of Sylvie's hand that lay, palm up, beside her face. She would wake in an hour or so, perhaps, stunned by the prospect of another day.

She woke at 10.30. Her hands were still lying open on the pillow at either side of her head, in what would have been a gesture of surprise or defeat if her face had carried one or other expression. But her features still held the neutrality of sleep and rendered the position of her hands meaningless. She turned her head, as her eyes opened, to look at the clock beside the bed. She was disappointed by the time. She had hoped it would be at least twelve when she woke. Today would be longer than she planned by an hour and a half.

Sylvie groaned deeply and raised herself on to her elbows, then sighed back into the pillow, turned on her side and curled her knees up to her stomach. She dragged the heap of blankets over the dark tangle of her hair, and closed her eyes to double the darkness. She managed to squeeze another half-hour of sleep from the day before the sound of a pneumatic drill forced her awake.

'Shit! Fuck! Fucking bastards!' she spat at the gas repair men. She might have slept for another hour, maybe more, if the fucking world didn't make so much noise. Why don't they leave me alone, Sylvie moaned inside the blankets. Why won't they let me sleep? Now, even if she managed to ignore the workmen and struggle back into sleep, it wouldn't be the deep oblivion she was after; she would be half aware of the day, out there, waiting to be lived in, and waking would be only a matter of time.

Sylvie lay in bed for another hour in a rage against the accidental, or not so accidental, interference of other people in her life. She savoured her unreasonableness. People going out in the morning, working in the streets — road menders, milkmen, postmen, dustmen — all of them clattering and shattering her sleep. Noisy fucking bastards, the lot of them. They didn't consider her. So they had lives to lead, work to do, so what? She didn't interfere with them. All she wanted was to be asleep. She wished they'd all die. She wished terrible accidents on them. She loathed them all, and their fucking, bloody, working lives.

She reached a crescendo of fury and then wept angrily at all the energy she had generated that she could do nothing with. It swirled around inside her with nowhere to go. Round and round, a whirligig of loathing and resentment. Each time it surged there was less room for anything else to survive in her: anything that resembled sanity, calm or pleasure cowered and shrivelled a little more.

Finally, a welcome numbness came, and feeling deadened enough, she got up.

This was how Sylvie's first day in her new flat began.

In his study above what was now Sylvie's living room Liam brooded about Grace's new employment. Yesterday morning's interview had been successful, and she had left at 8.30 this morning to begin her new incarnation as breadwinner. When Liam snorted the description at her from his side of the bed, she had calmly replied, 'Let's face it, Liam, you're not winning a lot of bread these days. We've got a mortgage to pay, you know.'

Liam had been a little taken aback by the modicum of wit she had suddenly summoned. The mildest of ironies had hitherto been a hidden accomplishment of his lovely but dull-minded young wife. He had been even more surprised when she suggested before she got up, without the slightest entreaty from him, that they make love by way of celebration.

'What's the matter? Don't you want to?' Grace had asked when Liam merely blinked at her.

'Who are you working for?' he demanded, narrowing his eyes at her once they had settled back to normal.

'Melville Harriman. I'm going to be his new PA. I told you last night. It's a PR company and Melville's the MD.'

'Dear God! You haven't even started work and you've already given up the English language.'

'What?'

'So how did you get to know this MH, the MD who does PR that you're going to PA for?'

'What?'

'I said, are you fucking him?'

'Oh, for Christ's sake, Liam.'

'I want to know if this bread you're about to win is going to choke me. I repeat. Are you fucking him, my dear?'

'No,' Grace snapped, jumping smartly out of bed. 'And I'm not fucking you, either.'

'Does this mean, now that we've uncovered your latent organizational talents, that you'll tidy up the papers on my desk and do some of the shopping, cooking and housework round here?'

The door of the bathroom slammed shut as he spoke, and then, a moment later, he heard the bath running. He continued in a defeated murmur to himself.

'No, I don't suppose it does. I expect Melville and his mobile dick will be keeping you far too busy for any of that.'

Now, it was ten o'clock and Liam sat, once again, in his study, considering this morning's lost sexual opportunity through the bottom of his first glass of whisky. He wondered if he wasn't just a little bit relieved at being deprived of making love to his wife when the suggestion had come from her. In any case, he knew all too well what a willing Grace meant.

He realized that in the excitement of Grace's new occupation (old, he corrected himself, an only too old and familiar occupation), he'd forgotten to tell her about the unspeakable Sylvie moving in. Well, if Moby Dick was going to pay his divine Grace for what she had previously done for nothing, then between her salary (salary of sin didn't sound quite right, somehow), Sylvie's rent (which he believed in like he believed in fairy gold), Daphne's rent (don't even think about Daphne) and his few pathetic writings, they might just have enough to live on.

But the list brought him out in a cold sweat. All those *people*. Suddenly a great population was going to be living in his house. Where was his solitude? What had happened to him and Grace locked alone inside the mansion of their misery? What had happened to the man who, failing God, failing self, failing Sophie and the kids, had decided to devote himself to the punishment of the flesh and spirit, with Grace as his chosen instrument?

Yes, all right, he had long ago understood that absurdity was the only road he could take, but this, now, was going too far. In the course of a single afternoon he was no longer just the sexual and spiritual clown he knew himself to be — he had, inexplicably, become a housewife and a landlady as well.

He lifted his glass in a glum toast to the God in Whom he could not believe, and hailed Him as the jokester Liam knew He was. Not so. Liam knew Him not at all. Or was it that He knew not Liam? Liam revelled in the delicious confusion of it all. The fact was, it rather looked as though his current condition was entirely of his own doing. He had the satisfaction of knowing that the circus in which he now found himself the sweeper of elephant shit was a creation of his very own. His choice of Grace's breasts as a fitting vehicle for his wizened soul had led him not by a simple route to a well-deserved stagnation, as he had thought, but to a multi-laned motorway that went nowhere — to the spaghetti junction of purgatory itself.

He tried, as an exercise in sobriety, to trace his way back through his metaphors, but got dizzy, and decided he was probably drunk enough to find the whole thing funny. He began to laugh, but didn't like the sound of it. Somehow the laugh was distorted by the alcohol in his bloodstream and came out very like a sob. It was too early in the day for tears. They were for later, for spilling over Grace's sweet feet. Best for last.

He was distracted in his meanderings by an excruciating noise coming up from the floorboards. He felt the floor tremble under his feet with the vibration from thunderous bass notes, as a recorded female voice ran up and down the musical scale, bemoaning her fate. She was accompanied in her wailing by an out-of-tune shriek from time to time at the end of a line, from a voice that was not on the recording, or very much in time with it, and which rose up from different places under the floor as its owner moved from room to room.

'... got NOBODY
... need some ... BODY
... Lord have MER ... CEEE
... ooooh I'm BER ... LUUUUE ...'

Sylvia continued to deal with the desolation of the morning, oblivious that her activities impinged in any way on her landlord upstairs. Sound helped sometimes. Whatever else she left behind at the flats of friends she had been staying with, she always took with her her portable tape machine and case of tapes; almost all of them women blues and jazz singers of past decades who had invariably come to a sticky end. The bluesy wail of female torch singers and their derivatives seemed to vibrate on exactly the same wavelength as the desperation and terror that throbbed away inside her diaphragm. Like a parent rubbing hard on a scuffed knee, the recorded sound seemed to override the inner soreness, giving a differently strong sensation in the same area of pain. It didn't always work. It helped sometimes if she howled, too, the songs giving her a safely limited structure for her cries:

'... got NO ... BODY
... need SOME ... BODY ...'

Like being your own parent and rubbing away the hurt. But sometimes she just couldn't fool herself into believing that someone was doing it for her. You can never really rub your own pain away; all the nerve endings finish up in the same place, back in your own brain. The result is just a confusion of sameness.

Today, turn up the volume and bawl her head off as she might, the trick failed. She punched the button on the tape machine and listened to the silence she had made. Silence like time. Time like space. Limitless. Unendurable. The next landmark: afternoon, tonight — hours, light years away, and anyway, only a prelude to more. *More* was the word that struck her rigid and dumb with terror. The sound of it: *more*. Long, low, sombre. The sound of the silence that was too much time. Here, alone, in her own place at last, *more* took over the space in the room that had been vacated by Nina Simone, and resonated dangerously, threatening to tip Sylvie's fear over the edge into full-blown panic.

'No more,' she whispered, like one scared to death.

A prayer, not defiance. She felt her heart pumping impossibly fast all over her body as if it had grown monstrous, and her inbreaths no longer reached as far as her lungs. She punched the tape button and the rasping cries of Simone returned:

'. . . ain't got NO . . . BODY . . .'

Nothing so far had happened this morning, except Sylvie's minor skirmish with nameless dread. She had moved from the bedroom to the living room three times, dealing with the music or simply altering her geographical position. Now, a little soothed by the music again, she began the task of getting dressed. A dismal, prolonged business because with each completed stage in the process she had to think about what was to be done when it was finished. And, in any case, the uncovering and gradual re-covering of her body involved a physical assessment.

Living in other people's houses meant eating from their fridges. While Sylvie sat on this or that sofa, worrying about what to do, or who to do it with, she ate as well as drank. She didn't sleep well, either, so there would be several visits to the fridge during the long wake of the night. Sylvie's weight increase provided a physical indicator of her mental state. She never dieted, but occasionally during the opening weeks of a new relationship, or while she was being enlightened with the Rajneeshees, she shed pounds, simply from eating a normal amount.

Sylvie pulled off her limp cotton nightie and, slack shouldered, dull eyed, gazed at herself in the mirror.

'Fat.'

She had to say the word, it wasn't enough just to experience the pain of her reflection. Look and say.

'Fat. Ugly.'

Naked, her flesh paid homage to gravity. It all sank downwards; her breasts, the rolls around her waist, her belly, the flesh of her thighs fighting for space between her legs. Too much of everything. She pulled on her knickers, the edges of which emphasized the bulge of bottom and thigh. When she snapped the hooks of her bra, her breasts conformed to an acceptable shape, but the lower edge of the bra cut into her flesh around her ribcage, making another contour where none should be. She pulled on jeans and watched her waist settle itself over the band as she zipped them up. Then a large jumper, loose and long enough to cover her hips and the undulations of her midriff. Finally, nothing was concealed; she was just a fat woman covered up. Who cares, she sneered at her reflection. What did she have to do with her day that meant it mattered what she looked like? What did she have to do, period? And then *more* was back again, as if it had never been away.

There wasn't much of a choice: either an active loathing of her physical self or the terrible mudflats of time with no horizon. And they both led back to each other in the end. Now she was dressed there was only washing her face and brushing the knots out of her dishevelled hair to keep her from the emptiness of the rest of her life.

When she had finished she walked into the living room and dropped heavily into the armchair. Her depression dropped down beside her and asked questions of her which she knew, from the years of hearing them asked, had no answer. Why was her life like this? Why was she so alone? Why did she feel so bad for so much of the time? She seemed to carry the misery of the world on her shoulders. And the why of it seemed insoluble. Her life moved from anger to despondency, to terror, or that familiar sense of doom – the unreasonable but certain knowledge that something awful was about to happen. The old name-less dread. Why me? She sniffed. Why does it have to be like this? And where *is* everyone? And why won't anyone help me?

But, as always, the questions remained surrounded by silence. There wasn't a hint of a reply.

I am Sylvie, she told herself in lieu of an answer. A heavy, dark thing, a nothing.

But today the complaints were wrong. Force of habit made them say themselves, but she did not have a blank day ahead of her. On the contrary, she realized from the depths of the armchair that suddenly seemed impossibly comfortable, she had far too much to do.

She had to sort out her social security and rent; she had to go to social services and tell them that she was permanently settled and wanted her daughter back; and she had to find a job.

Part Two

And the terror struck again. She closed her eyes with the un-manageability of all she had to do without noticing that her terror, only moments before, had been because she had nothing to do.

She was hungry. Well, it was practically lunchtime. She had noticed, on her way here yesterday, a fish and chip shop on the main road. She decided she needed something to eat before she began the awful tasks that lay ahead of her.

Sylvie returned with her parcel of fish and chips. The curtains were still drawn. She left them that way and turned on the lights, declaring it night, although the day was bright and sunny outside. As far as she was concerned, it would be night. She wanted its safety and comfort. It was no more than a hope, some atavistic memory of rolling a stone across a cave entrance and watching the fire spring to life. Safe at last.

Not so for Sylvie. The electrical brightness and the imagined darkness outside threw their own fearful shadow over her as she piled her fish and double portion of chips on to a plate and slumped with it into the armchair.

The emptiness grew inside her in spite of the food she stuffed into her mouth. The void expanded and offered her a vista, once again, of a lifetime, an eternity, of nothing. That was the fear; but, in truth, she knew she coped with that daily. There were ways of facing time. There was another fear, which combined with its impossible opposite, made *everything* intolerable, utterly insoluble. It was the terror of living, of doing anything, of filling the awful-enough void with activity. Between Sylvie's aversion to life and its doings, and her horror of what seemed an endless emptiness, there was no room for living at all. There was only panic that flickered madly between the one unspeakable option and the other. Somehow, the space between, which was where other people seemed to exist and get on with their lives, had been annihilated by the two monsters that fought for control.

This was how it was for Sylvie.

She had begun her day fearing the emptiness of the rest of her life. Now, the fear reversed. The thought of actually achieving the where-withal of a normal existence filled her with terror. What if they gave her the rent, a job, the child? Having got those things she needed to lead an independent life, she would then be obliged to get on with it, to cope like everyone else. She knew she couldn't.

70

Her head filled with images of things breaking down, or needing constant renewal – machines stopped working, sinks blocked and flooded, clothes needed repair and replacement, food ran out, a mouth that had to be fed every day, a body that grew and grew, to be clothed and cleaned, a voice that wanted things, stories, a cuddle, to know where something was. She wouldn't know where it was. Things would have to be put away in the right place so that they could be found again. Simple, practical activities that made life, in the long run, easier. But so many of them, so much, for so long. Day after day of being in charge of not letting things get out of hand. Daily routines, pushing the shopping trolley to the shops, school every morning if she got up in time, fetching every afternoon, in between sorting out, tidying up, renewing, going to work . . . For ever and ever, or until she was so old that there would be nothing left but waiting to die.

Sylvie looked around the room. Clothes, towels, sheets, most of them, so far, clean; things waiting to be put away lay on every surface. And she saw how it would be in just a few days' time. Newspapers to be thrown out, broken toys, dirty plates, overflowing ashtrays, empty wine and beer bottles, quarter-filled cups of cold tea or coffee. It wasn't that she wouldn't notice, at least some of the time, but she knew she wouldn't be able to do anything about it. Wouldn't know where to begin. And as it got worse, it would become all the more impossible. She had held off this nightmare by living a temporary life in other people's houses. They cleared up, paid the bills and kept everything going because they knew how to do it.

She didn't.

She wanted her independence, and her child, in an abstract sort of way, but she didn't want the reality of a flat for which she was responsible, or a six-year-old who needed . . . and needed . . . and needed. She told herself that she feared these things because she just couldn't cope with the practical attention they required. She hadn't the experience. She was ready to admit that, it was clearly true. But in her guts, where she didn't have to think or give names to the feeling, she just didn't *want* them. She wanted only to be left alone and not to have to do or think about anything. That was what the juices inside her screamed, when faced with the prospect of getting what every adult was supposed to want.

Fully inside her terror of a normal life, she shook with the horror of it, and knew what she really wanted: nothing, no plans, just a day-to-day vacuity. Until, of course, the thing came full circle and the horror of *that* overtook her to rack her with the other misery.

She put the empty plate on the floor. Not possible to be like this, to live like this. Not possible, at any rate, to allow the day to continue. She had no idea of the time, but she went to the bedroom, dragging herself slowly, like a wounded creature, and pulled off her clothes, dropping them on the floor and picking up the nightie she had discarded an hour and a half before. She crawled into bed, huddling beneath the blankets.

'Bastards. Bastards,' she whispered into her pillow. 'They're all bastards.'

And in seconds she was asleep. The rent, the job, the child would have to wait.

Sylvie fought her way through hours of excessive sleep. Sometime in the early hours of the next day she came fully awake, her body at least refreshed by fourteen hours of inactivity. Her mind howled, however, and demanded more unconsciousness. For a while Sylvie tossed and turned in the dark like a threatened rabbit desperately digging for a lost burrow. She gave up finally, and pushed back the covers to go in search of a bottle of Mogadon that she knew she had last seen in the bathroom, or possibly on the sofa under some clothes. In the living room, the bathroom proving fruitless, she heard the sound of pacing above her head. Slow footsteps moving up and down across the room upstairs. There were two floorboards that creaked each time a foot fell on them. Creak, creak. Creak, creak. The rhythm held. Six, seven, eight crossings and recrossings of the room.

She wasn't the only one awake, then. Liam couldn't sleep either. Well, serve him right for waking her up this morning, Sylvie thought. Maybe she ought to go and offer him a Mog. That would be neighbourly. What's he got to worry about, she grumbled to herself, spilling a tablet, and then, thinking about it, a second, into her palm and heading for the bathroom. But there was an unacknowledged comfort in the sound of the regular padding upstairs. The evidence of another life warmed Sylvie slightly, though she hardly realized it. The sound of human footsteps signalled that she was not totally alone in the world, and everyone else dead in their sleep, or gone away suddenly. She wouldn't wake to an empty planet where some cataclysm had happened and no one thought to tell her. Even for Sylvie, for whom other people represented most of what made her life insufferable, something was better than nothing at all, and footsteps in the early hours of the morning provided solace of a sort.

At last, Sylvie's pills began to take effect, so that in spite of her subversive anxiety ('they're not working . . . they're not working . . . I'll never get to sleep . . . never . . . never sleep'), she realized her body and mind had grown heavy, as if a soft, warm mist had descended, and she headed, semi-conscious and grateful, towards the tumbled haven of her bed.

Finally, Liam felt the stunning weariness of his unrequited middle-aged lust fall on him with the suddenness of a lift coming to a stop at the basement of a high building. He stopped pacing, drank a long draught of water and barely had time to get into bed before blessed unconsciousness brought an end to another of his days.

It took three days for Sylvie to gather the inner resources to go out and do what had to be done. Or rather to create the necessity. She was running out of money, and she had promised Liam that he could have the first week's rent before the weekend. Promises were easily broken, but she had to have money for food anyway. To get that she had to do everything else: tell social security that she was in permanent accommodation, get Divya back so that her social security benefit would increase, find a job so that she could have Divya back. Round and round. There was no way out of it, unless she could find another sofa to sleep on. But she discovered after a few phone calls that Sophie had rung people and told them she had organized a flat for her. Instead of offering her a bed, everybody congratulated Sylvie on having a place of her own. So there was nothing else for it, since she didn't have the energy to go away for long enough to be welcomed back to the sofas, she had to get on with her tasks.

*

Sylvie marched down the road, her thick black curls bobbing against her hunched shoulders as if set in motion by an excess of the furious energy that pushed her forward along the street. She had worked this energy up for a whole morning, pacing up and down, playing music as loud as it would go, banging drawers shut, before setting out and slamming the front door as hard as she could to give herself a final spurt that would last until she reached her destination. It was either that or slouch, drop shouldered and leaden, through the streets to occasional male cries of 'Cheer up, love, it may never happen!' These wouldn't be enticing calls. They were sneers from men who, having been rejected by or not daring to offer themselves to those they fancied on the street, could get their own back on a female too low in spirits to lift a haughty head and stare at them with contempt. The 'it may never happen' meant, in reality, 'it has happened, whatever brings a confident bitch down a peg or two, and we're delighted to see it'.

But protection against the cries of men in the street was only a side-effect, the build-up of anger and energy was needed for when she got to where she was going.

'Take a seat. We'll call you when it's your turn.'

It took an hour. Sylvie used the time to rehearse what she would say, over and over, and each time, as she imagined the answers, off-putting, downright rejection, the fury increased. By the time she was called, she had, in her imagination, been refused a dozen times in succession.

The social security clerk behind the glass booth, listening to her demands and tone of voice for the first time, registered that the woman was unreasonable, hysterical, and altered his manner and decisions accordingly. For Sylvie, however, this was not only the culmination of her fantasy rejections over the last hour, but, realistically, the latest in a long series of such scenes that went back years.

'I have a flat. *Permanent* accommodation. I need rent and I want my daughter back living with me, and I need a special payment for bedding and clothes. I want my benefit re-whatever you call it — assessed. Reassessed. Because my circumstances have changed. I'm going to have my daughter living with me. I need to be reassessed,' she repeated, shouting and tearful, banging her first on the ledge in front of the glass, as if the man behind it had already said no.

The youngish man closed his face into officialdom. He began any interview with a helpful look and a smile that did not encourage – that would be unrealistic – but showed willing. He was willing. But he had a ready mask when confronted by one of this kind. He opened the file in front of him as a matching action for the closing of his face, and leafed through the papers towards the end.

'You were here six months ago, Ms Johnson,' he said eventually, in a weary voice. 'According to your file, you said much the same thing then. My answers are going to be the same as Mr Smyth's. This is a social security office. We aren't responsible for returning your daughter to your care and control. You have to see social services about that. Your new rent will be noted and if we need to reassess your benefit, we will. But we cannot give you money as a single parent until your daughter is living with you, nor can we make a special payment under the circumstances – you don't qualify as urgently needy. So far as we are concerned, until the relevant authorities inform us otherwise, you are only entitled to a single person's benefit. Which you are receiving.'

'But I'm permanently settled. This time it's permanent. My daughter *will* be living with me. How can I get the things she needs unless you give me the money?'

He blinked at Sylvie.

'Have you thought of getting a job?'

'But I'll need the money while I'm looking for one. And I can only get a part-time job if I'm going to look after Divya. That won't pay for everything.'

The man closed the file.

'Well, we'll have to see, won't we? Get the job, go and see social security, and then come back to me.'

Sylvie was dismissed. She began to scream.

'I want my daughter back! I want money to take care of her! I want you to do something!'

The social security clerk controlled the internal tremor that afflicted him several times a day, whenever he was screamed at, wept at, or faced the fist of large, angry men through the glass barrier. He had learned techniques for calming his emotional reactions and keeping a visible control. He knew that he had nothing to say that could resolve any of this. He could only repeat, and then repeat again, if necessary, the facts that meant there was nothing, under the present circumstances, that he could do.

'You will have to go through the proper channels about your daughter, Ms Johnson. The rest will depend on our investigations. That is all we can do. Please stop shouting, it doesn't change anything. I don't want to have to have you removed.'

Not one word of this conversation was different from the last time she was here. She hadn't expected it to be any different, but for years now this had been the nearest thing she had to an occupation; the round of official interviews and arguments. It was what, when she wasn't doing nothing, she did with her time. The fact that this time she really did have permanent accommodation was a detail that she believed in possibly less even than the social security clerk. She sobbed quietly now, and the man pushed a box of paper tissues at her from his side of the counter.

'Why don't you try social services?' he suggested in a more kindly voice. He sensed now that she had used up the hysteria, that she was deflated enough to leave without any more fuss.

Sylvie stomped doggedly to social services.

'You don't have an appointment, Ms Johnson,' the receptionist concluded after checking in the book in front of her.

'I know that. I want to see my social worker. Or someone to do with my case. I'll wait.'

Sylvie looked at the clock on the wall. It was 3.50. She sat down on one of the plastic chairs ranged along the wall, and the receptionist returned to the magazine she had been reading.

At ten to five Jock Daneford arrived at reception looking harassed. He checked his watch against the wall clock.

'Sylvie, I'm sorry you had to wait, but I was with someone. What's the problem? I'm afraid I'll have to go at five on the dot.'

'I want Divya back.'

Sylvie stood with her legs braced, slightly apart, and let the rage gush towards Daneford from her dark, accusing eyes. Child stealer, they said.

Daneford sighed. Everybody sighed when they started talking to Sylvie. She thought suddenly and irrelevantly, why doesn't anyone love me?

'You know the position. Divya has to stay in care until we're sure you are in the right circumstances to look after her.'

'I've got a flat. I can stay there. It's permanent.'

The word had become a kind of open sesame by now.

'You've said that before. Who are you staying with?'

'I'm not staying with anyone. It's my flat. Two rooms and a bathroom, and a kitchen in the living room. It's mine, if I can pay the rent, which I can't if social security don't give me the money, which they won't if you don't tell them I'm having Divya back.'

'Why do you think you'll stay there longer than you've stayed anywhere else? How are you going to support Divya? Have you got a job? Have you arranged child-care?'

Questions, questions, questions.

'I can't arrange child-care until I've got a child. I'm seeing about all that. I'm getting a job. Part-time. She's my child. I want her back.'

'For the extra social security payment?'

'Why won't you believe me? I'm getting settled. I'm trying. Why won't you help me?'

'My first responsibility is to ensure that Divya will be properly cared for. Let's make an appointment for next week, and I'll come and visit you in your new flat. If you've got a job by then, we can discuss Divya's future.'

The minute hand clicked to the top of the hour. Daneford was so tired he wished he could just sleep for a week.

'I've got to go. Call me tomorrow and we'll make an arrangement. In the meantime, you'll take Divya out at the weekend, won't you? But don't make her any promises. All right?'

Sylvie had been standing biting the inside of her cheek.

'Fuck you!' Sylvie came to life. 'Stuff your visit. Keep the kid. I don't want anything to do with you, on her, or any fucking thing. You can all get fucking stuffed.'

Daneford didn't flinch as she shouted and marched to the door.

'Don't forget to pick Divya up on Saturday. She'll be expecting you. And call me tomorrow.'

The glass door swung shut before he finished speaking. He nodded to the receptionist, who raised her eyes and began to put on her jacket. Daneford wished her a good evening as they both came to the end of their working day. He held the door for her.

'Heard a new joke today, Jock.'

Daneford widened his eyes in a weary look of interest.

'What's the difference between a Rottweiler and a social worker?'

Silence.

'It's easier to get your baby back from a Rottweiler.'

Jock Daneford closed his eyes momentarily as he let the glass door swing shut behind him.

7

Crying

Someone was crying. Daphne clutched the wastepaper basket tighter against her chest and stopped on the bottom stair to listen. She thought of Eskimos and how they had dozens of different words for snow, each describing a particular condition. She wondered, tangentially, if there was a language which had no word at all for crying. Was there somewhere where people didn't do it? She promised herself that later she would take a look at the relevant section in the *Thesaurus*.

If the sound she heard coming from behind the door on the ground floor *were* snow, and if they were in Alaska, it would certainly have a special name. It was a crying of its own particular kind: small wet sobs, helpless, forlorn, as near to moaning as it could get without losing its mucous quality. The crier was almost lost in the crying. Though it was impossible to tell the age, the sex was clearly female. For a moment Daphne thought it was a child, but if it were, it was a child who had lost hope. Children cry to change things – but then, she supposed, so did adults, except when they knew that change couldn't happen. Mind you, children sometimes knew that, too, and this crying had the vulnerability of a small bird, a lost creature, of a child. There was a quiet terror about it.

Daphne was familiar with the sound of crying. She heard it often (though not as often as the other cry, at night, in the house, that she didn't like to think about at all). Two or three times a week she would be sitting in her attic and it would happen in the street. Now she thought about it, the cry in the street was different from the one she was presently hearing – almost the reverse. That one, in the street, was primarily terror, with an undertone of inescapable hopelessness. The terror made it a howl rather than a sob. She recognized it as the cry of a small child who, attempting to assert itself, had gone too far and driven a parent to the point where he or she says, 'Right, I'm going. I'm leaving.' And they walk away beyond the dawdling distance that a child knows can be caught up with. The howl from the child was the realization that it *had* been left. The worse thing in the world had happened, and it was alone for ever.

Daphne had spent weeks wondering why this particular mother and child parted company on the street outside her window with such regularity, causing the child's despair to carry through the air, up into her window and strike like a blade at the pit of her stomach. Finally, it dawned on her that there wasn't any child, or any crying, except what she could hear in her inner ear. She placed it in the muddled territory where ghosts, hallucinations and memory cohabit.

That there was this tangled place, Daphne didn't doubt. Nor did it bother her that it was inhabited by a mutually exclusive bundle of explanations. The rational, mysterious, psychological and psychic could all live happily together in Daphne's mind. It didn't matter what you called it, she still heard the child crying out in the street. She lived with it, and knew that it was something to do with her, and that it was nothing to do with her.

Logic was another neurosis Daphne didn't have.

But this cry that she heard as she had come down the stairs was flesh-real; it came from a creature of bone and blood. Although, as she stood listening, it had become clear that it was not the cry of a child, because now there was a child's voice soothing, comforting, but tinged with fear, and the crying continued above it.

'Don't cry. Please, don't cry. It's all right. I'll look after you,' the child's voice was saying to the sad, sobbing creature in the room behind the closed door that was dangerously near to the cupboard under the stairs.

The crying continued, and a rhythm developed between the sobbing and the comforting so that Daphne could almost see two people rocking together, back and forth.

'Oh, dear. Oh, dear. Oh, dear,' Daphne mumbled softly to herself, in unwitting counterpoint to the rhythm of crying and reassurance, holding the wastepaper basket with one hand and pushing the crown of her hat down over her head with the other as if she thought it were in danger of falling off.

*

Upstairs, flustered and disturbed, she poured herself a glass of sherry, and after a sip or two felt a little steadier. As she felt her stomach warm through with alcohol, she told God about the crying downstairs.

'That's a shame,' said God. He meant it genuinely, He didn't like to hear about unhappiness, but He was still a little wary, because although Daphne had explained about the human race, it hadn't stopped them making what they liked to think of as a joyous noise unto Him. So He added, 'Well, I hope you're not blaming Me.'

'No, dear,' Daphne reassured Him. 'I was just thinking how it makes me feel. Even though I've come over happy lately, there's still all this crying, and it does give me a bit of a twinge.'

'Well, you'd better see a psychiatrist or something. Unhappiness and twinges are more their line than Mine.'

'I was only *saying*,' Daphne said defensively. 'There's no need to be unpleasant.'

'Sorry,' God said unto Daphne. 'It's just that I'm in a broody mood at the moment. Couldn't we continue this chat when I'm feeling more sociable?'

Daphne left it at that and finished her sherry, though she couldn't help feeling that He might have been a bit more sympathetic. Even if human unhappiness wasn't His fault, it did no harm to anyone, not even the Lord, to be civil.

Daphne, having rather given up on God for the time being, lit herself a cigarette and turned instead to the *Thesaurus* for enlightenment. *Cry*, in the index, led her to the section *Human Cry*, just after *Stridor: harsh sound*, and just before *Ululation: animal sounds*. The section was too general for her needs, so she followed the reference number after the word *Lamentation* which had a section of its own. In it was *weep*, and she read what followed. It seemed to be what she was looking for:

> *weep, wail, greet* (what was that doing there?); *shed tears,*
> *burst into t.; give way to t., break down, cry, bawl* (that was better),
> *cry one's eyes out; cry out, shriek, ululate; sob, sigh, moan, groan,*
> *suffer; snivel, grizzle, blubber, pule* (she didn't like the sound of
> that), *whine, whinge, whimper.*

So, that was that. Somehow it didn't seem as satisfying as she imagined the Eskimo thesaurus entry for snow would be. And it displayed a decidedly stiff upper lip. *Snivel, grizzle, whinge*, indeed! Mr Roget obviously had an opinion about the virtues of self-control. Where, for example, was *have a jolly good cry*, the emotional equivalent of a nice cup of tea? She was sure any Eskimo worth his snow would do better. She was satisfied, though, to find her own thought processes vindicated with the inclusion – a nod in her, Eskimo-inclined, direction, she was certain – of *blubber*.

Daphne glanced at the previous section. It was *Rejoicing*. She'd eat her hat if that Roget didn't approve of rejoicing, provided it wasn't done with an unseemly excess of emotion. Before that, was *Dejection. Seriousness*. Ho hum. A pattern. Good, bad. Up, down. High, low. Hi ho. She flicked to the beginning of the category: it was entitled *Personal Emotion*. Yes, quite. So, how did it go?

> *Joy. Suffering. Pleasureableness. Painfulness. Content. Discontent.*
> *Regret. Relief. Aggravation. Cheerfulness. Dejection. Rejoicing.*
> *Lamentation. Amusement. Tedium . . .*

That would do, thank you very much. It was getting tedious, Daphne thought, no longer amusing, and she was beginning to regret she had started on the painful business of personal emotion because she could feel dejection, to say nothing of aggravation and discontent, setting in with a vengeance.

She dropped the book into the newly emptied wastepaper basket.

'Silly old bugger,' she said. 'About as much use as God on a broody day.'

It probably wasn't Roget's fault, though. All the roller-coaster feeling: feeling good, now feeling bad . . . Whoops! Here we go feeling good again. It wasn't Roget's invention. You couldn't blame him that people liked to think in pairs, any more than, according to God, you could blame God. Someone ought to write a thesaurus of in-between words that lived in the fuzzy middle between one feeling and another, which was where most people lived, most of the time, Daphne thought. Where were all the definitions for feeling middleish? Perhaps everybody felt middleish all the time, but when they went to the *Thesaurus* to find a name for what they were feeling, all they could find was happy or sad, so they had to suppose they felt one of those instead, and then there they were, in a condition of either euphoria or despondency, whatever they thought they felt to start with.

She wondered if she ought not to offer this idea to the sobbing woman downstairs, who might not feel so awful after all, but perhaps just didn't feel deliriously happy, and couldn't find a name for her condition other than miserable.

Daphne shook her head at herself. Better not to interfere. And, in all honesty, she doubted from the sound of it that the woman sobbing felt middling about anything.

She reached down and took up the *Thesaurus* she had thrown away. If she was going to write the Book of Love and Liam, she'd need prompting for all those words on the tip of her tongue that flatly refused to be remembered as soon as she wanted to put them down on a piece of paper. But, when she thought back to her writing days, she recalled that she had never once found the word she wanted in the *Thesaurus*, and usually forgot the sentence she had intended to write in the first place while she was looking it up, so she threw the book back into the wastepaper basket and emptied her overflowing astray on top of it.

Her thoughts on the subject of the *Thesaurus* done with, and her cigarette finished, Daphne could no longer avoid opening the door to her attic room. She had known since she sat down with her sherry that someone was outside, standing quietly, waiting for her to come out.

She knew it wasn't Liam. If it had been footsteps on the stairs which alerted her, they had only impinged on her inner ear. Whoever it was had crept up the stairs tiptoed and shoeless. That was hardly Liam's style. And if it wasn't Liam she didn't want the privacy of her attic invaded. But the fact was she *knew* someone was standing outside, and her solitary comfort was breached by her sense of being waited for.

Daphne poked her velvet-hatted head cautiously around the door she held a quarter open against the intruder. In fact, no one was standing, waiting outside her door. Divya was sitting quietly on the top step of Daphne's landing, leaning against the banister. She had been looking directly at Daphne's door. Now, without moving her gaze, she looked straight at Daphne, her face expressionless.

'Can I do something for you?' Daphne asked, narrowing her eyes in what she hoped would be an off-putting, witchy way. Divya seemed to be unmoved. She stared at Daphne as if *she* were intruding on *her* privacy.

'I'm just sitting here. Why can't I sit here?'

Daphne forgot about the invasion for the moment and was caught up in the thrill of debate.

'Who said you couldn't? Did I say you couldn't? You can sit where you like. None of my business. All I said was, can I do something for you?'

'No,' the child said, still with an expression that suggested that Daphne's appearance had spoiled her examination of the door.

'Good. That's all right, then,' Daphne said and, retracting her head, she closed the door.

'Huh!' she said to herself with a little sniff, as she sat down again at her desk. 'Huh!'

She pulled the Underwood towards her and got from the drawer the sheet of paper with the single sentence *Her life had been a closed book since 1955* and the number – *1* – in the top left-hand corner typed on it. She rolled the paper into the machine, wedged her hat firmly down on her crown and wrote:

Now Dermot had pierced her solitude.

She sniffed and exed out *pierced her solitude* and typed *come into her life* instead. Then after a moment staring at the page, she crossed out what she had just typed and wrote something else.

Her life had been a closed book since 1955. Now Dermot sat in the room below hers, little knowing that soon he would be flicking through her pages.

She stopped and smiled with satisfaction at her work. So here was the beginning of her first book for thirty-five years. She had a great urge to pop on her coat and go to the telephone box at the corner of the road to ring her old publisher and let him know his forthcoming good fortune. Then it crossed her mind that perhaps Whatshisname had retired. Someone new would be sitting at his desk. She felt sorry about that. He'd been a nice old thing. But what an opportunity for

some bright young spark. Not only a new book from Daphne Drummond, but the chance to reprint the other three. A publishing coup, it
would be. A sensation. Daphne half recollected a writer who had all
but disappeared and then made a great splash by suddenly publishing
a new novel after years of silence.

'Oh, my Lord,' Daphne whispered to herself in excitement and
almost bit her tongue because she didn't mean it like that, and didn't
want to interrupt His Broodiness. She visualized the new book, with a
smart modern cover, her name written large on the front and the
spine. She saw it multiplied in bookshop windows, and herself signing
copies as people handed them to her, smiling gratefully. Cuttings
would come in the post. Young men would interview her reverentially.
They would take her photograph.

DAPHNE DRUMMOND WRITES AGAIN!

She'd offer that to the brash young men if they didn't think of it for
themselves. It would be fun, and what was wrong with a bit of fun,
she asked herself, as she experienced something niggling at the back of
her mind. So what if she'd only written two sentences so far? Hadn't
all her books had only two sentences to begin with? And why shouldn't
it be good enough? And why wouldn't anyone want to read what a
forgotten old woman had to say about love?

Daphne's smile faded. She stared at her work for a long time and
then abruptly ripped the sheet of paper out of the typewriter, crumpled
it up, threw it into the wastepaper basket and put another clean one
into the Underwood. She typed the number – *1* – in the top left-hand
corner and wrote:

*Alice's life had been a closed book since 1955. Now, Michael had come
into her life. He sat drinking, in his study below Alice's attic. He had,
as yet, no way of knowing that he would fall in love with her. But
Alice knew.*

Daphne nodded slowly at the paragraph on the paper, her face still
serious. She had the first paragraph of a novel that she hoped to write.
With any luck it would be more honest than the last three. That would
do.

Daphne sat back, and then had another thought. She took out a pencil and a pad of plain paper from the drawer. There were – she counted – forty-four words in the paragraph. She made some calculations, based on a daily word rate of a hundred and multiplying by thirty. She thought that a hundred words a day was a nice, manageable amount. That made three thousand words per month at the rate of a hundred a day. Multiplying by twelve gave her a total of thirty-six thousand words a year. She thought back and remembered that seventy to eighty thousand words was the approximate length of a novel. Call it seventy thousand, there was no need to make things very difficult for herself; she could say what she wanted to say in seventy thousand words, surely. She did a bit more arithmetic. If she wrote a hundred words a day, every day, she would finish her novel in two years. It was possible that she might miss a day here and there, but there was an extra three thousand words to allow for that.

It worked out perfectly. In two years she would have finished her novel, just as she was ready to make her move. She was more than satisfied with herself. It was a realistic plan. Her hat and the novel would mature together. Everything would be ready at the right time. How handy.

Daphne, already thinking creatively, suddenly had a new concept: she would buy herself a little motorized caravan with the advance – surely she would get enough? Her bagladydom would not be compromised by that. She wanted mobility, and becoming a baglady wasn't intended to be a punishment. She had no desire to be cold, wet and miserable for the rest of her days. Daphne approved the notion of becoming a baglady with a van. There was no reason why she couldn't stop and rummage through skips and rubbish bins for useful items in proper baglady fashion. Old tyres, wire coat-hangers, almost empty tins of paint, discarded hubcaps, would not have to be overlooked. She had no particular feeling about waste or recycling, or anything like that, but she was pleased that she would be less likely to come away empty-handed from her rummaging – she hated disappointment in all its forms – and she liked the bang-up-to-date modernity of the idea. A mobile baglady sounded properly vigorous and up to the minute. She fancied herself with her foot well down on the accelerator (it was true, she would have to learn to drive), speeding across the country, racing up and down motorways, waving at the other drivers as she overtook them. She would be a Boadicea of a baglady. An ancient warrior of the road. A modern wanderer. She hoped they made the caravans with automatic windows and lots of switches and buttons. She wanted the very latest technology at her fingertips. Daphne was going to be in the vanguard of bagladydom.

She longed to share her plans with Liam, but he wasn't quite ready for them. The time would come, of course, but she would have to take things gradually. He wasn't as adapted to the modern world as she was. It was something he had yet to learn. One of many.

However, for all her reading, writing and arithmetic, and her plans for the future, Daphne had not quite dislodged the knowledge of the little girl who was, she was certain, still sitting outside her door and making her feel, very much against her will, quite uncomfortable.

'If you think I'm a sweet little old lady who'll give you biscuits and orangeade, you're quite wrong,' Daphne announced as she opened the door fully and stood on the threshold of her attic with her arms folded.

Divya looked unconcerned.

'I don't like biscuits and orangeade.'

'Well, that's good, because I'm not going to give you any.'

'Good,' the child said, turning her gaze away to the window on the half-landing below her.

'Well . . . good,' Daphne responded feebly, wondering what to do next. Retreating back into her attic and closing the door behind her was an admission of defeat, but she felt at a loss standing full square in the doorway, looking as though she meant business, but having none to conduct. The child, clearly, could sit where she was all day, staring into the distance. Daphne tried to relax her posture by leaning her shoulder against the doorframe in something of a slouch, so that she looked, she hoped, more like someone just hanging around, waiting to chat to passers-by.

'So who are you?' Daphne tried.

Divya didn't look at her.

'I live here,' she said.

'So do I. That's a coincidence, isn't it? Have you lived here long?'

'I live downstairs with my mother. I came yesterday.'

'I've seen her coming and going. I didn't know she had any children.'

Divya gave Daphne a withering look.

'Where have you been staying, dear?' Daphne asked.

'None of your fucking business.'

Daphne warmed to the sullen little girl, even as her toes itched to kick her downstairs.

'I used to live downstairs, you know,' she said casually. 'When I was your age. When I was a little girl.'

It was clear from Divya's lack of response that she cared less about Daphne as a little girl than she did about her as an old woman, but after a moment of silence, she spoke.

'Did you hear the crying?'

'Yes. When I was emptying the wastepaper basket. It was your mother, wasn't it?'

Divya glared at her.

'I mean the other crying. Did you hear it when you lived down there?'

'There was just my mother and me. What other crying?'

Divya shrugged.

'Just some crying, sometimes. On the landing outside. I've heard it twice. But my mum says there's nothing.'

Daphne felt uncomfortably that she knew what Divya meant, but pushed it firmly out of her mind.

'Have you looked?'

'I couldn't see nothing, and the crying stopped when I opened the door. Doesn't matter.'

'What's your name?'

Divya snapped back into sullenness.

'Why do you want to know?'

'Well, I only thought, if you were going to sit there a lot, I'd have to step over you when I wanted to go downstairs. I thought it would be nicer if I said, "Excuse me, Whateveryournameis" instead of just "Excuse me."'

Daphne beamed expectantly in the silence, but nothing came.

'My name is Daphne,' she added. 'So you can say, "None of your fucking business, *Daphne*" in future. It's more neighbourly, don't you think?'

'You're potty,' Divya snapped.

'Go on, try it: "You're potty, *Daphne*."'

Divya's face quivered ever so slightly. A smile very nearly threatened the corners of her mouth.

'My mum was upset this morning,' she said in a tone that was less harsh.

Daphne scratched her hat.

'Well, it happens, dear,' she said. 'I used to cry sometimes. As a matter of fact, I used to cry a lot. But I don't now.'

'Why not?'

'Because I've become happy,' Daphne stated matter-of-factly.

'Stupid,' Divya said, equally matter-of-factly.

'No, I'm clever. Being happy is a jolly clever thing to do, so I must be clever. Not many people can do it, I can tell you. Well, it's been delightful talking to you, dear, but I've got work to do now. I expect we'll bump into each other again.'

Divya watched Daphne give her a little wave and turn back into her room, closing the door behind her. She hugged her knees up tightly to her chest and continued to sit on the top stair, dividing her attention between the window on the half-landing and Daphne's door.

Daphne, try though she might, was unable to get the thought of Divya out of her mind. It annoyed her, it wasn't what she wanted. She had just got things so well worked out. Her tasks: Liam, the book and getting ready for bagladyhood. They were enough; just right to occupy her for the next two years. They were to be her only concerns. She was happy and productive at last. The newcomers downstairs were no part of her plan.

Daphne looked grumpily out of her attic window on to the disordered patch of front garden that no one cared for. Her eyebrows stretched towards each other, making deep vertical folds in the skin between them. Her lips pouted crossly and the nostrils at the end of her sharp nose flared as she snorted her annoyance.

She pulled off her hat and examined it. It was coming on very nicely. There were shiny spots all around the brim and the crown was streaked with grease. She stuck it back on her head, and pulled it down over her brow with both hands, swivelling it to get it firmly wedged.

What worried her more than the fact that Divya and her mother were extraneous matter in the house where she and Liam were going to find love were her feelings about the child with the mother who wept. She most certainly didn't want those feelings, thank you very much. She had better, happy, future things to contemplate. She did not want to think about what she thought about that sullen, rude, sad child who pretended to stare out of the window. And she had absolutely no desire to concern herself with the strange question Divya had asked about the mysterious crying in the hall on the ground floor.

Too late.

Too late.

And just when everything was going so nicely.

She knew what the crying was. She could see she wasn't going to get away with thinking happy, future thoughts exclusively.

The cupboard under the stairs. Oh, dear. Oh, dear.The cupboard under the stairs. Someone once – before Daphne and her mother lived there – had put a door across the triangular space created underneath the rising staircase. Someone who thought what a good idea it was to do something useful with it. A nice little storage cupboard, you could never have too many, big enough for brooms and mops and half-used tins of paint. Big enough for a small child. But that wasn't what was intended. The door-maker had a practical, economical turn of mind.

Whenever Daphne was locked in the cupboard she would try to fend off the dreadful blackness by imagining its maker. It was a man, though perhaps the idea for the cupboard would have come from a woman.

She pictured a nice, large man with a bland, pleasant face and big hands, who found it easy to be amused. The corners of his eyes and mouth were always close to smiling, even while he was concentrating on measuring and cutting wood, or holding nails between his teeth as he hammered others into the framework. He was in shirt sleeves, a stripy, collarless shirt, and braces held up his corduroy work trousers. He liked to do things right, this door-maker. He wanted things to fit, even if no one else would notice a small gap here or there that let the light in. He liked to work with his hands. It pleased him to do useful things.

Daphne came to love him. She knew how sad he would be to know the use to which his handy cupboard was put. She saw how he would look at her when she summoned him up to tell him what had happened, and his nearly smiling mouth and eyes would droop and glisten with pity. It was all wrong, it was wrong, she could almost hear him say. But she didn't want him to blame himself. Little as she was, she knew it wasn't his fault. He hadn't *meant* his cupboard to be put to such a purpose. He had children of his own. Daphne knew how he held them in his strong arms and swung them around, laughing at their shrieks. Handfuls of squealing children being swung safely in the big, smiling man's arms. But he always looked at her so sadly, shaking his head at his own helplessness. He could build cupboards and swing his children, but ghost-creature that he was, he could only look at Daphne with his incorporeal face set in sorrow and wish he hadn't made everything fit so tightly and the lock so strong. And then he would go, or fade rather, into the blackness that seemed to move forward of its own accord to swallow him up, and Daphne would be left all alone without even a kindly ghost for comfort.

Then she would lose control. The blackness was a beast. Terror came. She would curl up with her cheek on the floor at the bottom of the door. The tiny gap that allowed the door to open and close without scraping the floorboards let in the merest sliver of light. Daphne would put her face to it as if her desperation could make her flat, dimensionless, like a sheet of paper, and allow her to slide out. The amount of light was so small that it didn't affect the total blackness in the cupboard, it was almost as if a yellow line had been painted on the floorboards beneath the door that extended no more than an inch beyond it.

Daphne would beg to be let out, calling through the crack to the only person she had to call to.

'Please, Mummy. Please, please, please . . . Mummy . . . Mummy . . .'

But all that happened was that the crack of light disappeared as her distraught mother pressed the snake-shaped draught-excluder along the base of the door, and then there was the sound of the living-room door being slammed shut against Daphne's diminishing cries.

And then there was nothing but waiting.

And then there wasn't even that.

Daphne learned the full meaning of helplessness during her times in the black cupboard under the stairs on the ground floor of that house, though it wasn't until later that she put the word to the experience. It was not then, at four, five and six, part of her vocabulary, even though it was a large part of her existence.

It was only at the very beginning, the first two or three occasions she was incarcerated, that Daphne truly believed each time that she would be left there for ever. She was so young then that the thought 'until she died' could not occur to her – she had not understood about death yet. So *for ever* meant exactly what it was supposed to mean; an unending stretch of time into unimaginable blackness.

Her demented mother, crazed by the taunting of demons, would pick her up under the armpits and deposit her on the floor in the cupboard.

'Devil ... you little Devil ... You have to be put away ... put you in the cupboard ... keep you away from me ... Devil, with all your voices and your faces ...'

The door would click shut, the key snap the lock in place. She had been put into a cupboard in the dark, and the door shut on her, and why should it ever open again?

When it happened, her mother was not her mother. A change would come over her face, like a curtain that swished across her features and left behind a terrible fear in her eyes, and a twisted mouth, the lips working against each other, the teeth biting them so hard they bled. If she could have trusted her *mother* to come and take her out of the terrible black place, she could not hope that the changed person her mother became – all of a sudden, out of a queer silence that later she learned to recognize – would ever think of her again once the key had secured the door.

Hardly out of infancy, Daphne knew no hope, but that, perhaps, was not the worst. Later, repeated experience and the ability to recognize her mother in both states let her suppose that eventually the strangeness would pass and she would indeed be released. But what that told her was that it would inevitably – *inevitably* – happen again. She *would* be let out but by the same understanding, she would be put back again. And that was possibly worse than hopelessness. She hardly knew. Was the inevitability of *more* worse than the hopelessness of nothing? It was to be many years before she gave up lurching between the two and found another path to tread. It had happened late, very late; but it had happened, she had got away from that cupboard and the repeating blackness of her life.

And now, five decades later, the ground floor had another mother and child, and there was crying in the hall again, and she, Daphne, who had finished with all that, had to go back into it, and listen.

Daphne tried to find some happier memories to counter her deepening gloom. She had lived with her mother for fifteen years. The demons came at intervals, so there were times when everything was all right, or right enough. But all Daphne could remember was the cupboard, as if the blackness in there had blanked out any light at all from her past life.

She reached for moments of quiet. She knew her mother had not been cruel, only mad. There had been smiles and cuddles, stories and mealtimes. It was a bad business in those days, being a woman alone with a child, but there were moments of love between them. Daphne knew there had been, but only in the thinking part of her head. Memory had lost everything except the dangerous silence and ensuing madness. It seemed to her so sad that she could not remember anything good about her mother. It was as if a beautiful painting had been lost in a fire and there was nothing more than a pile of ashes to indicate that it had ever existed.

As a young woman, Daphne had pursued the darkness, perhaps because she had lost her memory of the light. As a child she had sometimes crept into the cupboard of her own accord, as if she had come to need the blackness. Later, after the poor creature, her haunted and distraught mother, had opened her veins to let the demons run out of her, Daphne launched herself into the world of Bohemia. An orphan, a waif of fifteen, who scribbled sadness on exercise paper, she took to the pursuit of the dark as if it were her own lost country and she an exile fighting to get home.

It was a well-populated land. In London, Paris and Berlin there were plenty of people who loved to gaze into the crevices and rat holes of despair. They found Daphne there and taught her how to re-create the darkness – how to use sex as if it were a cup of poison, how to make misery physical, with a suicidal excess of drink and opiates. She didn't need much tuition, she had a knack for it. Death was a dark glory, a pose for most of them, who were only passing through. It was a pose for Daphne, too, but it summoned the reality she had known. She was not equipped to play games with darkness and death. She wore black. Everyone wore black, but Daphne had real blackness inside. When her friends moved on to a more frivolous view of life, Daphne was stuck. She was an embarrassment to them. She did not behave properly; she cried when crying was considered inappropriate, she slept with everyone but was stupid enough to get pregnant. It was no longer fashionable to have babies that died. The times changed and people left their cupboards, but Daphne's was still locked, and she hadn't realized that everyone else had had the key inside with them all along.

Silly girl. Foolish girl. Craving unhappiness and finding it all too easily. Well, that was enough now. Daphne shook herself. She had given up unhappiness. Finally, she had had enough of it. And only just in time. She would have no more to do with it. Daphne Drummond no longer wanted to be miserable. She had decided to take all her unhappy decades and crush them, like the paper on which she had written her sad little stories, into balls between her palms. She would learn to juggle with them; two, then three, then who knew how many, throwing them up and catching them all. She would paint them bright colours and balance them on the end of her nose. She would enjoy herself during her final decade or two, she had told herself.

But she was shaken by the discovery that the blackness hadn't been dispersed by the brightly coloured balls and her determination to keep them flying about in the air. A small child with a weeping mother had brought the blackness back so vividly that Daphne now strongly suspected it might never have really gone away.

Well, the child and her mother were not Daphne's problem, Daphne told herself sternly. No, not at all. But perhaps the mysterious crying was. For all her refusal to acknowledge the closed door on the ground floor, it was a fact that she had come back to live here. Was it the old longing for the dark reasserting itself? She sensed sabotage close to home. She had dismissed misery from her life? Then why was she living here where the memories were suddenly so strong, in spite of her determined rejection of them, that they made sounds out in the world which even other people could hear?

Daphne considered her two-year plan. Loving Liam, writing the new novel, buying the caravan thing and taking off on her wanderings. All very well and good, but things were not as simple as they had seemed. Her new-found *joie de vivre* was looking like no more than a thin pie-crust with a decidedly murky filling. Did one have to go on being haunted for ever by ancient accidents? Was it not possible to say no, at long last, enough of that, and laugh a little at the end?

'Oh, dear. Oh, dear. Oh, dear,' Daphne moaned softly to herself, clutching her black velvet head in her hands and rocking softly back and forth. 'This is an awful nuisance,' she muttered in her small, nearly 69-year-old voice. 'An awful nuisance.'

8

Liam Dreaming

There was a cold spot at the north pole of Liam's head. His fingers, reaching up to investigate, found smooth skin where they had expected to find hair. Their further exploration traced an intriguingly perfect circle of hairlessness at the top of his cranium.

Head cold because no hair to keep it warm. Twenty per cent of body heat lost through top of head – and that through a head fully equipped with insulating thatch. Liam's arctic circle.

But I am not a bald person, Liam thought. Not even balding. Something's happened. Time suddenly alarmed him. What had he been doing when he first noticed his chilly pate? There *was* nothing before that. Nonsense. Always something before something. Life's like that. One thing follows another. What was before, then? *Nothing.*

A new chill, this time of fear, rushed through him. Lost in time. It occurred to him to check the rest of himself. He looked down. Bare feet in open sandals poked out from dark-brown material that reached to his ankles.

Oh, oh. Strange.

What's happening? Think harder. Make the brain work. Work. Work. Or else. Before the sense of coldness at the top of his head, he was . . . he was . . . he was . . .

. . . heading, finally blessed with exhaustion, to bed.

To sleep.

The terrible anxiety was dissolved by a rush of relief that spread through him as if it were life-giving stuff pumped by his heart. I am asleep, he understood with gratitude. It was a reprieve. I am dreaming, he dreamt. Thank God.

It was all right now. He gave himself permission to continue the dream. But consciousness would not leave once it had been summoned.

He continued to dream, but also continued to be aware that he was dreaming. His rational mind ticked away, making sense of the images his dream self concocted.

So. Tick, tick, tick. Sandals, habit, tonsure. The sun shone a cold bright spring light, but he was in shadow. The chill his skull felt radiated from stone: flags beneath his feet, vaulting above his head, slabs of cold stone walls running beside him. The sun, shining through open arches separated by fluted columns, cut diagonal lozenges of light into the shaded flagstones.

Cloisters.

There was silence, except for the ringing flap, flap, flap of his leather soles against the stone. In the centre, the bright, midday-lit lawn. Green. Soft grass, tended lovingly, but not crushed by feet. An oak in the centre. Old, gnarled, deformed into a twisted beauty by time. Thick trunk, spreading canopy, brilliant with new leaf growth. The base, where trunk met lawn, wide and solid. Unseen roots spreading well beyond the edges of the green. Very likely beyond the cloisters. Quietly, invisibly, under foot, under stone. The secret network that was the power beneath its visible manifestation.

Liam's rational mind watched Liam the dreamer walk slowly through the cloisters, his tread as calm and evenly spaced as the cloister columns, or the gentle beating of his quiescent heart. It was all peace. He was all peace. Time had forgiven him and gone away. Only the rational mind knew about past and future, but, awed by the inner silence, kept its knowledge to itself, not wishing to disturb such serenity.

Searching for the certainty of God, he whispered to himself so that the dreamer should not overhear. Walking at a measured pace, keeping quiet, maintaining, with the gentle rhythm and silence, an open place, available, though not striving, to be filled. This was his task, he told himself, the dream monk's timeless task. No hurry, no expectation, no fear.

Liam's rational mind basked in the tranquillity of his dream, as if it were sunshine and he a holiday-maker who knew he had to make the most the foreign heat. He willed his dream on, savouring everything, paying attention to small details, noticing corners and crevices, because, apart from the pleasure of doing so, he knew the dream would continue while he held its parts in his gaze. He was not inside Liam the dream monk, but floated a little above and behind him, like a shadow, or an echo, peering, as it were, over his shoulder so that he got a similar though not identical view. The non-dreaming Liam saw what the dream one saw, but a little aslant. It could not be avoided, he could not become the reality of which he was a shadow, so he couldn't see through those eyes. But it was close enough, and the extra awareness of being in, but not of, the dream was a sort of compensation for the slight twinge he felt at being a little to one side.

There was no one else in the cloisters apart from Liam and his shadow, no sound even of life and activity behind the walls. Liam the dreamer found nothing strange about this; dream creatures know no strangeness. His shadow noticed, not being of dream substance, but understood the nature of dream and simply enjoyed the improbable solitude. He was happy to follow close behind the other as he walked unhurriedly, going nowhere, around the echoing cloister.

Liam longed not to wake up, but the longing itself indicated that he would – that he was already waking. Time took on the nature of loss as the dream faded and he struggled for more of it against consciousness. He wanted to perambulate for ever with his dream self in the quiet place that required only that of him.

At the foot of his bed a black-eyed creature stared at him, its head dropped to one side, on to a scrawny shoulder, as if it thought a different angle might make more sense of what it saw. Liam stared back for a moment, still not quite out of his cloister, before the shock of the intrusion hit him.

'You were crying,' Divya said. 'I've never seen a man cry.'

Liam automatically touched his lower eyelid; it was damp.

'What the hell are you doing in my bedroom?'

Divya shrugged, unperturbed.

'Just looking.'

Liam sat up, still shaken. He gazed at the apparition. Divya was wearing a pair of her mother's size fourteen jeans, pulled up and belted with a scarf around her armpits, and gathered round her waist with another scarf. Her lips were painted twice their natural thickness in vivid crimson and her eye sockets ringed with black kohl, like a startled racoon. Two bright red circles indicated her as yet unformed cheekbones, and made her look as if she had just received a grave insult. Liam did not want this replacement for his cloisters.

'You live downstairs. You can't wander into other people's rooms. Your place is downstairs. Go away. Where's your mother?'

'Why were you crying?'

'That's none of your business. I wasn't crying.'

She regarded him with a look that suggested he was very stupid.

'Yes, you were. My mum cries. I don't cry. Crying's for babies. It's silly. It's silly when grown-ups cry.'

'No, it's not. People cry when they're unhappy. People are entitled to cry. Aren't you ever unhappy?'

Divya seemed to have a talent for engaging people in unwanted disputation.

'It's none of your fucking business.'

'Well, then, what I do when I'm asleep is none of *your* fucking business. Or being in my room. So clear off, little girl, or I'll tell your mother.'

'You can't, she's asleep. She doesn't wake up till late, unless some fucker wakes her up.'

'Well, I can tell her later.'

'She won't care. So there!'

'So there, yourself!' Liam snapped back.

Divya poked out her tongue. Liam responded with his. They were at stalemate.

'You're a horrible little girl, aren't you?' Liam lifted himself to sitting position.

'So are you.'

'Don't be ridiculous.'

'Don't you be ridiculous.'

Liam's eyes clamped shut in a massive blink.

'What's the matter with your face?'

Liam took a deep breath.

'I'm going to get out of bed now, and I've got no clothes on, so you had better leave right now.'

'So what?'

It occurred to Liam that he wasn't actually awake, that his cloister dream had turned into this nightmare of six-year-old dialogue. It was the only reasonable answer to the mystery of his participation in it. He decided to make himself wake up and disappear the small monster at the foot of his bed.

It didn't work. She was still there. He was awake.

Divya was used to wandering around large houses where the rooms belonged to no one in particular for very long. Fostering had not worked for her, so most of her life had been spent in community homes. In the beginning there had been too much coming and going from Sylvie's various set-ups for her to be settled with a family, and by the time it was decided to stop letting Sylvie have her because the disruption was too great, she was not a child who could easily be placed. She seemed to have started talking tough as soon as she started talking. A variety of weary child-care workers speculated whether her first words had been 'Shut up!' or 'Mind your own fucking business!'

The description 'impish' came to the most kindly disposed minds when they saw her; but 'satanic' had also been used. At six, her coal-black eyes gleamed a warning that she'd better not be messed with. She had Sylvie's dark, wildly curly hair that her carers kept short, though it remained a chaotic mop, to make the regular delousing sessions easier.

Finding a private space of one's own in a large house with an ever-changing procession of children going through it was no easy task, so Divya had solved the problem by taking all the space to be hers. She would wander in and out of rooms regardless of their purpose or ownership. It didn't matter to her whether they were other children's dormitories, public areas like the kitchen or television room, or the office; as far as she was concerned, they were all hers. She was oblivious to the notion that other people's possessions marked their territory. She had been there before most of the others, children and staff, and the place belonged to her. She would make this point by curling up to sleep in beds that were not hers, or walking into the office in the middle of a staff meeting, and squatting on the floor with paper and pens she found by rummaging through the desk drawer, while the assembled adults stared at her, uncertain how to assert their authority when she didn't even acknowledge their existence.

She was known as Goldilocks, not merely ironically for her black hair, but also for her capacity to use things that were not hers. Mostly, she was indulged by the staff and some of the children. They would groan impatiently at the sight of her mess of hair poking out from beneath the wrong covers, and a member of staff would come and carry her back to her own bed. When she interrupted meetings, the staff would point out that the meeting was private, just as a gesture, and when she ignored them, get on with their business as if she wasn't there. Occasionally, there would be a resident who could not cope emotionally with a small child who seemed to deny them their space. She was hit from time to time, but violence appeared to have no more effect than ignoring her. She was just as likely to end up in the attacker's bed the following night. The workers learned to keep an eye on her and recognize who was likely to become aggressive as a result of her behaviour. She never thanked anyone when they rescued or protected her. It was as if she noticed nothing outside her own desire to be here or there or wherever. Someone likened her to one of those cartoon creatures, Mr Magoo, they suggested, who causes chaos wherever he goes — houses collapse, people crash into things, objects fall from great heights just after he has passed by — but he carries on in complete ignorance of the destruction in his wake.

Liam stared at the child at the end of the bed, done up like a harlot, dressed like a clown. Her domestic inexperience looked like, and perhaps was, imperviousness to the world beyond her own physical boundaries. Liam had a sense of something minute and alien under the masking paint and baggy clothes. He wondered if there was something wrong with her. Was she retarded in some way? Her emotional blankness reminded him of what he had read of autism. But, at the same time, there was something intelligent, *accountable* about her that made him ask the question, 'Is there something wrong with you?' aloud. It did not seem to be a question that Divya could, or cared to, answer. She stared back at Liam, and swayed from one foot to another.

Liam remembered the inherent madness of children. They did not live altogether in the same world as adults: growing up was the gradual migration to the world of the sane. Naturally, it depended on how you looked at it. From the child's point of view . . .

But he decided that he had no obligation to look at things from a child's point of view, not being one any more. His relativism did not go that far.

'Go away, right now,' he said briskly, making it clear that he would take no further disturbance from the child.

'The woman upstairs doesn't cry,' Divya said, ignoring his instruction.

'What woman? What are you talking about?'

'The old woman. She's happy. She never cries any more.'

Liam was alarmed suddenly at the thought that if the child were roaming about the house she might come into the room when he and Grace were . . . He was distracted by the thought that he could find no word for what he and Grace might be doing. It was the first time for years that he had looked at the two of them from the distance of another pair of eyes. It was never *he and Grace*, it was only *him doing something to Grace*, or *Grace refusing to let him do something*, so in his mind they never made love, or fucked or anything that two people might do with each other. It made the notion that they could be overlooked by the affectless gaze of Divya all the more terrible.

'You are not to roam about this house. Do you understand? I'm going to speak to your mother. You must stay on the ground floor. You are not allowed in the rest of the house.'

He spoke deliberately, threateningly, marking the end of each word with an extra widening of his eyes.

Divya couldn't have cared less. She was immune to the fury she caused in others. This house was no different to the others she had lived in: not hers, but all of it her territory. She was a wanderer within the enclosing walls of wherever she happened to live. There was no heart to the house for Divya, for all that the two rooms on the ground floor were supposed to be her new home, containing, as they did, her mother. The fact of living with a mother was all but lost on her as an indication of home. It was a sign she had never learned to read. So the lack of partitioning walls in the house that Liam couldn't afford to, or didn't care to, convert meant that access to the stairs and other rooms made all of it her territory.

The open structure of the house didn't affect the adults' territorial sense in the same way. They had already learned that they belonged where their possessions rested. For Daphne, her Underwood made the attic her place. For Liam, Grace and the tears he had shed for her made the middle floor his.

But nobody thought of the house as home. Daphne's home was in the future, travelling in her van. Liam's home was Grace's body, wherever it might be. Grace's home was with her current lover. Sylvie's home was somewhere that belonged to someone else. And Divya had no thoughts of home at all.

9

A Home Visit

Sylvie was not managing. Jock Daneford had written a memo to his senior explaining his concern and asking for a case conference.

In the car, on the way to visiting Sylvie and Divya, Jock allowed himself a secret moment. His social worker carapace fell away and he heard himself think what he couldn't even whisper during his working day. After twenty-five years' experience of trying to patch up the disordered and dangerous remains of families, he had concluded, in his most interior, private self, that it was not that there were problem families, but that *families* were the problem. He was of the opinion that *all* children should be separated from their parents at birth. He let himself go further: what he actually thought was that they shouldn't even be born at all.

But Jock was no revolutionary. He was merely in a condition of quiet despair. He had no alternative social form in mind, only the certain knowledge that the greatest disservice that humanity could do to a human being was permit it to be born. This was not something he could discuss with his fellow professionals. It was not something he even discussed with himself. It was simply what he knew. For twenty-five years he had walked in and out of rooms, flats and houses, trying to contain the damage that parents did to children. He wasn't pointing an accusing finger at anyone – he had no doubt that the parents had been equally damaged in their time. Whenever he saw reports of famine and disaster, which were invariably accompanied by pictures of children suffering, he had a vision of innumerable millions of ordinary-looking front doors behind which were children suffering purely from the effects of being born and brought up by other people who had themselves suffered those effects. Starving children could, with no more than a decent degree of goodwill, be fed. What about the others? What about the unrelenting but low-level misery that was the lot of all the children? Years and years of it. Who could help them? And how? Jock couldn't, even though it was his job. Take them away or leave them there: it made no difference, the damage went on. The children suffered pain with families, and loss without them — even if they were physically or mentally better off.

Jock was tired. He stayed in social work because he was tired, and because something in him said he had to confront the reality that others wouldn't, if only to bear witness to what he knew and almost everyone else chose to ignore. He didn't blame them, either. It was intolerable listening to the misery, having it roll around inside your head and knowing that there was nothing to be done about it. He wondered at his capacity to live with the intolerable. He wondered for how much longer he could bear it. Certainly the noise in his head got louder, the sound of low-level sobbing, like a terrible tinnitus that no one could hear but himself. But what else was he fit for after all these years?

The years of helplessness had taken their toll. Now, when he had a new case, he never had the slightest doubt that whatever he did would be the wrong thing, or at least not the right thing; because the right thing was simply not available as an option. Increasingly, Jock had gone about his work wrapped in a cloud of desolation, which seemed to thicken with the passing years. His only hope was to reach retirement before the cloud was so dense he would see nothing at all.

Jock stood in the centre of Sylvie's living room. The curtains were drawn, but a beam of daylight cut through their not quite closed centre, lighting a stream of dust motes that danced in the gloom.

'Where's your mum?' he asked Divya, who had led him in here after opening the door.

She was wearing a bright-green sweater that reached her ankles and concealed her hands. She had to keep pushing up one sleeve to find the biscuit she was eating.

'In bed. She's asleep.'

It was 11.15.

'Why aren't you at school?'

'Mum said I didn't have to today.'

'You're supposed to go to school every day. Are you ill?'

Divya looked sulky and didn't answer.

'Can you go and wake her up? Tell her I want to see her. Please.' He smiled at the child who merely stared at him without moving. 'Please,' he repeated quietly.

Divya turned and opened the door of the bedroom, disappearing inside and closing it behind her.

Jock removed a plate with the remains of a fried egg on it that was perched precariously on top of a pile of dirty clothes on the sofa. He put it on the table on top of some unopened bills, and pushed the clothes to one side so he could sit down. The room smelt of stale food and the cigarette ends overflowing in unemptied ashtrays and saucers which lay dotted around the carpet. The place was not just untidy, it was filthy. The sink in the kitchenette in the corner of the living room was filled with dirty dishes, and the grimy lino dotted with bits of food. Not one surface was free of a burden of displaced matter: piles of dirty clothes, magazines, half-eaten biscuits, unopened letters, mostly with window envelopes. Everything was where it was because it had been pushed aside to make room for something else that didn't belong there either.

Jock tried to sigh a great weight off his heart and failed. Pieces of a Monopoly game which would never be played again were scattered round the room: cards, tokens, miniature houses and hotels, all over the place. Jock bent and picked up a silvered token – a tiny top hat – lying at his feet. The box was lying upside down under the table. Jock started to get up to put the token into the box, but stopped himself. It would have taken the best part of a day to find the rest of the game. He dropped the token back on the floor where he found it.

Jock tried to remember about the importance of living with a real parent, but he was sabotaged by the thought of Divya waking up and beginning her day in this dismal room. He suffered from an excess of imagination – and, in fact, his heart sank not so much at Divya's morning vision of her home, as Divya's vision filtered through his own heart and mind. Was it better than being in the over-efficient cleanliness of a children's home? It would be, Jock supposed, making an effort, if there was warmth and affection to be had. Untidiness, dirt even, didn't matter very much, if there were emotional ties, a sense of belonging, of being cherished. So said the psychology component of his social work training, trying to assert itself. But, Jock wondered, heretically, how could anyone feel cherished in a place that was not itself cared for?

Jock had been brought up hard, in grinding urban poverty in the north of England, he and his sisters. His mother had a fierce pride in keeping things nice against all the odds. She had done battle against dirt and squalor; it had been her way, and they had known it was an expression of love for them all. She hadn't the time or the temperament for demonstrations of love, but none of them ever doubted she cared. He wondered why they were so sure of that. Kisses and cuddles had been rare events; he couldn't remember his mother reading to them at night, or praising them for their smaller achievements. But his mother's love for them had been certain. It was part of the air they breathed, and as unquestioned. He knew the shine on the rickety table at which they ate, and the scrubbed floors, had come to represent her pride and hopes for her children. It did not have to be that way for everyone, he understood. People expressed love in different ways, he told himself, and children almost always understood the intention if it was there, he thought, trying to offer himself comfort.

But, still, his over-identifying heart sank at the squalor surrounding him.

Divya came out of the bedroom.

'She's getting up,' she told Jock and went into the little kitchenette to fill the kettle.

'I'm making her tea,' she explained.

She had to stand on tiptoe to reach the tap. Jock watched her plug in the electric kettle and find a cup in the overflowing sink, which she rinsed with water and dried with a teacloth stiff with dirt.

'How are you settling in, Divya? Do you like living here more than the home?'

'What's it to you?'

'I'm in charge of your welfare. I want to know you're getting on well. It's a long time since you've been in a home of your own. Do you like it?'

'Don't care,' Divya shrugged, tipping the old tea bags into the sink on top of the dirty dishes. 'There's an old woman upstairs.'

'Yes?'

'Nothing. She doesn't cry.'

'Oh? Why not?'

'Dunno. She says she doesn't. She stopped. She's happy because she's clever.'

'Do you cry?'

'No.'

'Who cries, then?'

'None of your fucking business. He cries.'

'Who?'

'Upstairs. The man. When he's asleep.'

'Are you still doing your wandering about?'

'None of your fucking business.'

She poured the boiling water into the teapot while Jock forced himself not to go over and do it for her. Jock tried to think like a trained social worker, and conjure an assessment from his observations. Making a cup of tea for her mother was, in itself, something. It was not something she could do in care. The kids had their share of chores, there was a rota requiring everyone to do something useful towards the upkeep of the house. It was supposed to make the children feel they were responsible, that the home was something like home. But it was nonsense. Now Divya was living, and in a small way co-operating, in a household. She was doing something for someone. Learning the give and take of a one-to-one relationship must be important, Jock told himself, even while he winced at the thought which had come into his head with neon-lit quotation marks.

Sylvie opened the bedroom door and stood for a moment, still adjusting herself to being upright. She sat heavily on a pile of magazines on a chair by the table, and rested her head in her hand.

'I've got a rotten headache. It's those sleeping pills. Divya, give me a couple of aspirin. Where's the bloody tea?'

'Aren't you sleeping?' Jock asked.

'Not without the pills. I get tired during the day so I have to sleep, and then I can't at night.'

'What happened to your job?'

'It didn't work out.' She lifted her head and glared at Jock as if she had only just realized he was there. 'What's this, the third degree?'

'It's my job,' Jock said quietly. 'Divya ought to be at school. Is there somewhere she can go for a bit while we talk?'

'Go out and play,' Sylvie told Divya, who was just delivering the tea and aspirin. Divya's face remained tight and expressionless as she turned towards the door.

'See you in a little while,' Jock said as she left. Then he turned back to Sylvie. 'So why isn't she at school?'

Sylvie shrugged.

'I can't get up in the morning. She's all right.'

'She's supposed to be getting an education. Do you think you're coping?'

'I don't know,' Sylvie said dully.

'I have to make a report for the case conference.'

'So, make it. I don't care.'

'Do you still want Divya to live with you?'

'How do I know? You're the policeman. You know everything. You decide.' Her aggressive tone dropped suddenly and was replaced by what were more like private thoughts. 'Everything seems to have got on top of me. Maybe she ought to go back to the home.'

There was a silence for a moment and then Sylvie spoke again as if she were talking to herself.

'But what would happen to me? What would I do?' She looked up at Jock plaintively. 'She's my daughter, of course I want her, but it's very hard to manage. Couldn't you get someone to help me?'

'Let me talk to Divya and see what she wants,' Jock said finally.

He couldn't believe he should allow the child to stay. Sylvie was depressed and, if not a danger to her daughter, dangerously incompetent. His concern had to be for the child. It was probably true that Sylvie needed Divya if she was going to get out of bed at all, but it wasn't what children were for. In his heart – social work theory apart – he doubted if the bond between them was the love the theorists rated so highly. It was dependency he heard in Sylvie's voice, and it was a dependency going in the wrong direction. But what would the child feel about being taken away again? It would have to be final this time. God knew what she felt now – so much damage had been done already.

He left Sylvie near to tears and went to find Divya. She was sitting on the stairs outside the door.

'How would you feel about going back to the home?'

An impossible question.

'Nothing.'

'Do you want to stay here with your mother?'

An impossible question, but one that Divya knew the correct answer to.

'Yes.'

There were a number of reasons for this apparent affirmation of family. In the first place, Divya preferred this house over the home because there were fewer people in it, and none of them were children. She didn't like other children; those younger than her whined and cried and made a nuisance of themselves; the older ones bullied or ignored her.

Another strand of reasoning was that no one told her what to do, hardly. She didn't have to go to school very often, and no one told her to tidy up. No one told her anything much, and she didn't like to be told.

The other reason for her saying yes to Jock's difficult question was much less accessible to Divya's understanding. Divya's *yes* had come from a mixture of obligation and a sense of how things were supposed to be. It was more a reaction than a thought, and hardly qualified as a decision. Somewhere lodged in her six-year-old head was the idea that children *should* live with their mothers, and therefore she was supposed to say yes when asked if she wanted to. Her beliefs about the proper place for children were curiously similar to current social work ideology. Six-year-olds are as vulnerable to received opinion as anyone else. She had no recollection of happy families. Sylvie had never been more than occasionally and casually affectionate: birthday cards, awkward weekend visits, sudden embraces when Divya's presence in Sylvie's life represented living happily ever after with her current man. There was not even any accumulated habit of living with her mother to explain Divya's obscure feeling that if she had a mother, she ought to live with her. The thought of staying with Sylvie did not make her happy, there was merely a notion of what was fitting making it difficult to say no. It was an instinctive push towards what everyone, including Divya, regarded as normal.

There was one other motive for staying which she couldn't have explained if anyone had asked. Divya was a cross, deprived and sullen child who remained at a great distance from other people. If some children craved affection and relationship when they had not had them, others, like Divya, rejected closeness for the same reason. But she knew her mother needed her in some way. She would have felt bad if she had walked away, even if she wouldn't have felt particularly sad. When Sylvie collapsed in tears at her own inability to cope, diffident Divya found herself obliged to put an arm around her mother and comfort her. In the short time they had been living together, Sylvie had become Divya's burden. To leave her to her own devices, not to help her get up in the morning, not to help her into bed and find her sleeping pills in the evening, would have been to desert Sylvie. As Divya imagined leaving with her little suitcase, she felt as she would have felt walking away from a helpless puppy that could not fend for itself. Divya could not have named, or even described, the discomfort this imagined desertion imposed on her, but it was strong enough to make her answer yes, and thus allow Jock to convince himself that his own unorthodox thoughts on the well-being of children were without foundation.

A need to belong and a feeling of well-being are not one and the same thing. Divya knew she was supposed to belong somewhere, and by all the accounts she had come across, the right place was with her mother. But Divya's decision was not an indication that she felt being with Sylvie was where she would be happier than anywhere else. In fact, the only emotion she felt as she told Jock she wanted to stay with Sylvie was a sort of dread. And in this there was a direct connection – a growing bond – with her mother. The bleak feeling Divya experienced was Sylvie's incapacitating nameless dread, in its infancy. It was a bond which Jock, had he been aware of it, would have been happy to sever.

Jock, however, at the moment, was more than willing to be reassured by Divya's assurance that she belonged with Sylvie, because his dissenting views were moving him ever closer to what he feared might be breaking-point. He didn't question her *yes* too closely because she reiterated the wisdom at the core of social work theory, and relieved him of his burden of doubt. Out of the mouths of babes, he thought, with some relief. What he found distressing, he concluded as the curtain came down over his deepest doubts, was no more than what *he* found distressing, and nothing to do with the probably inalienable bond between mother and child.

Jock took Divya's *yes* as balm for his nagging conscience, and when the case conference opened he would tell the interested parties that, in his opinion, the child should stay with the mother, despite the problems, because, on balance, the risk to her emotional life of being parentless was greater than the danger of neglect. It was what the conference would want to hear, and it was what Jock the professional wanted to believe. Everybody's best interests would be served.

PART THREE

10

Liam Throws in the Towel

Grace was never home these days. The child bride turned personal assistant had an infinity of business lunches, meetings for drinks and professional dinner parties to attend. Sometimes Liam saw her in the morning, but only blurred, through one half-opened hung-over eye as she called goodbye to him from the door of the bedroom. She was never back before midnight, and Liam, drinking as determinedly as ever and getting older by the second, was rarely able to stay conscious across the cusp of night and day.

Liam knew that Grace was lost to him. He knew their house of lust had become no more than a dormitory, and an overcrowded one at that. It would be only a matter of time before old Moby Dick Harriman persuaded her to leave her comic and pathetic husband. Liam was not in the slightest degree surprised. The end had been clear from the beginning – perhaps it had been the only point of the beginning all along. Certainly, Liam had been drinking himself into numbness, ready for this moment from the day they had moved in together. He had had his bout of middle-aged excitement and now it was over, along with everything else.

He sat at his desk and stared beyond the half-full bottle of whisky at the pile of water-stained and crinkled papers in the middle. There were letters requesting articles for anthropological journals, and four books he had been sent to review. The deadlines for all of them had long passed. It was three months since he had been asked to do anything. Hardly surprising when he had not managed to do what had been asked in the first place. There would be no more work. There would be no more income. At the bottom of the pile a bank statement told him by how many thousands of pounds he was overdrawn, and next to it – curled by Daphne's washing-up water – a letter from his bank manager informing him his cheques would no longer be honoured.

Liam hadn't bothered to dress this morning. He sat at his desk in his old Paisley dressing gown, barefooted and unwashed. He wondered if he would ever get dressed again. He couldn't think what for. All he had to fill his day were fantasies, and clothes were a positive hindrance to the kind of fantasies he liked best. Today he would concentrate on revenge, he decided. He would deal out death and vengeance until alcohol submerged his mind once again into a parody of sleep.

He was doing quite well. Melville Harriman, the big fish and Grace's new boss and lover, lay on the floor of his high-tech office bleeding gently into the plush beige carpet. He was stark naked and blood trickled from several ragged punctures dotted around his torso which Liam had made with a metal kebab skewer he had brought with him after rummaging through a drawer in the back of his mind filled with sharp and deadly utensils. It was deadly unsharp, excruciatingly blunt, with just the right degree of rust, and twisted in the centre so that, with the proper kind of screwdriver action, it would produce extreme and extraordinary pain. Melville the whale was going to bleed slowly to death through his holes, on his office carpet, with just a spot of ptomaine poisoning as a finishing touch.

Liam sat in his dressing gown and watched with quiet satisfaction as the sea monster writhed in agony and Grace flung herself at Liam's feet, seeing the error of her ways. He was unforgiving and regarded his naked wife (he had found them *in flagrante*, of course) with con-tumely. But then he lost it. He couldn't possibly stare coldly at Grace on her knees, bare breasted, in front of him. He reached out to stroke her lovely, weighty tits and before he knew it, Blubberman was on his feet, fully healed, his holes miraculously plugged, and sauntering from the room with Liam's lost darling on his arm. Liam was left with his hand extended, caressing air.

Liam knew this kind of loss of concentration to be his downfall. His monkish fantasies were just as much at risk from it as his murderous ones. He was a dilettante in every respect, he concluded gloomily.

Grace was going, and her absence opened up the prospect of the rest of Liam's life. Once he had been a wanderer in the East, concealing his search for God or Purpose with an academic calling. The burden of his Protestantism had, in the end, denied him the orgy of meaning that others found in the sixties. Once, he had known he was destined to be something special in the world. But time had slipped away, and revealed his intelligence to be only ordinarily good. He recut his cloth and became a happily married man whose sense of emptiness was no more than a conceit. He was a spiritual exile, yes, but one who had found a land of milk and honey to comfort him. He made delightful babies with his delicious Sophie and grumbled happily about the lack of light. No one had taken him seriously, and he hardly believed in his dissatisfaction himself. Sometimes Sophie laughed, and called him Eeyore, and he loved being her grumpy, lovable ass. And then he had seen Grace's breasts through gauzy cotton and his life had come to an end. There was no sense to be made of it. His spiritual emptiness had turned upside down, and underneath was nothing more than a longing for a pair of tits. Nothing more and nothing less. He threw everything away for them, as he hadn't done for God. God, after all, was a risky bet; Grace's breasts were there, firm and certain. He could have those, and they fitted the space he had imagined was reserved for God — miraculously, you might say. So it had been goodbye to everything, and those who had laughed at his mumbled dissatisfactions in the midst of his happiness were unable to comprehend his solution. He asked them to take his tawdry desire seriously. This is something I must have, he explained to those whose lives he had broken. Now he had had it, he understood what he had been after in the first place: a real exile, a desert created by the contempt of others. He had taken the path that ensured he would end up nowhere. He had destroyed the happiness of others because he had been determined to destroy his own happiness. That had been the aim, not merely the effect. Now, he was at the nowhere, and the imminent loss of Grace seemed not just inevitable, but desirable. Good. It was done. Over. He would not get dressed again.

Liam stood up and swayed slightly before pointing himself in the direction of the cabinet in the corner of the study where the drinks were kept. There was a full bottle of Cointreau, and one of sherry, but no more whisky. He opened one of the drawers of his desk and rummaged around in it, finally finding what he was looking for. It was a credit card, the only one that had not been stopped. He had been keeping it for an emergency. He found the number of his local wine merchant and dialled it.

'Yes, just one case of Bell's . . . by credit card.'

He read out the number on the card in front of him.

'No, I want it delivered. This afternoon will be fine. Thank you. Thank you very much.'

He put the phone down and, clutching the half-empty bottle of whisky under one arm, made his way to the bedroom to await delivery.

By mid-afternoon there was an empty bottle of whisky that had rolled under his bed and eleven unopened bottles in a case next to it. The twelfth was open and being cradled in Liam's arms. He had forgotten to take a glass to the bedroom but decided that, anyway it was easier to drink lying down straight from the bottle. Now, it was precisely positioned on his chest, within easy reach of his mouth, and he sipped at it with the concentrated stare of one who had an arduous duty to perform.

Daphne called a rousing 'Yoo Hoo!' as she popped her head around Liam's bedroom door, having failed to find him in the study. Liam was lying in bed with an empty bottle balanced on his chest. He was not roused by Daphne's reveille, but his eyes unglazed slightly after she had been bending over him for a few moments, her face inches from his, sniffing his outbreaths, like a cat.

'What *are* you doing, Liam?' she demanded, straightening up and putting her hands on her hips.

Liam took a long time to answer. His eyes swivelled into some sort of focus and he stared balefully at Daphne. It took several more moments before his brain received the meaning of her words, and then several more before he could organize sense and a sentence with which to answer her question. He wanted to answer it, because it was unsatisfactory that only he should know what he was doing. He wished to publish the new solution to his condition.

'I am committing suicide,' he said in a slow slur. 'Now, I would like to be alone.'

'Don't be ridiculous, Liam,' Daphne said with a click of her tongue.

'Always been riduc . . . always been. Can't be helped. There it is!'

His head lolled to one side and he groaned at the way the world tipturned as a result of his movement.

'You're a terrible nuisance, Liam, you really are.'

Liam mumbled his agreement.

'You'll have to sober up because I've got exciting news for you.'

Liam groaned again. What news could be more exciting than his suicide? The world had gone quite mad.

'I've adjusted my plans. It's all going to be all right, dear.'

Liam stared at her and blinked. It was Daphne at the other end of the undulating tunnel.

'Oh, go away. I don't want to talk to you. I'm committing suicide, for God's sake.'

'Well, dear, there's a few things I could tell you about God, so you better wait until you're in a fit state to hear them before you do anything for His sake. Now, stop being so silly. It's all going to turn out wonderfully. I can't imagine why I didn't think of it sooner.'

Liam focused on Daphne again, this time taking her in. The hat was still on her head – had it taken root? She was wearing a suit made out of a pinky-orange material. The short jacket finished at her hips and was pinched in and straining at the waist. An enormous violet fabric flower flopped from one wide lapel. The skirt was straight and so tight as to allow only mincing steps. It stopped at her knees, just below which were a pair of stiletto-heeled black patent-leather boots. She looked as if she'd had a lot of bad luck at a jumble sale.

'My business suit, dear,' she told Liam, noticing his fixed stare. 'Because I'm going to do business. Lots of business. Now, please make sure you're sober when I get back.'

She took two bottles at a time from the case by the bed and poured them out of the bedroom window on the unkempt flower-bed in the front garden below.

'Can't do much harm,' she muttered. 'They're all dead anyway.'

Liam was paralysed and unable to do anything about Daphne's sabotage of his suicide bid. He had to make do with calling her names, in a weak, ineffectual tone of voice.

'Fucking bitch. Stupid cow. Leave that alone. Don't touch . . . How dare you? I'll kill you . . . I'll bite you to death. Drive a stake through your heart, breathe garlic all over you. Leave my whisky alone . . . It's mine . . .'

'There, there, dear,' Daphne soothed. 'You'll feel better this evening. Well, perhaps not better. You'll feel terrible of course. But I'll come back with such a wonderful surprise that you'll forget that you wanted to be dead. Bye for now. And don't do anything silly, will you?'

She beamed at him and left.

Liam wept sixty-proof tears at the way in which life would keep getting in the way. He had had such a satisfactory solution. And now, instead of being dead and gone, he was no more than dead drunk, with a hangover to face. He had a hasty change of plan. He decided that as soon as he could walk, he would kill Daphne and spend the remainder of his life having a well-deserved rest in solitary confinement in a high-security prison for very dangerous men indeed.

Daphne went about her business with a will. If the cold hand of past misery was not to clutch at her heart again, she had to activate her plan and find a way out of the house where sorrow seemed endemic. Why wait, was the radical thought that had come to her.

She stood at the reception desk repeating her name as the young receptionist blinked at the apparition in front of her.

'Daphne Drummond, dear. Drummond. Now I want to see the person in charge.'

'In charge of what?' the perplexed girl asked.

'Of everything. I suppose David Middleton isn't here any more?'

The girl behind the desk looked blank.

'Who?'

Daphne shook her head at such ignorance.

'One of the very greatest editors in Britain.'

The girl shook her head.

'Oh, never mind. Just get me someone in charge. Tell them Daphne Drummond wants to speak to them.'

The receptionist dialled a number and tried to convey with her tone of voice that a mad woman was in reception. She repeated the name three times as the voice at the other end asked, 'Who?' at first with incomprehension, and then with a hazy memory, and finally with in-credulity.

'He says go up. It's on the top floor. The name's on the door,' the girl said, still mystified.

'What name is that, dear?'

'George Maynard.'

George Maynard was waiting in the doorway when Daphne arrived, breathless, at the top floor.

'Daphne Drummond? I can't believe it. I thought you were dead.'

'Well, as you can see, I'm not. Mind you, those stairs made it a close thing. So who are you, then?'

Maynard introduced himself as editorial director to the firm of Steppings and Wolfe, and drew her into his office. Daphne sat in the chair he offered. Her boots creaked as she crossed her legs.

'Are you sure you're the man in charge?' Daphne asked.

Maynard was in his early forties, but managed to look little more than thirteen. He was very tall and thin, and appeared to have an excess of elbows and lower limbs which he seemed ill at ease with, as if they were constantly threatening to go out of control and make off in several directions at once. His fresh-faced public schoolboy looks did not please Daphne, who remembered her old editor as a much older, more solid, gentlemanly sort of person. In fact, he had been the same age as George Maynard when he published Daphne's books. Daphne always had trouble with the peculiar effects of the passage of time.

Maynard gave her a slightly apologetic grin.

'Look,' he said, and pointed towards the ceiling of the opposite wall. Long-sighted Daphne saw her three novels lined up on the top shelf. 'Out of print, I'm afraid. But it's an amazing coincidence, you turning up like this, because I had Virago on the phone only last week asking about the rights.'

'Who?' asked Daphne.

'Virago. You must have heard of them.' It was clear that Daphne had not. 'They're a huge success. Publish dead women writers . . .'

He blinked at the living woman writer in front of him, and Daphne watched his cheek flush a charming schoolboy crimson. He went on hurriedly.

'Well, I was saying at the weekly editorial board meeting that maybe we ought to think about reissuing them ourselves. And now, here you are. You're not dead, are you?'

'No, dear,' Daphne said kindly, sorry for the knots the young man had got himself into. 'So David has retired?'

'Ages ago. I think he died. What? Ten years ago, it must have been.' He allowed himself a small moment of surprise at how quickly time was passing.

Daphne said, 'Oh' quietly to herself, and fingered the velvet brim of her hat in her bereavement.

'So what happened to you? You just disappeared, didn't you? Like Agatha Christie. Very dramatic.'

'Not quite like Agatha Christie. She didn't know where she had been, and I do. Now, dear, I'd like to discuss a little business with you.'

George Maynard waited expectantly. He felt excitement scratching at the back of his skull like a cat trying to get at a bird it sees through a window-pane.

'I'm going to write a new book. A novel. It's called *Happily Ever After*. You can reissue the old books in the meantime and get everyone excited about the new one. Now, what I want from you is an advance of however much one of those mobile caravan things costs.'

The name *Jean Rhys* went up in lights in front of Maynard's eyes. A new novel by a lost author was almost as good as a lost novel by a dead author. His heart began to beat faster as he thought of the marketing opportunities.

'Daphne, that's wonderful. How much have you written?'

'Forty-four words, if you don't include the title, and it's coming on very nicely,' Daphne said with a beatific smile.

Daphne explained herself to the bemused editorial director. Her plan was to travel about in the mobile caravan thing. She had had enough, for reasons that she wouldn't go into, of living in houses, thank you, and had decided not to wait any longer before making her move. The reason why George Maynard would benefit from making this possible with an advance on a novel of so far forty-four words (plus the right to reissue the old ones) was that this was how she would gather her material. She planned to take her lover with her. *Happily Ever After* would develop as it was lived.

'A lover?' Maynard asked, his gaze fixed on Daphne's preposterous hat.

'Yes, dear. He lives downstairs, below my attic. He's in bed at the moment, recovering from an unsuccessful suicide attempt with a case of whisky. So I've moved things forward a little. He'll see things differently when we're on the open road.'

'So he's not actually your lover, then?' George asked, having lost all sense of propriety.

'Well, not just at present, dear. But he will be.'

'Daphne,' Maynard said thoughtfully, 'I wonder if you shouldn't be writing your autobiography. All that missing time, and wonderful period stuff before you stopped writing ... It would be a very good basis for reissuing the old novels.'

Daphne shook her head emphatically.

'No dear. We must stick to fiction. Otherwise, it'll be impossible to tell the truth. If I have to keep typing "I", it'll be sure to come out wrong. But don't worry, everything will be there. And a glorious climax. Love and freedom ... geriatric sex ... the open road ... destiny ... all that sort of thing, George, dear.'

George Maynard thought hard. What he had sitting in front of him was a publishing coup. Daphne was the stuff of PR dreams: feminists, feature writers, biographers, TV producers (documentary and drama), the old, the young ... Who wouldn't be interested in her? It wasn't usual to give advances for a manuscript of forty-four words, but what a thing, to have been responsible for a new Daphne Drummond novel after all those years of silence. And if an autobiography would have been better, he could make sure that the biographical material was pushed to centre stage. And what about a stage play? A film? George's mind raced. What was a few thousand? If she couldn't get the book together, he could have it ghosted.

But what if she disappeared again? No problem. He'd pay for the van thing, and then offer a monthly cheque for a year or so. She'd have to keep him informed of her whereabouts and the progress of the book if she wanted the cheques. He was not entirely motivated by the commercial potential; it would amuse him to finance Daphne and it pleased him because, as one of the last of the independent publishers on the face of the earth, he could bloody well do what he wanted, without having to get the agreement of some faceless financier who was more interested in breakfast cereal on the other side of the Atlantic Ocean. There was pressure on him, at the moment, to sell out. An American conglomerate had decided that a prestige British publishing house would look good in their annual report. It would be a strike for the independence of Steppings and Wolfe; a very satisfying way of thumbing his nose at Walter S. Kretsky and telling him exactly what he could do with his cornflake dollars. Yes, he'd do it, if only to show that he was free to take the publishing risks for which his house had once been famous.

'All right, Daphne,' George smiled. 'I'll tell you what we'll do.'

Daphne was not entirely pleased that George wouldn't give her a cheque there and then. He insisted on a contract being drawn up. She was to find the caravan ('Second-hand, please, but you can have it looked over by the AA'), and he would stump up for it. She would then receive a monthly cheque for £250 for twelve months, in the first instance, for expenses and so forth. Probably it would be a month before the legal department of Steppings and Wolfe had a contract ready to sign. Did she have an agent? Well, never mind, they'd manage without, *and* it would save her ten per cent.

'A month?' Daphne asked, incredulous.

'That's double quick by publishing standards,' George explained.

Daphne decided that, although this was not a perfect arrangement, it was workable. In any case, she supposed Liam would need a little time to be persuaded to settle his affairs and get ready to leave. It was best not to be too precipitate; she didn't want him to feel rushed. In the meantime she would find a caravan, buy lots of typing paper, some of that new liquid stuff for making corrections, and open a bank account. But first there was another errand to run.

Dr Meades smiled a polite welcome as Daphne entered her surgery.

'Well, what can we do for you?'

She consulted the open file on top of her desk. It was empty except for Daphne's name and address on a blank sheet of paper.

'We don't seem to have any notes on you.'

Daphne sat with her big plastic handbag on her lap. She liked the look of Dr Meades, who was a plump middle-aged woman with ruddy, unmade-up cheeks, a peasant-print dirndl skirt and a pair of sensible leather sandals and thick support tights. A nice sort of woman, Daphne decided, although speaking for herself, she infinitely preferred her own patent-leather boots.

'I haven't been ill, dear, not for a good long while. No reason to bother you. I know how busy you are with the halt and the lame.'

'Well, how can I help you now?'

'It's rather personal, dear.'

Dr Meades smiled encouragingly, while enjoying Daphne's improbable hat.

'You see, I'm just about to embark on a love affair. It hasn't quite begun yet, but it will be . . . well, frankly, quite a passionate business.'

Dr Meades's face retained its amiable smile. Only her eyes widened to take in Daphne's information.

'An affair? I see . . . well . . . how can I . . . ?'

'I've been doing a little reading down at the library about what happens to the female body after menopause – of course, I got all that over and done with ten years ago. No trouble at all. But I understand from a very good book I found – the Boston Women's Health Collective, it was – that the walls of the vagina get thin, and that during the sex act there's often trouble with lubrication. Too much fucking friction, as it were, dear.'

'Yes, yes, I see,' Dr Meades said with extreme seriousness. 'There can be a certain lack of lubrication . . . Have you experienced any difficulty?'

'Well, my dear,' Daphne smiled, settling comfortably in her chair. 'I haven't actually *done it* with anyone for twenty-five years, so I can't say positively whether lubrication's a problem or not. Naturally, I've masturbated up a storm, but I never bothered much with the internal stuff, just stuck to good, old-fashioned steam-driven clitoral stimulation, you know? So lubrication hasn't been an issue, you see? But now that I have, or will have, a lover, I want to make sure there aren't any unnecessary technical problems. Passion's a delicate business, isn't it? No need to put obstacles in its way.'

Dr Meades took a deep breath.

'Well, Mrs Drummond . . .'

'Miss, dear . . . Miss Drummond. I never married. But you can call me Daphne.'

'Thank you. Well, Daphne, I think what you need is an hormonal cream. You just apply it before intercourse to the walls of the vagina. Or your . . . lover . . . he can do it for you. That ought to do the trick.'

Dr Meades pulled her prescription pad towards her with a light heart. She would spend the rest of the day smiling and humming happily at the thought that she had eased the difficulties of post-menopausal love for Daphne and her passionate paramour. It wasn't every day, or even, sadly, every week, in her hectic urban practice that she had the opportunity to give such simple satisfaction. When Daphne rose and thanked her, Dr Meades shook her head.

'No, thank *you*, Daphne. And do come back and see me at any time I can be of assistance.'

Liam had spent the day sliding in and out of sleep. He would have preferred to be awake, in spite of his thunderous headache, because the dreams were dreadful. Sometimes it wasn't clear when he was awake and when asleep. He would think he was awake, his head banging, but then he'd hear the sound of weeping, someone crying in the house, and it wasn't him. He might have supposed it was the child who lived downstairs, or Sylvie, but oddly, he didn't. It was his certainty that it wasn't either of them, nor him, which suggested to him he was not awake. But then, was he dreaming his headache as well?

As days went for Liam, this was one of the worst. His drunken, hung-over dreams refused to allow him to wander in peaceful cloisters, but made him live through his most dreaded fears. At one moment Grace, suitcase in hand, walked out the front door. This torment wasn't enough for his psyche, however. It repeated Grace's exit over and over again, like a record that had got stuck. His cries of 'Don't leave me, don't go!' rang in his ears as the door slammed and slammed again on his happiness. Sometimes he dreamed, with relief, that Grace was in bed with him, but when he turned his smiling face towards her and extended his hand to caress her breast, she became Daphne, grinning like the Wicked Witch of the North, and his hand found only flabby, drooping flesh, as she whispered, toothlessly, 'Darling . . .' into his ear. He woke up with a scream in his throat, but then the crying started and he feared this current condition was *sleep*, and the Grace/ Daphne business *real*, and for a terrible moment he was unable to move his head to the right in case what he saw was the old crone, in fact and indeed in bed with him.

Liam was right to be sceptical about his condition. Eventually, between the crying, Grace leaving and Grace lying next to him in bed, he turned his head, and found Daphne smiling at him from the other pillow. He turned away, blinked hard, and tried again. She was still there. It must be a dream, he told himself, in spite of the very real thumping headache he had, because Daphne appeared to be lying there, grinning up at him from the adjacent pillow, with the black velvet hat on her head. But, after a couple more turnings away and a good deal of blinking, he was forced to consider the possibility that he might not be asleep, and that Daphne was, in waking fact, in bed with him, hat, ancient drooping flesh and all.

Admitting it as a reality, however, didn't stop it being a nightmare.

'Daphne?' Liam croaked, hoping that he wouldn't hear his own voice which would prove he was dreaming.

'Darling.'

A terrible thunder rolled and cracked inside his head.

'Daphne, why are you in my bed?'

He spoke like someone who, after an accident, notices that his left leg is lying several feet away from the rest of his body and asks in shocked politeness what it is doing over there.

'It's all sorted out, Liam. Everything is going to be all right.'

He didn't want to know. The crying started up again.

'Who is that crying?'

Surely now his dream state would be revealed.

'Can you hear it, too? That's me, when I was a child, locked in the cupboard under the stairs. Take no notice, dear. We're going to leave all that behind us.'

Good. He was dreaming after all.

So why didn't he wake up?

'Get out of my bed!' he yelled, heaving himself off the pillow, determined now to rid himself of his nightmare. But at the peak of his bellow, the lightning that so inevitably follows thunder lit up a forked path of pain down through the top of his head, and he fell back on to the dented pillow with a groan hopeless enough to make the Lord Himself weep.

11

Sex

It had been more than two decades since Daphne had touched naked human flesh other than her own. The ache of abstinence had not seemed worse than the ache that resulted from the repercussions of love, and Daphne had learned to live with it. Actually, it had passed, that longing, after a comparatively short time. It had surprised her, she who had needed other human bodies merely to feel alive, at least for the duration of the love-making. Daphne had been fucked by anyone who had crossed her path from the age of fifteen, until in her prematurely haggard, vodka-drenched forties, she could no longer find anyone who would take up the offer. So for the past twenty-five years the only body to which she had access was her own; and for twenty of those years she hadn't minded very greatly.

Looking back, she wasn't at all sure she had ever liked sex much. The truth of it was she needed someone to hold, especially at night when the black silence reminded her of the cupboard. She wanted to hear the sound of someone breathing in the same room, to feel a warmth radiating from a sleeping body beside her. Through all those raging years she fell asleep next to a seemingly endless series of lovers of either sex, like a child who had climbed into bed with its parents after waking alone from a nightmare. Sex was incidental, usually no more than a grunting, writhing, sweaty business that paid for the companionship. Once or twice, though, it had been different — twice, in fact: once with a man, once with a woman. Out of the whole nameless, faceless parade only two names and faces stuck. It didn't seem much for a sexual lifetime, but when each relationship happened it had seemed to Daphne at the time to be much more than she could manage. On both occasions she had wished the anonymity back again, until the enchantment took hold, and she couldn't wish for anything but more. Daphne was the most passive of sexual partners, permitting the use of her body, being simply available. Those who bedded her took what she offered and left it at that. But the man and the woman she remembered had used her passivity as a channel, a pathway, to her desire. They had poured passion into her until it met her own, hiding away, uncertain, cowering for fear of meeting derision. Each of them had brought Daphne to the edge of herself, and taught her how to want and take from the bodies of others. It had been delicious sex for its own sake. When, in her celibate decades, she felt a longing, it was a longing for that − for the taking rather than the being taken.

She might have lived richly inside the bubble of passion with either of them for a good long while, but the pall of blackness descended on her finally, and it was stronger than the power of their love. A terrible, inexplicable sourness took her over and she punished each of them viciously for what they had not done, until they had to leave or risk their sanity.

Daphne had learned that it was possible to find joy in other people, but it was a lesson she hadn't wanted, knowing she couldn't sustain the pleasure. What was the point of knowing about something when you couldn't have it? But now she was ready. The lesson sat waiting for twenty-five years, simmering quietly in the back of her mind, and now she was ready to use her information. All things had their time. The time for Daphne's passion had come.

'Think of it as an adventure,' she had told Liam, after returning from her businesslike afternoon.

'I don't want an adventure,' he had wailed, feeling Daphne's fist close around his shrivelled member.

'All right, think of me as helping you,' she suggested helpfully, while her fingers gently pumped, pressing and loosening around the spongy penis as if it were a lump of clay she were moulding in readiness for shaping into . . . she hadn't yet decided.

'Don't help me,' Liam howled. 'I don't want helping. Leave it alone.'

But Daphne wouldn't take no for an answer.

It was strange, but Liam seemed unable to move his arms to push her hand away, or his body to get as far from her as possible. He felt as if he were tied down. He couldn't remember a hangover as bad as this.

In fact, he was tied down. Daphne had bound his wrists and ankles to the bedhead and footboard. Liam was splayed like a spatchcocked chicken, face up, his body wide open in invitation, each limb secured by one of a colourful variety of dressing-gown cords and ties. It came as some relief when Liam realized that his paralysis was a genuine physical immobility and not just the result of his hangover. But only for a moment, before the absurdity of his situation came clear to him. Finding absurdity in his everyday existence had once been very much to Liam's taste, but something had happened in the past few years to his sense of humour. It was not what it had been.

'You're raping me!' he yelled, straining his head as far as it would go off the pillow so that his sandy-lashed, red eyes bulged, and thick ropes stood out on either side of his neck.

'Well, I'm trying to, dear, but you're not being much help. Don't worry. Relax. I'll manage on my own. You'll be pleased in the end, just see if you're not.'

Daphne wasn't concerned about Liam's flaccid condition. She knew that, under the circumstances – drink and the unusual sexual situation – she wasn't likely to get his full attention. Engorgement was probably out of the question, but she was prepared to wait. She liked what she had: the naked, alcohol-bloated, sexually wilted body which she was free, by virtue of his bondage, to explore at her leisure.

It wasn't only Liam who needed time. Daphne had to adjust, too. She needed to renew her familiarity with the naked human body – someone else's – and to reacquaint herself with her desire. She was an explorer, noticing things as if for the first time, and yet feeling a tinge of recognition, like a child taken to a place it had been once in infancy, long before memory was sharp. She went slowly, one sense at a time, so as not to be so overwhelmed that she got confused. She explored the feel of Liam's body, loosening her grip on his still shrunken penis and stroking his balls, his thighs and his belly with the tips of her fingers and the flat of her hand.

She began to get the feel of his landscape, different from her own, though the components were often similar. She noted the lack of smoothness, especially in the soft parts, belly and balls, which were covered with hair as if to compensate for their feminine texture. She liked the contrast between the outside of his thigh, which was hard muscled, and the inside, which yielded to her touch. Her fingers travelled around Liam's body and caused a reaction in her own. She felt a precise connection between her fingertips on his flesh, her brain, and the tightening in her throat, chest and lower abdomen. An old channel was reactivated, and desire ran its familiar route from out-there to in-here.

She looked, smelt, tasted; and all the sensations were sharp and known, like old clothes suddenly in fashion again. She nuzzled his groin and then, recollecting, his armpit, and came over dizzy from the taste and odour of human crevices: salt, tangy, murky secretions, caught and held in the coarse tangles of russet hair for her to savour.

Daphne continued her leisurely inspection, making little noises of recognition and pleasure. She compared and contrasted, touching complementary parts of her own body as she came to rest here or there on Liam's various places. She touched her own breasts as she caressed his, feeling both their nipples come erect at the stimulation; she caressed her belly and his, her thighs and his, her pubic mound and his, and increased her own excitement with the confusion she created in her brain. Sometimes, it was unclear whose body she was touching with which hand; sometimes, it was difficult to tell which body responded to touch, and which to touching.

It was twilight in Liam's bedroom, the time when lights are switched on to confound the death of hope that the gloom incites. Liam felt the lack of light strike at his heart as he was forced to submit to his examination. Since he had no choice, he stopped struggling, realizing that it was useless and only exacerbating the discomfort from his nearly unbearable hangover, but he continued to voice his protests. He was a victim of a devilish twilight assault, spellbound into immobility while the succubus had her way with him. A dirty net curtain lay between his eyes and the world he could no more than fuzzily perceive, which was only partly due to the coming of night. His voice sounded in his inner ear as if it were submerged in the mushy matter that was the interior of his skull.

'Don't do that! Stop it! Don't touch me! Leave me alone! Will you leave me alone!' came thickly from Liam as Daphne went on with her

132

investigations. He felt, at first, hideously vulnerable, used, at risk from whatever terrible whim might come to the black-hatted crone grazing over his unprotected, naked body.

From time to time, as she bent to sniff or lick, Liam felt the brush of the velvet brim of Daphne's hat across his flesh. It made him shudder even more than the fleshy touch of her fingers, or the wetness of her lips and tongue. But, imperceptibly, the shudder turned into something more like a shiver, perhaps a quiver; a kind of tiny electric tremor that trilled in the base of his spine. Something confusing began to happen to his body and his mind, although, in his semi-comatose state, he was no longer entirely sure which, if either, was which. He suddenly found himself caught up in the pornography of bondage and reification that was being acted out on him, but it was as if he were voyeur rather than a participant. He began to feel the appropriate responses of a consumer enjoying a pantomime of lust designed to inflame the passive observer's sexual temperature. He continued to experience the feel of Daphne's outspread fingers poking and kneading curiously at his flesh; the throaty, appreciative noise she made as she inhaled his private scent; the sight of her loose-fleshed, sagging body kneeling over him; the stale lavender-and-sex smell of her growing desire.

And, quite abruptly, his vivid, squirming disgust at all this turned round to face him and smiled a smile of unconscionable lust. Disgust did a *pas de deux* with desire, until they were twisted together as indistinguishable sensations that changed the tone of his voice and the syntax of his protests. Now, he heard himself moan: 'Don't ... Stop ... Don't ... Leave me ...' and the intention of his words was no longer clear, either to the mad old woman in the filthy velvet hat who was assaulting him or to himself.

Was not this the very apotheosis of Liam's craven sexuality? What was being on his knees in front of the sumptuous beauty of Grace compared to having his desire subverted, wrenched from him, by a crone of a creature far beyond his sexual pale? If Grace was a brick wall against which his longing banged its head, Daphne was a siren, singing her spell, demanding and getting a longing whose existence he could not have imagined. He saw her aged body with a clarity that should have been impossible in the failing light. He strained against the bonds that held him in place, no longer in an attempt to escape, but wanting to explore the loose flesh around the neck, to weigh the drooping breasts in the prickling, sweaty palms of his hands, to caress the fallen buttocks and the hanging folds of her belly with his mouth. Liam was, by the time Daphne laid herself down full-length on top of him, sobbing with the need to reach out and touch: a very Ulysses whose Penelope had become no more to him than an outworker for the garment industry.

It is said that anyone in a sufficiently weakened condition, mentally and physically (and a hangover as a result of attempted suicide by alcohol will probably do) can be made to believe anything. And it is not impossible that desire is a form of belief. Liam's altered sexual consciousness might well have been described by those qualified to describe such things as a typical example of conversion syndrome. Had his converter had other interests, he could, in his state, have become a convinced born-again Christian, or an old-fashioned Marxist, or a devout pigeon fancier.

But the true believer intent on conversion is not inclined to think in terms of syndrome; it is quite likely that a genuine conviction is necessary on the part of the converter if a powerful and sudden change is to be effected. Daphne was, in all innocence, a true believer in her love for Liam, and as such, in equal innocence, took instinctive advantage of his malleable condition.

Still, the question remains as to whether any of Liam's previous desires represented a choice of his own free will. Liam himself in his more philosophical days would have doubted it, and sneered, 'Free will? All very well, my dear, but about as likely as a free lunch with Milton Friedman.' Is a passion, a sexual obsession, ever anything other than a conditioned response whose origins are to be found in some long forgotten childhood trauma that only ten (or fifteen) years on a couch would bring to light?

Had Liam's passion for Grace been a mature, considered decision, or was a switch flipped at that moment in the seminar room when the lights were turned on and Grace's breasts were exposed to the glare of Liam's subterranean need?

And what of Sophie? Now, *there* was a grown-up, mutually satisfying relationship, surely? Well, perhaps. But what did mature happiness do for Liam? It made him long for something he could not have, and he chose God as his unattainable object – at least until Grace came along and proved to be more immediately unattainable. Liam could only damn and blast his wandering soul that would not live contented in his apparently contented breast.

Whatever the cause – psychological syndrome, chemical alteration, true passion or soul recognition – Liam's eyes were now opened anew. It was a fact. A present fact that made the past irrelevant. Tied up, dehydrated, exhausted, miserable; all of a sudden he was in thrall. He desired Daphne's naked and passionate old body, and he could not remember ever before desiring anyone with such an overwhelming need.

So much for memory.

So much for choice.

Liam had always dreaded the effects of time. Specifically, he dreaded decay and death. More specifically, he dreaded facing his own decay and death, looking into the near future and seeing nothing, just the mouth of a black tunnel gaping at him, saying, 'That's it, you've had your lot. And what was *that* all for, then?'

Sophie had been his amulet against the fear once his attempts at a mystical assault on the citadel of entropy had come to nothing. She had done well, making a quiet sense of the senseless for Liam. There were breakfasts in the morning, babies made, two people working peacefully in different rooms, knowing that they would hold each other when night came. A fine order had been established; as much, perhaps, as anyone could hope for. But it hadn't worked for Liam.

The order had become routine, so that the edges of excitement had rubbed off and left him only happy and comfortable with Sophie of whom he wanted more – unhappiness, discomfort, if necessary – anything, so long as the present was strong enough to keep him from brooding on the passing of time. And the babies grew and reminded Liam of the very thing he was trying to put out of his mind – change, decay and death. He watched their triumphs with a sinking heart. The first blemishes on their perfect skin made him want to weep at the loss of purity – bumps and bruises made by the irresistible desire to get about alone in the world; drops of blood seeping from scratches and cuts that were necessary accidents as they pushed themselves beyond their current manipulative capacity. The birth of his last child had struck gloom in Liam's very bowels. He watched the new life fighting its way out of Sophie's body, battling for the light and air, and all he could think about it was that he had helped make something that would die. He had created death.

So, on to Grace. Forget babies and routine. Go for proximity to young flesh that seemed to push the very air aside to take its place and space in the world. He kept her by him at any cost, his new amulet: youth, ripeness ready to burst, so that when the fear grasped at him he could bury his face in Grace's breasts and hide from the old ogre, who would not see him in that magical place that defeated death. But he had found, as he nuzzled the soft buoyant flesh, that thoughts of time still came to him and presented him with the image of Grace old, of her tits fallen, of his hiding place found out. He became tormented by the time that was drifting inexorably by. Every day, hour and minute that passed caused him pain. He touched Grace and ploughed into her body with increasing desperation as if it were quicksilver that would disappear on contact. And Grace added to his problems by not being content to be Liam's fleshy saviour, as if such a role were not supreme. She kept trying to be what she called 'a person'. If Liam had wanted a person he could have stayed with Sophie. Why couldn't Grace see that?

Liam's arrow of time had always been the old Newtonian single direction. His universe was the same as Newton's and respected the Second Law of Thermodynamics where everything tended towards disorganization and disintegration. Order to chaos. A force meets a billiard ball, and the billiard ball moves in the opposite direction. The billiard ball never hits the force and weakens it enough to turn it back the way it had come. Or something like that. One way. Young to old to dead.

But now another direction had become available to Liam, through the determination of Daphne. He saw how it might be possible to start at the other end, with the decay already set in, and observe the signs that led backwards in time, to youth, beauty and order. He would trace origins from the contours of age, and work back from now to then, to find what was inherent, what was untouched. He would discover something within decay that defeated the vandalism of time and the obscene graffiti it scored into human flesh. Death may not yet be defeated, but the power of ineluctable time might be weakened by a close and loving scrutiny of its effects.

Daphne lay with her cheek and one side of her hat flattened against Liam's pounding chest, resting a little from the force of her rediscovered lust. She noticed the change in Liam's heart rate against her ear but thought it was only the beat of her own madly pumping organ being diverted through the echo chamber of Liam's rounded belly.

'Darling . . .'

Daphne blinked. Someone had said, 'Darling.' She had heard it, and if she wasn't sure whose heartbeat was whose, she was certain that she hadn't uttered a word. She lay very still, breathing shallow, like someone hearing a sudden noise in the middle of the night and waiting to hear it again in order to assess whether it was just the settling of the building or a living danger to be confronted.

'Darling . . .'

There it was again. Quite clear and out there in the world, although her cheek picked up a simultaneous vibration from Liam's chest. Daphne lifted her head and scrutinized Liam's face.

'Did you say something?' she asked warily, narrowing her eyes.

Liam's eyes were damp. Well, that wasn't unusual, especially after he'd been on a bender. But the look in them was very odd indeed. Longing, she would have said if anyone had asked.

'Darling! Darling!' he half sobbed, half sighed, arching his neck in a hopeless attempt to reach Daphne's unreachable lips.

There was no doubt about it.

'Do you mean me? Are you talking to me, dear?' she inquired, wondering if she hadn't tied his restraints too tightly and perhaps caused a lack of oxygen to the brain. Liam's deep sighs raised his belly and unbalanced Daphne, who slid sideways and rolled off Liam's body, landing next to him on the bed with a small bounce. For a moment she was breathless, both from the sudden change in position and her recent sexual reawakening. Then she sat up straight backed, placed both hands firmly on either side of the brim of her hat as if she were expecting a strong wind to blow up at any moment, and stared down at him, astonished, waiting for enlightenment. She noticed, out of the corner of her eye, something very like signs of life in his previously quiescent penis.

It's one thing to get carried away on the wings of an emotion and fling oneself bodily towards the object of one's love – it's quite another to have one's love respond, against all the odds, in kind. Daphne had made no plan for the immediate aftermath of a successful seduction. In her mind, there was the naked encounter with her re-strained and reluctant object, and then, as in a film cut, the two of them speeding (she didn't know where) together in her mobile home, baglady and lover, happy as pigs in shit. She had omitted to think out a route from the one scene to the other. She had certainly never pictured Liam's moment of capitulation.

Daphne placed her lips lightly against Liam's mouth. She applied no pressure, only leaving them there by way of a test to see if what she thought was happening was indeed happening. Liam's mouth opened. His whiskers parted and a dark groan rumbled from his depths. Daphne applied a little pressure, just to make sure, and for the first time in two and a half decades found a tongue other than her own investigating the inside of her mouth.

Liam's probing and alien tongue in her mouth was more startling than any other penetration she had imagined during her solitary fantas-ies of loving Liam. She had spent many lonely hours in her attic imagining intimate encounters in as much detail as memory would allow, but she had forgotten the shocking intimacy of the intimate encounter between mouths. She pulled away from Liam with a small 'Oh' of surprise at the sensation that rippled through her; a sharp something that took her breath away.

To call what had happened merely a kiss was like the Victorians discreetly covering table legs for fear of inflaming the imaginations of the young. The kiss was almost too intense to bear, with all the mixed pleasure and promise of its softness and tension, its wetness, textures and tastes.

'Oh, Liam,' Daphne breathed again.

'Untie me.'

Liam's investigations were even more detailed than Daphne's. It was as he thought; Daphne's body was a time machine. Liam discovered he could move at will from the present to the past or future. Like a child playing in a sandpit, he could build structures and then see them crumble into the essential flowing substance that could be anything or nothing – only stuff that ran like dry water between his fingers. He kneaded Daphne's soft, fallen breasts, empty sacks, and knew what they had been, saw them, felt them, as they once were, and loved them for their then and their now. They were also pleasing to his touch. He allowed his mouth and fingers to delight in their spongy texture, while his mind rebuilt them as he knew they had been. He pored over Daphne's body like an historian finding a primary source: his imagination fired with the business of re-creation; his senses thrilling to the feel and smell of the aged parchment which was a pleasure in itself. He traced the prominent veins in her legs with his fingertips, following their route, and stroked the creased flesh of her loose-muscled buttocks with a gentleness that made Daphne fill with pride at her time-marked flesh.

'I'm so glad you like my body, Liam, it's been the work of a lifetime.'

Liam pressed his wet whiskered mouth against Daphne's concertinaed abdomen. That was exactly what he had discovered – the lifetime that lived vividly in the folds and creases of her ageing flesh. It was more sensual than anything he had ever imagined. So much; so very much. So much more than the tenuous thrill of firm, young flesh, whose only promise was decline. This was everything, the body of a lifetime, touched and weathered and fuller with whatever it was he needed than anything he had known. He was beside himself with happiness.

'I am beside myself with happiness. Thank you,' he said solemnly, looking along up Daphne's body to her face on the pillow.

'More like between my legs with happiness,' she chortled. 'Is it all right down there? It might be a bit drier than you're used to, but I've got a nice tube of cream from the doctor if we need it, dearest.'

He didn't seem to hear her. He was suddenly riveted by her face. It was as if he had never seen it before. And it was true; he had never really looked at Daphne. He shifted his position to see better. Her skin was mottled with red patches from broken veins beneath the surface;

tiny tributaries ran off them to either side like delicate tracings on a map. He took in the vertical lines around her mouth and the dark shadow on her upper lip. Her small, barely lashed, grey eyes, too, were surrounded by lines which, like those around her mouth, had come with the years of laughter and crying that stretched the delicate skin until it was no longer smooth and uneventful. He saw simultaneously the face she had had when he was twenty, ironed out, a silk-cheeked beauty whose strong nose and slanted eyes made her more than merely lovely. Now that time, unhappiness and alcohol had worked on it, it had moved and was still moving towards another kind of beauty, which Liam longed to watch develop. He didn't fear decay in Daphne when he looked at her and saw what she had been and would be; he was excited by the workings of time that took fresh-faced prettiness as nothing more than raw material for the real face it would become.

Liam's conversion was complete. With the aid of Daphne's lubricating cream he made slow and deeply concentrated love to her, a new kind of love, for him, that was far removed from the thrusting desperation of sex with Grace, or the almost orientally distanced sensuality with Sophie. He didn't have to cheat time now; he could savour it.

It had been everything she had dreamed about, Daphne thought to herself when Liam shuddered into a deep sleep. All he had needed was to be made to concentrate on what she had to offer, and then, *of course*, he had seen and loved her as she knew he must. She was very pleased with how things had gone.

To tell the truth, she had been a little anxious about tying him to the bed. She *thought* it would turn out all right, but she hadn't been altogether certain that waking up to find himself bound hand and foot wouldn't put him in the wrong frame of mind. It seemed, however, that everything was working out just the way she had planned.

This was a great lesson, she thought, about life and the novel. When she was asked to give lectures to aspiring writers in the provinces, this would be the core of her message. All her previous novels had followed from the events of her life, so that, in effect, she did no more than edit experience into an acceptable structure. The new novel would be different; planned bit by bit by living it out, as if life were a notepad on which the structure of her fiction would be sketched. A much more satisfactory arrangement, as events had already proved. Why make her novels follow the vagaries of life, when life itself could be the first draft and therefore subject to her wishes and decisions? I will choose to be happy and to have Liam love me, she had thought. And here he was beside her, snoring rhythmically inside the crook of her arm: her lover, her man, her darling. The book was as good as half written. She may have left it a bit late, the taking charge of her life, but she had the hang of it now.

Daphne let sleepiness drift over her, as she attended to the half-forgotten feelings of being a sexual creature after so long. She tingled from the crown of her hat to her ingrowing toenails. Even if she had, sensibly enough, put away her conscious craving for the touch of another, her body had kept the memory of being loved – like it had held the memory of the steps up to the front door – imprinted quietly in its very cells. Desire had not disappeared, but been stored like furniture in a warehouse, ready to be dusted off and used. Youth and age had nothing to do with it; love had gone dormant, but it remained serviceable.

Daphne felt a damp trickle of Liam's semen between her thighs and sleepily followed the route of countless sperm making their way through her vagina, up into her 68-year-old uterus that, after so many years of inactivity, had once again contracted with orgasm as if it had been no time at all since it had last been called on to respond.

She looked down at her ravaged old body and Liam's plump middle-aged one, and chuckled at the joke life had been saving up to tell her. She thought, as she drifted off into delicious sleep, that it was one of the funniest and most delightful jokes she had ever heard.

12

Everybody Dreaming

It was dreamtime in the house in which Liam, Daphne, Sylvie, Divya and, possibly, Grace lived. Everyone was asleep (except for Grace, who was asleep, but elsewhere), each for their own reason: exhaustion, satisfaction, medication and, in Divya's case, a not yet altered response to the coming of the darkness.

Everybody passed through phases of REM sleep which brought with it dreams, though, naturally, not necessarily at the same time. An experimenting angel gliding silently through the house, gazing at the faces of the sleepers, would have noticed darting eyeball movements beneath the closed lids, indicating that the subject was telling him or herself a story; or, depending on the angel's academic persuasion, that the brain was discharging excess electrical energy and, in doing so, randomly firing memory cells that seemed, to the sleeper on waking, to make a narrative of sorts.

It was dreamtime for Liam, who, on the whole, thought of dreams as messages from the soul — or spirit — or psyche, if anyone insisted. He was back in his cloister, walking the weathered stone in solemn, measured steps. It was all silence and meditation, and waiting for the word of God. This time there was no dreaming self observing him. He was at peace, at one with himself, until he noticed something odd about the quality of his tread.

It was more slap, slap, slap than flap, flap, flap. What he saw when he looked down at himself was not his feet but his naked belly. His paunch, covered with pale, curling hair, naturally endomorphic but coming dangerously close to downright fat as a result of his drinking, blocked his view of his feet. He didn't need to see them now, anyway; the view of his gut told him what he needed to know.

His feet, like the rest of his body, were naked. He had nothing on;

no habit, no sandals, nothing. He walked the cloister starkers. In the nude. Somehow, in the way one only can in dreams, he simultaneously saw his back view. A vision confronted him of protruding buttocks to match the swell of his gut, and substantial thighs the insides of which rubbed together as he walked. The excess pounds wobbled as the slap, slap, slap of his soles on the stone juddered his flesh. The sudden shame of finding himself naked in broad daylight rose up in him like milk filling an empty glass jug. But there was worse than shame.

Adam knew his nakedness before the sight of the Lord and was ashamed, so Liam's embarrassment had, at least, a notable precedent. But there was nothing in Genesis about the shrivelling sense of one's own absurdity, never mind in the sight of the Lord, but in the sight of oneself. A mortifying vision of his own ludicrousness tinted the whiteness of the milk in the glass jug with the vermilion flush of blood. The solemnity of his meditative progress around the cloister was stripped bare, and made ridiculous by his baggy, bouncing bum and the small thing between his legs that bobbed with every step like a pom-pom on a woolly hat.

Liam heard God chuckling. He wasn't surprised; he didn't merit the wrath that Adam had elicited.

'Will you look at that, for heaven's sake?' the Lord gasped between His convulsions. 'And people say I don't have a sense of humour!'

Liam tried to hide his absurdity from the sight of the Lord, but there was nowhere to go. His dream architect had omitted to provide doors out of the cloister through which a mortified monk might run. There was no way out of Liam's Eden. And, anyway, where *is* there to hide from an all-seeing, all-laughing God?

'I'll tell you one thing,' the jovial Jehovah boomed to His attendant seraphim, as Liam attempted to cover the full-frontal knock-kneed nakedness with his hands (but God, being God, like dreams, could just as well see the back view). 'Whoever said that I made man in My own image needed his eyes testing. If I could think of anything they've got down there that I'd want, I'd sue for misrepresentation.'

The experimenting angel, having noted Liam's eye movements, would know that he was dreaming. She would have seen Liam's face twitch once or twice and watched him toss about, first one way, then the other, taking most of the duvet with him. She would have made note of a grunt and then a groan. But of the content of Liam's dream she would know nothing. There would be no more than a series of superficial fidgets to be indicated on the celestial graph paper. She might have woken him and asked him for his side of the story, but, apart from the fact that she didn't exist, that's not what experimenting angels do. It isn't part of their remit; not how they conduct their business. So Liam was spared the extra embarrassment of having his post-orgiastic, nocturnal humiliation known by anyone but his Maker.

So much for post-coital bliss and the state of Liam's soul – or, if anyone insists, his psyche.

It was dreamtime for Daphne, who thought of dreams as *extra*, and hoped they would be fun, though the truth was that sometimes – often – they weren't. The bad ones began with the dark. Not the dark of lying awake with the lights off, but the dark of being asleep and knowing there was no light. That was where her dream began, when, after she fell asleep, satiated from love-making with Liam, her eyeballs began to move under their lids in the characteristic manner of REM sleep. The darkness surrounded her, palpable as a threat which she strove not to identify, knowing that when she did she would have to acknowledge that she was once again locked in the cupboard under the stairs.

Finally, there was nothing for it but to admit it, for where else was there such terrible darkness? At least the cupboard was confined to its bounded space; there was an outside, even if she couldn't get there. If it wasn't the cupboard, then the blackness was infinite – no one else, no where else, nothing. A world of nothing without end. It was better, then, to be in the cupboard.

Daphne clutched her hands to her head against the rising terror, as if she would keep the panic from exploding through her skull. But instead of the childish pigtails that belonged to this moment of the dream, she felt the soft velvet of her hat, which seemed to have come with her from the waking world. It had, perhaps, developed an organic attachment to her head that wouldn't allow it to be separated from her even by the miasma of dreams. The velvety nap conveyed comfort as Daphne stroked it, and the hat itself seemed to keep the panic down. What else are hats for? As her fingertips played over the material they felt not just its softness, but also its colour. The dense black velvet was blacker that the blackness in the cupboard, but it was not a fearful blackness. Its quality was of the consolation of a darkened sky pierced with the pinpoint glowing of a multitude of stars. The hat's blackness was night, wrapping around a sleeping child who knew a good morning would come sooner and better for stillness and rest.

To her astonishment, Daphne felt the terrible darkness recede as the velvety black from her marvellous hat took over. Now her only problem was that Liam had turned over and taken most of the duvet with him.

It was not magic, the alteration of the recurring dream, just small bursts of extraneous electrical energy firing neurons: dreamstuff. An accident that turned the regular nightmare into something better. Or so the most reductionist of experimenting angels would have said. What she would have said about the accident of regular nightmares is the stuff of another story.

It was dreamtime for Sylvie, who preferred not to think about dreams at all, and was only grateful to be asleep. The best time in the world was that moment, as she lay in bed waiting, tense with anxiety that sleep would never come, when the pills began to work. A mesh curtain, soft, silver grey, came down like a blanket and smoothed out the wrinkles in her mind and the clenched muscles that, even lying in bed, were painfully tight, protecting her from expected but undefined blows. Everything began to go loose and, with gratitude to the drug industry, Sylvie knew that oblivion was on its way.

And that, she hoped, was that until morning, when the dismal business of starting again started again. If she dreamed, she had no recollection of it, ever. The pills seemed to take care of the problem of a night-time existence – bad enough having to have a daytime one. Thank you again, Roche Pharmaceuticals Incorporated.

Of course, like everyone else, she had REM sleep, although it was less frequent than the others. So it was very possible that Sylvie had her dreams, and the angel would probably make the assumption that she did. Whatever they were, it was likely that they would be as frantic and desolate as her waking life. Sylvie assumed so, and was very pleased not to have to remember and, therefore, experience them.

Best not to think about them, they were sure to be unpleasant. A relief, too, for the observing angel, though she probably wasn't aware of her good fortune.

It was dreamtime for Divya, who had no fixed ideas about dreams, but dreamed densely in vivid technicolor, nevertheless, and woke with them imprinted on her eyelids as if she had spent all night in the Ritzy of her mind.

Divya liked her dreams, which were populated with a large and regular cast of characters. There were two main groups which each had a separate dreamspace of their own: the Divyas and the Worms. Divya could never decide which she liked best. Usually, each morning, she best liked the group which she woke with the memory of.

The Worms were worms. Quite small and white, like elongated grubs. They lived in Divya's stomach and played out their existence with reference to that environment. It was a life lived in Divya's hazily understood internal organs. The worms were a family: mother, father and several baby worms, and their existence was completely ordinary, except for the peculiar fact that it was lived out in a universe enclosed by Divya's skin. Of course, *completely ordinary*, for Divya, was what she had heard or read about *ordinary*, and had little, as a result, to do with her actual life. The children worms went to school (buses took them via her circulatory system because she'd learned about that in school); the father worm went off to work with a briefcase, somewhere in the centre of her chest; and mother worm stayed home, cleaning and baking in the unpromisingly wet and sloshy domestic sphere of Divya's stomach. A fight between the children worms resulted in the bubbling, curdling noises that often came from her belly during the day. Stomach aches were from mother worm having a good spring-clean. They lived on what Divya ate, waiting for the food to arrive through the chute of her oesophagus. Sometimes they liked what was delivered, sometimes they didn't. Nothing extraordinary ever happened in the life of the worms. They just lived their day-to-day existence, as normally as abnormal young Divya could imagine.

That night, it was the Divyas' turn or, at least, they would be the dream that Divya had before she woke, and thus the one she would lie in bed and remember the following morning before she got up.

The Divyas were, of course, Divya, but multiplied. But although they were Divyas, none of them, apart from one, was *exactly* her. She watched their story unfold for the night, settling down as if she were seeing an episode of her favourite series on television.

Tonight there were a bunch of them, twenty or so. They lived on the same street and inhabited the same school playground, the two venues where all the Divya dreams occurred. It was the playground this time; a large tarmacked space that had white lines painted on it for hopscotch, netball, as well as several indefinable patterns that were not immediately identifiable with any game in particular.

There was another group of characters who belonged in the Divya dreams. They were men in dark suits. There was one man for each of the Divyas, and their job was to assist in their contests; for the Divyas were always pitting themselves against each other. This was where the strange lines of the playground came in. Intricate games with machiavellian rules set Divya against Divya, and the forfeit for losing was undefined but truly terrible. There was no harmony between these Divyas, and nor were the men in suits quite what they pretended to be. All, except one, gave hindrance dressed up as help to their assigned Divya. They were not friends at all, but sinister presences. Only one Divya had a man in a dark suit who really helped, and she was the *real* Divya – or so she seemed to the Divya who was doing the dreaming.

Divya's man whispered his suggestions while Divya carried out a complicated series of manoeuvres which were certain to gain more points than the deceived Divyas, and thus avoid the awful consequences of losing. There was no real tension in the dream, just the dogged working through of tests, the outcome of which was certain, since the Divya who was most Divya knew that her man told her the truth, and that the others were deceivers. It was simply a matter of completing the course.

Finally, the main Divya won and a riot ensued as the other Divyas surged forward to attack her. The dreams always ended like this – with the Divyas battling it out, thick black hair flying, faces scratched and bleeding, shins kicked and bruised. They fought until the confusion was so great it made Divya wake up. But she woke with the knowledge, every time, that battle scarred as she might be, she had come out on top. It never occurred to Divya to wonder what the Worms thought of all this violent activity in their universe. They were a different dream for a different day.

The experimenting angel would have noticed how Divya always woke with a slight smile on her lips — a smile that was notably absent during the rest of the day.

It was dreamtime for Grace, too, but since she was in another place she was not part of the angel's observations, so what she thought about dreams and their content would not have been recorded, and so was neither here nor there — rather like Grace's current position within the house.

Only Jock Daneford was not asleep; he hadn't been sleeping at all well lately. But since Jock was neither asleep, nor, like Grace, within the actual boundaries of the angel's investigations, his thoughts were not considered.

It's possible that an angel less earthbound in her approach to experimentation than the one under consideration might have thought about the slumbering consciousness of one other party present in the nighttime group: the house itself. There would be no eye movements to note, of course, but in the disturbed silence of human sleep, regular breathing and snoring, there were other sounds. Creakings, sighings, groanings, rustling: small but definite noises that, funnily enough, sounded very like the sounds the people made while they were asleep.

Perhaps some other angel with a different set of parameters might have concluded that the house was dreaming, too. After all, it had a history; it had grown and changed; time and people had impinged on it; energy, in the form of electricity, hummed through connective wires in its walls. If dreams were the dispersal of excess energy, why shouldn't the house have its dreams, and react in whatever way it could, with pleasure or fright, at accidentally stimulated memories?

But such a notion would be too fanciful for a rigorous angel, familiar with the human rules of categorization, who regarded anthropomorphism as second only to moral relativism in the hierarchy of cardinal sins.

People were people. Houses were houses. And angels were angels. Any other approach to being was fit only for children, the soft-headed and a handful of novelists who were more to be pitied than blamed for not knowing any better.

13

Grace Drops By

Daphne spent her first few minutes awake recollecting the events of
the night before. She kept her eyes shut, the better to enjoy the
memory. Liam emitted deep and regular snores from his side of the
bed, so Daphne could tell he was still deeply asleep. She was pleased
about this because, for the moment, it put off the slight nagging worry
she had about Liam's frame of mind when he woke up and found her
next to him in his bed. She was certain that their night of love was to
be more than the single desperate act of a drunk and hopeless man,
but she also knew that there might be an initial resistance to the new
situation.

It was a well-known sign of men's incomplete emotional make-up
that they took some time to acknowledge their commitment, even
when it was already a *fait accompli*. Daphne knew it to be the nature of
the male to try to escape the inescapable, and that Liam would be, in
this, a man among men. Escaping from something was one thing, but
what they thought they were escaping *to* was a mystery, probably
especially to them. *Freedom*, they would say, and invariably said, but
that was no more than a two-syllable *Homo sapiens* version of 'Ug'.
Very homo. Very sapient.

Not that Daphne hadn't done her fair share of non-commitment.
She had to admit that she had probably been *Homo sapiens* along with
the rest of them, until the idea of freedom had suddenly redefined
itself in her sixty-ninth year, and flashed its new version up, laser
bright, in her mind. Freedom, she had decided, was anything at all
provided it was uncircumscribed by the razor wire of safety and
propriety, when it became nothing whatsoever, no more than a two-
syllabled grunt of discomfort.

With her eyes still shut, Daphne extended her arm under the duvet and felt for the soft inside of Liam's thigh to quell her abstract anxieties with warm flesh. What she found under her palm made her feel like the witch who inhabited the gingerbread house in the wood adjacent to Hansel and Gretel's cottage. Too skinny, too smooth, she thought, alarmed. Had Liam wasted away during the night? Liam's thigh this morning was all hard bone and scrawny tendon; there was no flesh at all for a hungry old witch to get her teeth into.

Cautiously, she opened her eye nearest the side of the bed that Liam occupied. It registered the slender, sleeping form of Divya, black hair amok on the pillow, thumb stuck in her mouth. Daphne opened the other eye and raised her head in order to take the situation in thoroughly. It was true. Divya was squeezed between Daphne and Liam, who was still asleep and snoring, but pushed to the very edge of the neither queen- nor king-sized double bed. Her hand rested on the skinny thigh of Divya. Daphne was at least relieved of the fear that Liam had undergone a terrible transformation during the night. That was something.

Liam himself was no longer in a state of nature in his cloister, the butt of a joke between God and His angels. He was currently standing on the edge of a massive clifftop with the boiling sea crashing against great rocks far beneath him. He was Icarus now, and on the very verge of challenging gravity, or God, depending how one looked at it (God was never very far from Liam's dreams). At the same moment that Daphne raised her head to get a good look at the interloper in the bed, Liam stepped off the edge of the cliff and realized, just before the other leg left its mooring, but too late to do anything about it, that he had, inexplicably, forgotten his wax and feather wings. He fell, plummeting like a lead bullet towards the cruel granite and foam that waited to receive him, and, with a jerk that almost lifted him off the bed, woke up, just before he rolled off his tiny portion of the mattress.

For a moment he was stunned, still tensed against the breaking of his bones. Then he understood he was awake and his eyes focused on the company that was gathered in his bed.

First Daphne. The essence of the previous night came back to him: the drunkenness, the hangover, the bondage, the final lust before losing consciousness. Daphne was half sitting up in the bed, her hat still on her head but lopsided from sleep, blinking at him. Liam blinked

151

back, undecided about his reaction. Then his eyes fell on Divya, lying on her back, her wide-spread legs having caused Liam's near tumble.

He could make no sense of this at all. He wondered if he shouldn't have risked the terrible fall from the clifftop in preference to the prospect that the current waking world held out to him. But the easy way out was no longer on offer. He had rejected it, not knowing, as his cunning psyche or demon did, that the alternative was much worse than an ordinary horrific death.

'Oh, Jesus,' he groaned, clutching the edge of the bed. 'Oh, Jesus.'

'We've got a visitor,' Daphne explained, her eyes as wide as Liam's.

'I've got a bedful of visitors,' Liam croaked, not so much to Daphne, but to the voice he thought might be coming from inside his extremely painful and unhappy head.

The front door slammed. Footsteps on the stairs indicated it was someone coming in, not someone going out. It was eight in the morning. Daphne knew it was not Liam; Liam knew it was not Daphne; they both knew it couldn't be Sylvie, who would still be in the middle of her night, or Divya, who was snoring quietly between them. They kept perfectly still, frozen like a stalled film, as the footsteps grew louder and stopped on the landing outside Liam's bedroom door.

The film moved only one frame as Grace opened the door and entered, then it stopped again so that the tableau now contained three immobile adults and a sleeping child.

The movie was restarted by Daphne.

'Hello, dear. This is a surprise, isn't it?'

It wasn't clear to anyone present who Daphne was suggesting was the recipient of the surprise. It didn't matter, at least it got things going.

Liam said, 'Grace' in a voice that was still a groan, but lacked any definite intention.

Grace stared at the threesome in the bed that had been hers until the night before. She had come with a mission and a speech that she had been carefully rehearsed in by Melville Harriman. It carried her forward in spite of the shock.

'I've come to get my things. I'm moving into Melville Harriman's flat. I want a divorce, but if you refuse to give me one I'll just wait until I can get it on the grounds of separation. I love him, and he loves me. Melville, I mean.'

This had no effect on anyone for the moment. The plan had been to say her piece and then gather her clothes together, refusing to utter another word apart from 'My solicitor will write to you about it' in response to anything that Liam might say. Grace and Melville had ruled out the possibility of violence. They had decided, after much discussion, that Liam's languid character precluded an actual physical assault. Even so, Melville had insisted she make the visit first thing in the morning so that Liam would be predictably hung-over rather than unpredictably drunk.

Grace's set piece hung uselessly in the air like a knock-knock joke at a siege. Once again Daphne came to the rescue.

'That's a jolly good idea. Best thing for everyone, I should say. Don't you think so, Liam?'

Liam merely continued to stare at Grace in the doorway.

Grace, who according to the plan should have been efficiently bustling about the room putting clothes into a suitcase, remained where she was as if, the rehearsed speech being over and done with, she was now free to take in the extraordinary sight before her eyes.

'Liam?' she said, with a genuine question in her voice.

It crossed her mind that it was possible that it *wasn't* Liam. Perhaps she was mistaken. She might have come to the wrong house. She might, given the improbable vision in front of her, have come to the wrong planet, the taxi being a space machine and not the black cab it had appeared to be at all. Anything was more possible than what she was seeing.

'What did you say?' Liam asked her, knowing that she had said something of importance which he had somehow omitted to listen to.

It did seem to be Liam. It was his voice, and it looked like him. Grace couldn't remember what she had said. She couldn't exactly remember what she was doing here. She was unable to answer Liam's question.

'She said she was going to go and live with Neville Hurrying, dear. She's come to get her clothes,' Daphne explained, helpfully. 'You just carry on, dear, don't mind us,' she added to Grace with a kindly smile.

Liam turned his attention to Daphne. He looked at her for a long moment. He appeared to be thinking hard, like someone in the middle of an exam. Liam was trying to comprehend this waking world which had none of the logic of his dreams.

'Your hat's crooked,' he told Daphne.

It seemed, having taken all the circumstances into account, the only appropriate thing to say.

'Thank you, dear,' Daphne said, adjusting it.

'Liam!' Grace screamed, no longer asking a question.

Divya woke up and looked around her: at Daphne, at Liam, at Grace. Obviously, they were having a meeting. She was used to grown-ups having meetings.

'Where's my mother?' she asked Daphne, whom she decided was in charge.

If her mother was the only one absent, then the meeting was probably about her. It must mean that Sylvie was in trouble, which was worrying to Divya, who sensed change in the air. Nothing lasted for very long, she knew. She was hardly surprised, but she wondered dully what this would mean for her own future. Where would they put her now?

No one took any notice of Divya's question, which also didn't surprise her. She was often ignored. On the whole, she preferred being shouted at, or even hit.

There was nothing about this situation that was to Liam's liking. Grace wanted a divorce. She was taking her lovely body off to someone else. One of the things Liam didn't like was the fact that, in spite of all the time and effort and the catastrophe he had made of his life on behalf of Grace's body, he was able to contemplate its loss without feeling anything very much at all. He should, at the minimum, feel devastated, desolate, without hope, if only to justify his enormous emotional, physical and financial expenditure. What was all that misery for – his, Sophie's, the children's, Grace's, even – if he didn't care that Grace was going to leave him?

Something else Liam didn't like followed from the previous thought. He considered the possibility, with Grace gone, and his mistake acknowledged, of begging Sophie's forgiveness with all the tears he deserved to shed, and asking her to take him back. He knew immediately she would refuse. She was settled with David and had lost all trust in him. But Sophie's refusal to take him back was not what disturbed Liam. It was his realization that he didn't mind. In fact, there was a sense of relief.

What could all this mean? How was it possible for him to see the two women who had meant everything to him for so long disappearing from his life, and to find it perfectly acceptable? There was not so much as a flutter from his aching, sentimental, obsession-drenched heart.

Which brought him to the third aspect of his morning's events which was not to his liking. He didn't mind losing Grace, and having irrevocably lost Sophie, because he was engaged elsewhere. When he turned to look at Daphne he felt the old tautening of his throat, his loins and his uncontrollable heart. It was as unmistakable, that physical reaction, as it was ridiculous. His eyes told him it was ridiculous, this daft old woman with her crooked hat and time-worn face, her flabby-skinned shoulders naked, her limp tits covered by the duvet she held up in a mockery of modesty; but whatever his eyes told him, they were the same eyes that sent the signal which caused the rest of his body to contract with excitement.

He was in love with Daphne.

He didn't like that at all.

'I am in love with Daphne,' Liam heard himself say in answer to Grace's question.

Liam's statement addressed Grace's unformed question, but certainly didn't answer it. Grace's stunning and stunned grey eyes merely got wider and more perplexed.

'Yes,' said Daphne, reinforcing Liam's declaration with a quiet confidence all her own. 'It's true, he is.'

It was true. He was. God knew how, or why, but there was no question about it. It was like a migration. Passion had picked up its suitcase and headed for a new destination. It was the same passion that had searched for God as its ultimate mate, and, not finding Him, Her or It, had fixed on Sophie, and then Grace, as fitting its hungry hollow space with as near precision as humans, having irregularly shaped bodies and souls, were likely to come.

Sophie had been a companion in every way, but passion was a jealous lord, and wanted it all for itself. It had rejected Sophie who had filled Liam's life so satisfactorily, and turned to Grace whose charms were solely limited to passion's domain. To hell with Liam's happiness, that wasn't the project at all. And now Daphne. What was it she had that overrode Liam's single-minded desire for Grace?

Liam had not the faintest idea, except that she had none of the qualities of his previous objects of desire. Passion, still sulking at God's refusal to come out and play, had chosen to hang out with perversity, making the worst of a bad job. Passion and perversity were an unpredictable pairing; a dangerously capricious duo. A sudden fixation on the unlikely and the impossible was, perhaps, only to be expected.

It came to Liam that he had never, not for one moment, been in control of his life, and that, equally, he hadn't made a single real decision, however it may have seemed to him at the time. Liam heard himself declare his love for Daphne to his former love, and realized as he spoke that he was master of nothing; on the contrary, he was at the mercy of dark, joking demons, who were his real self far more than his supposed self had ever been. *Wanting* had always been in charge, with the aid of biochemical minions which Liam had considered merely his servants. But actually, he could no more say no to his desire than stop enzymes pumping into his stomach to digest food, or adrenalin rushing to make his heart pound at the sight of what he had no wish to be deflected by.

Liam felt cosmically sorry for himself. And why shouldn't he? It wouldn't make any difference one way or another, but he felt somebody ought to sympathize with his situation, and he was the best person to do it with the wholeheartedness required. Self-pity was a nicely overwhelming emotion which allowed him to feel the collapse of his life like a brick wall falling on top of him, without having to consider the consequences, which were, in any case, unimaginable.

The situation confronting Grace was, visually powerful though it may have been, incomprehensible to her. Several possible explanations rushed through her head, but only the sexual ones made enough sense to stay. It seemed more likely to Grace that Liam was guilty of child abuse than of having sex with an old woman. But if it was true, what would Daphne be doing in bed with them? *Perhaps the two of them were* ... But Divya didn't look abused, she just looked sleepy, and Liam had said, 'I'm in love with Daphne.' Grace tried to think of other things the phrase might mean, but there was no ambiguity in the statement. It had to mean what it appeared to mean, but, for Grace, it *had* no meaning if 'I' meant Liam, and 'Daphne' meant Daphne, and 'love' meant what she thought it meant.

There was no place in Grace's understanding of the nature of the world for such a statement. She had not thought very much about beauty as an abstraction, so she hadn't dwelt on the slightly curious fact that old *objects* were considered beautiful often because of the signs of time rather than in spite of them. In the realm of practical beauty she knew that youth, firmness and slimness were the constituents of what was desirable. She was those things, and she was desirable – which was another thing she knew without surprise. There was no possibility in her mind of there being anything else to be desired. She had read, of course, during her time at college, suggested chapters of books criticizing such a limited description of beauty, and, at the time, she agreed with the arguments, as far as she understood them. They seemed to say it was unfair on women who were not young, firm and slim. Grace saw it was unfair. But what could you do? That was how things were, and, well, there it was. As a novice feminist she did her best to be aware of how lucky she was to have youth, and an attractive body to go with it. She practised sympathy for those who were not so fortunate. And although she knew in principle that she would age, and her body would inevitably change, she never *really* believed it any more than she actually believed that one real day, at one real moment, she would die.

So Grace's reading, as a student, had not helped to broaden her view of the nature of desire and its objects. Indeed, the books seemed to confirm what she had already experienced: that she would be the object of desire for men of all ages, and others who were older, fatter and flabbier would not.

Therefore, what could Liam possibly mean when he said he was in love with the naked old woman who was sharing Liam's bed?

Grace could not take in what her eyes and ears were telling her. There was something wrong with a world which gave out such messages. Everything had seemed normal when she woke up this morning beside Melville, and it had stayed that way until she walked through the door of the room which had, only the day before yesterday, been her bedroom. The answer was, obviously, to leave and return to the world where things were normal and the way everyone — men, feminists, adolescents, magazine editors, manufacturers, advertisers, scriptwriters, novelists — expected them to be.

She decided to leave her clothes where they were for the time being. She would phone next time and make sure that everyone was out before returning to get them. With a renewed sense of purpose, she swivelled on her heels and left the room where the world wasn't normal, closing the door quietly but firmly on the small group of people who watched her in silence from the bed.

Grace was as sane a young woman as ever had been born on the planet.

14

Divya and Daphne
Make Breakfast

Sylvie was probably not sane. Not if sanity means that a person can look at their behaviour and its effects, and adjust it appropriately if it makes life impossible to live. On that definition, Sylvie was not sane.

She was perplexed by the way the world seemed to be and unable to make any connections between her behaviour and life's impossibility. But even if she had made the connections, it was very unlikely that she would have been able to make the necessary adjustments.

She was closer in some ways to those lower orders of creatures who, finding the world impervious, for some reason, to a piece of instinctive behaviour, nevertheless continue uselessly to do what no longer works until they drop dead with exhaustion, or a predator comes along and gobbles them up at its leisure. They, and Sylvie, were restricted to set forms of activity that they were unable to alter to take account of the current circumstances. The animals were like this because they did not have enough brain power to give them a degree of autonomy from their inbuilt behaviours. This was not true of Sylvie, who had all the brainpower needed to think a way through most of the difficulties the world placed before her. Why she was unable to do this was a mystery, most of all to Sylvie herself, who could not understand why it was that everything that life required of her was simply *impossible*.

She no longer wondered much about this mystery, however. She had given up even the small amount of effort she once made. Now, life was on top of her, and she felt it to be so in a quite literal way. She experienced living as a terrible burden that sat on her head, shoulders and chest. She went about, when not lying in bed, actually stooped; her head bowed, her shoulders rounded, her spine curved with the weight of all the things she could not manage. She looked, always, as if she were walking into a wind.

But she lived with the weight, she did not think about it much. For most of the time, now, her mind was occluded by a dense, grey fog. Very occasionally, she made an attempt to enumerate the problems, just to list them in an orderly fashion, but almost instantly crimson and white flashes tore through her head, and the problems, now an undifferentiated and insupportable mass, poured like molten shit over any embryonic coherent thought which might have been struggling for life.

The only thoughts that lived vividly were 'I don't understand' and 'Why, why, why?' and 'I hate them/her/him/it'. The why of it had no answer, not for Sylvie, nor for anyone who tried to work it out on her behalf. There had been no simple, terrible trauma in her early life, only a suburban ordinariness, damaging enough, perhaps, but which millions of other people had survived. It was as if she had incrementally let go of the capacity to deal with the day-to-day business of living. Somewhere during the period of drifting and wondering what to do with herself, which all her contemporaries had experienced, she had lost the knack of doing what had to be done, and enough people and passing cults had taken her in to make it unnecessary for her to try. Helplessness had become a mode of existence which worked well enough not to bother with more difficult routes. Perhaps Sylvie's condition was no more than a character trait of mild laziness which, reinforced over the years, had become a prison with unscalable walls. But to call it laziness is not to suggest a moral judgement. Sylvie truly could not think of any way of being different. And she was as unhappy a person as there could be; at the bottom of a spiral of helplessness and unhappiness that, like ecstasy, could only be experienced and never effectively described.

Most people have times when things, as they say, get on top of them. When a door on chaos opens a crack and they see muddle pressing through the gap, threatening to spill into the world of orderly process they have made for themselves, and undo everything. Lives are knitted to a pattern, but, as any knitter knows, even the most complex weave is only multicoloured threads that, once undone, are nothing but a tangled mess. Most people need to keep on knitting like crazy to stop everything falling apart. It's the story of social organization. The threads, potential chaos though they are, must be continually patterned, but the threads themselves are necessary.

'What you need ...' people advise others who are going under. 'What you need *is a job*.' 'What you need is a flat of your own to run.' 'What you need is *a husband/wife/lover to care for*.' 'What you need is *a child*.' And, usually, just some of these components of normality won't do. People with a job, a house, a companion, will be told they need a child; *that's* what's wrong. A woman (or a man) with all those things but without paid employment will be told that getting work will sort things out. There have to be enough threads to make the pattern complex enough to keep the fabric solid.

But all this depends on a sense of normality. It requires a focus on an ideal, a feeling of what is right and proper. Sylvie had none of this. It so happened she had some of the parts of the pattern – a flat, a child – but it was accidental, and she was still surprised that she should have either: neither at home in one nor at home with the other. Sylvie's expectations were not exactly beyond the norm. She expected other people to have the things that added up to normal. Indeed she required it of them. It disturbed her to find people who did without them, and they were people she avoided. It was grown-up to be part of a household, a worker, a parent. *They* were supposed to be grown-up; *she* was not. She did not feel like one of the grown-ups. She depended on others for that. Which put Divya in a curious position. Sylvie was a child who had a child, and she knew it was not appropriate for her. The things which held other people's lives together could not help her; they did not serve the same function.

Currently, Sylvie's mind was clogged with rage. Once again, someone had slammed the front door and woken her up. She looked at the clock. It was just gone eight. She became hysterical with anger. Whoever had woken her should die. They should fucking die. Run over by a lorry; fall under a train; get cancer.

Her resentful fantasies stopped her from getting back to sleep.

'Fucking cunt!' she shouted to the empty hallway, waking herself irrevocably.

She lay in bed for a while, feeling her heart pound. She had a headache and her mouth was dry from last night's Mogadons. She called out to Divya, who would still be asleep in the next room. There was no reply. She called louder, yelling her name. She had to have a cup of tea. She howled Divya's name with such force her lungs couldn't cope and caused a fit of choking and coughing that made everything worse. All her anger now focused on the child who refused to answer her call, until she had accumulated enough angry energy to fling back the bedclothes and stamp into the next room.

The room was empty. The duvet was crumpled up at one end of the sofa, and the bit of crocheted blanket Divya always slept with had gone.

Sylvie sank on to the sofa and pulled the duvet tightly around her, hugging it against her chest. She was miserable. There was a whole day ahead of her, and nothing special about it, nothing to do, which was both a relief and an intolerable threat. It was an unthinkably long time to wait until night came. She tried to cheer herself up a little with the promise of a nap during the afternoon. Well, a good, long sleep, actually.

She supposed that Divya was around somewhere. She was always wandering around, sitting on stairs or in corridors, or being nowhere so far as Sylvie was concerned until she turned up. Sylvie wished she was there to make her a cup of tea. Putting the kettle on herself seemed like too much of an effort. She looked around the living room and the adjoining kitchenette. There were two levels of mess: one her own, the other Divya's. Sylvie's mess was like background noise, she hardly noticed it. It consisted of the usual mounds of washed and unwashed clothes and sheets, which occasionally she put into different heaps with the intention of putting one lot away and taking the other to the launderette. Usually she put off these activities for so long that the piles got muddled up – a not too dirty sheet was put on her bed, and the soiled one thrown on the mound of clean stuff. The overflowing ashtrays, old cups of coffee with grey scum attached to the side and greasy plates in the sink made it all the more difficult to contemplate washing up. On the table, in a small space surrounded by clothes and tapes, was a pile of letters; some opened, others still sealed in their window envelopes. Next to them a bottle of milk had solidified and looked too unpleasant to touch, let alone empty.

All this was, however, familiar landscape, and her own. But Divya's mess was different. It was not that there was more of it than Sylvie's; there was considerably less. But it was not of Sylvie's making and, being other, it seemed to make the ordinary intolerable. There was no more than a scattering of stuff; dirty knickers, taken off and left on the floor here and there; a few piles of discarded clothes; some books; sweet papers; a half-empty box of Sugar Puffs lying on its side under the table; coloured pens dotted around, separated from their tops; comics lying open on top of washing. On its own, Divya's mess would have taken an efficient half-hour to clear up, but to Sylvie's eyes it was this mess which made it impossible to do anything about the state of the room. Without the superfluity of Divya's stuff, the chaos would have been manageable. So it seemed to Sylvie, in spite of the fact that the living room and kitchen had been an undealable-with mess since the third day of Sylvie's occupancy, long before Divya and her detritus arrived. But Sylvie had no recollection of this. Throughout her life, what was impossible *now* was worse than was impossible *then*. And it was always now, and never then. The inexorability of time was what most marred Sylvie's existence.

Sylvie was as exasperated by Divya's slovenliness as any house-proud mother might be who had drummed the virtues of good order into her child to no avail. But Sylvie grew monsters easier than most, and Divya's disorder became a considered malevolence, a deliberate aggression which, added to her equally deliberate absence now, when Sylvie needed a cup of tea in bed, made a demonic sprite of her ordinarily untidy daughter. It was not *fair* when things were so difficult for her anyway, that she should have to put up with this, too; this extra burden. Why would no one help her? Why did they deliberately make things impossible for her? She could have managed all right, if it wasn't for having the child. It was too much to ask of her. It wasn't fair. It wasn't fair because *she* needed help, *she* needed looking after. How could she be expected to manage to look after a child as well?

But, as always, there was no answer to this, beyond the unreasonable expectations of the world, and wrecking rage and misery continued to twist and sour her insides as if she had swallowed something corrosive. She pulled the duvet tighter around her, feeling herself diminish from the inside out. The mess out in the room seeped into her head until the physical landscape which she saw through her eyes was the inextricably muddled contents of her mind, and what she experienced as her mind was the hideously macaronic jumble of the room in which she sat.

The door on Sylvie's chaos opened wide, and the mess poured into everything and everywhere. She sobbed pathetically on the sofa.

With Grace gone, Liam turned his attention to Divya.

'And what are you doing here?' he demanded.

'Sleeping.'

'This isn't your bed. You live downstairs.'

This didn't have the same undeniable logic for Divya as it had for Liam. She stared at him.

'When did you come up here?' Daphne asked.

Divya shrugged.

'I don't like the crying.'

'Who? Your mother?' Daphne asked cautiously.

'No. The house.'

'I see, dear,' Daphne said, apparently prepared to leave it at that.

'Well, I don't,' Liam snapped. 'What is she talking about?'

'The house crying, dear,' Daphne explained. 'It does, I'm afraid. I don't know what can be done about it. An exorcism, perhaps.'

'The house is crying?' Liam asked carefully, trying to get things clear. 'A ghost?'

'No, I think it's more of a memory. Actually, I don't think exorcism would help. I don't know what you can do about memory.'

'I find drink works wonders,' Liam said glumly. 'You should have poured my whisky down a crack in the floorboards, instead of watering the plants with it.'

'Don't be silly, Liam.'

'I beg your pardon, my dear. I was only trying to help. It was my pitifully ineffectual attempt at participation in this new world I've woken up to, where houses cry and everybody sleeps in my bed. I don't seem quite to have got the hang of it yet.'

'I'll get you an aspirin, dear,' Daphne said gently, and reached down to the floor for her skirt and blouse. 'Come along, Divya, we'll make some tea. Liam's not feeling very well this morning.'

'Daphne?' Divya said as she was laying out the tray for Liam's tea and aspirin.

Daphne was pleased to hear her name.

'What is it, dear?'

'Why does the house cry?'

'Well, it's my fault, I'm afraid. I lived here when I was your age. I told you that, didn't I? My mother wasn't well, you see. Sometimes she had terrible frights and got confused and put me in that cupboard under the stairs. I cried a lot in there. I suppose the sound got stuck, or something.'

'It is like a ghost, then?'

'Well, I suppose it is, if you can have ghosts of people who aren't dead. And why not? Or perhaps it's the house itself. Perhaps it caught my unhappiness.'

'That's stupid. Houses can't be unhappy. They're just things.'

Daphne poured hot water into the teapot.

'I don't know,' she said thoughtfully, giving the idea proper consideration. 'Perhaps things soak up very strong feelings from people.'

She glanced at Divya who gave her the kind of look that Leonardo might have given the Schoolmen.

'And perhaps they don't,' she added, hastily. 'You know, Divya, one of the things I really like about being old is that I can think all kinds of silly thoughts, and not be in the slightest bit embarrassed about thinking them. There's something for you to look forward to. Still, silly as my thoughts might be, you hear the crying, don't you?'

Divya wanted to say something about how it was all right for *her* to think odd thoughts, but it was the job of grown-ups to put them out of her mind. But the thought was only lodged in her in the form of discomfort at Daphne's words; she had no language for her abstracted notion of what was fitting.

'My mum says I'm hearing things. She says there isn't any crying and I'm just making it up to drive her mad.'

This wasn't quite what she had wanted to say, because her mother's denial of what Divya knew she heard did not comfort her at all, any more than adults who took her childish thoughts at face value. It also brought up another concern. Divya felt a pull inside her between betrayal and need. But she couldn't stop herself speaking of it to Daphne.

'She cries all the time.'

'Your mother?'

Divya nodded and looked at an invisible spot on the floor in front of her.

Daphne looked at the same spot. She reminded herself that she was happy. That she had got what she wanted. Liam loved her. Everything was going the way she wanted it to. Divya's situation was not her problem. The fact that they were in the same house was nothing more than an accident and it was not necessary for Daphne to feel anything about Divya's difficulties. She reminded herself again that she was *happy* now. Happy ever after.

But the spot on the floor that they both stared at opened up to become a black hole filled with the anxiety and misery of being a child in the inadequate care of a hopeless adult. It was not Divya's feelings alone filling the hole; it was simply *what it felt like*. For all of them. The black hole belonged to them both, and also to the nameless, countless others. Daphne's heart ached with her old unhappiness that lived on in Divya. Happy ever after or not, Daphne knew exactly how it was to be the little girl who helped her lay a tray for her lover, and it filled her with misery like molten lead. Wishing she didn't know helped her not at all.

'You have to know what you know. There's no being picky,' she told herself firmly.

'What?' Divya asked.

'I said, you have to know what you know. There's no getting away from it, dear.'

'You say funny things, sometimes.'

'And some of them are true, dear. I wish I could be sure which were which, though.' And as if she had heard and interpreted Divya's thoughts on the unsatisfactory nature of grown-ups, she added, 'This will disappoint you, but it seems to take a lifetime to get grown-up, and even then, it's only now and again. But,' she hurried on, realizing how alarming that must sound to a small child locked into helplessness, 'even when you make mistakes, it's still better to be in charge of things. It does get better, Divya, eventually, I promise you that.'

Daphne reminded Divya of the fairy godmother in a film of Cinderella her mother had taken her to see when she had her one weekend. They were both daft and not like other people she'd known, and she had been greatly encouraged, the night before, when she climbed into bed with the sleeping Daphne and Liam to find that Daphne kept her soft, squashy hat on even when she was asleep. Of course, Daphne hadn't made any magic, but sometimes she sounded as though she could. Not that Divya wanted to go to a ball in a glass coach and dance with a prince, or anything. She had a kind of wanting place inside her, but she hadn't worked out what it was wanting, yet. She thought a fairy godmother might tell her, and she was fairly sure some kind of magic would be needed to get it, whatever it was. She had hopes of Daphne, mostly because, although she didn't understand much of what she said, she felt she *almost* did, or that she might, some-time.

'You say funny things, Daphne,' Divya said again, buttering the last slice of toast.

'Thank you, dear,' Daphne smiled, pleased, in spite of her resistance to knowing the child's unhappiness, that they seemed to be friends. 'Now, I'll take this up to Liam, and you better go downstairs and get ready for school. Your mother will be wondering where you are.'

Divya looked at Daphne as she opened the door for her.

'I don't like my name.'

'It's a pretty name.'

'It means Divine Love. My mum said.'

'Well, that's nice. There's nothing wrong with that.'

There was a bit of a silence while they both looked at each other, each knowing that both of them knew what was wrong with it, in all manner of ways.

'Perhaps you ought to think of another name, a sort of private one, you like better. We could keep it just for us. But Divine Love's not bad as something to aim for,' Daphne said, in a way that Divya almost understood, as she started to make her way upstairs with Liam's break-fast.

15

Plans for the Future

'Now that we've got ourselves nicely sorted out,' Daphne said, handing Liam two aspirins, 'I think we ought to have a word about Divya.'

Liam swallowed both his pills and gulped down a tumblerful of water.

'I wonder if you could explain to me exactly how we've got things sorted out. I'm sorry to be obtuse, but I'm having a very trying morning, what with one thing and another.' He winced.

'Well, dear, I love you and you love me . . .'

'Di dum, di dum, di dum, di di,' Liam intoned with all the rhythm he could muster. 'I used to be an intelligent person – not in matters of the heart or scrotum, perhaps, but in most other areas of life, I was considered to be an almost clever member of the human race.'

He looked mournful.

'Well, of course you are, my love. No doubt about it. Very intelligent. You don't have to worry about that. We can have all kinds of interesting and very intelligent conversations when we're travelling together. We can talk about human nature, and discuss the mysteries of time and space. And you can tell me all about primitive societies and the way they're different, and the way they're not. As a matter of fact, dear, you won't find me completely ignorant of anthropological ideas – I read some of your old papers when I was rummaging around in your study, and jolly interesting and intelligent some of them were, too. And then I'll make comments and observations, some of which will surprise you with their insight. Mind you, there will be others – observations – that won't be so clever, but think how much I'll learn during our chats about life. No, you mustn't worry, we'll have a tremendously intellectual time of it.'

Liam allowed the bit about rummaging in his study to pass without comment. He knew he had only so much energy available. He had to pick his way carefully through the confusion and only use his limited resources to cut a path towards something which made sense. That was the most urgent task: making sense of *something* – anything would do for now.

'What do you mean "when we're travelling together"?' he asked carefully.

'That's what we're going to be doing. Didn't I mention it? Surely I did? I could have sworn I had, but perhaps I only thought I'd mentioned it. I've had so many conversations with you when you weren't there, I get confused sometimes.'

'Didn't it bother you when you didn't get any answer from me when I wasn't there?'

This, he knew, wasn't strictly to the point; it just slipped out.

'Oh, but you always answered me. They wouldn't have been conversations otherwise, would they? I'm not as stupid as all that.'

'Did I say anything interesting?'

'Masses, dear. As you said, you're a very intelligent man. Of course, it's not the same as the conversations I have with God, but then they they wouldn't be, would they? Mind you, you're both very grumpy individuals, so you've got something in common.'

'God,' Liam said, unable not to notice that he was almost enjoying himself.

'God,' Daphne repeated. 'Come on, eat your toast, you'll feel better for it.'

Liam remembered the path he was cutting.

'Go on about the travelling.'

'I went to see my old publishers – not that my old publishers are still there.' She remembered that David was dead, and had to blink a sudden sadness away. 'Anyway, this nice young man liked the idea of my book of love, and wanted to reprint my old books. He was *very* pleased to see me. So he's giving me an advance, and I'm going to buy a . . . motor home, I believe they're known as in the trade, and we'll travel about together as I write my book. We could go' – she thought for a moment and then said in a tone of discovery – 'anywhere. Wherever our fancy takes us.'

She smiled triumphantly at this realization of complete freedom.

'What book of love?' Liam yelled, having forgotten their previous, less than amiable conversation on the subject; but it only gave him unnecessary pain, so he spoke in a softer tone. 'I'm writing a book about love, not you.'

'No, you're not, you're thinking about it. I've already written fifty words of mine. But that's all right, you can write one too. They're not very likely to be the same, are they? Anyway, mine's going to be a novel. About you and me, and our love affair. I can't imagine there'll be a problem about it; after all, everyone writes books about love all the time, and no one seems to mind. The more the merrier, if you ask me. Of course, we'll have to have two typewriters, but that's not a problem, we can take one end each of our motor home . . . ' – she paused, pleased with how natural sounding this technical term had become – ' . . . as studies, and meet in the middle for lunch and lust.'

Liam shook his head in confusion. It didn't help to clear it, so he shook it longer and more slowly. This also didn't help. His life, after all, was in ruins. But then, it had been in ruins for as long as he could remember; for several years, anyway. This was just a different kind of ruin. More total, perhaps, but certainly more entertaining. He felt slightly better for that thought; a little more able to move towards the crux of the issue.

'Daphne,' he said, quite severely for someone so hung-over. 'I don't want to travel in a . . . motor home. I've got a house. I live here. My wife has just left me, for a . . . a . . . big fish. My life is a wreck.'

Daphne took his hand in hers and patted the back of it encouragingly.

'Exactly, dear. Your life *is* a wreck. Do you like this house?'

'Well, no, I hate it, but that's not . . . '

'Do you have any work?'

'No, but . . . '

'Do you love me?'

'Yes.' There was a pause while the shock of his affirmative rang in Liam's ears. He continued after a moment. 'But you must see . . . ' – he tried to explain the absurdity to himself as much as to Daphne – '. . . that I'm not in a rational frame of mind. Neither of us should trust my emotions. It's all very well for me to say I love you . . . to feel it,' he acknowledged with a massive scrunching of his face. 'But, we must ask ourselves, my dear, how real is it? How can we make plans on the basis of a sudden emotional explosion?'

'I've already made them, my dearest,' Daphne told him, unfazed by Liam's common sense. 'There's nothing sudden about it, actually. I've known for months that you would love me. It just took you a little longer to find out, that's all. Anyway, it doesn't seem that there's much here to hold you, so what possible objection could there be to travelling? What's the point of standing still?'

'For one thing, it's less exhausting than moving. And what about my children?'

Daphne waved her hand in the air.

'We can come back to London quite regularly, and they can come and visit us. I get on well with children – and, think of it, dear, they'll have a stepmother and a granny all at the same time. Isn't that nice?'

'Oh, Daphne,' Liam groaned softly, and pressed his other hand on top of the one patting his. Mad though it was, he felt his heart bursting with affection for her. But was it anything more than just the kind of warmth he might have felt for a sweet old aunt? It was, because beneath the swell of affection, desire began to stir again, mixing like a heady cocktail with the memory of his seduction by her the previous night. There was a bountiful affection and plentiful lust, neither of which, to his knowledge, had been present together in him since he had left Sophie. With her, he had called the combination love; why not with Daphne? What was missing that made it something less? Admiration? He was full of it, listening to her peculiar but efficiently laid plans. Humour? That certainly wasn't missing, once he had his ear in. If all that didn't add up to love, then it hardly mattered, because he had called much less love. What he had felt for Grace had never been more than desire, mixed with a penchant for hopelessness. He had given up everything for that. And now, here was Daphne, dotty, maddening, but capable of making him, in the midst of the worst hangover in his entire existence, want to hug her and feel her queer reality pulse against his tired flesh. He wasn't even sure if he didn't feel that with her, he *might* write a book. If it wasn't love, it was enough.

'I love you,' he said, and reached out to pull Daphne towards him.

'I know, dear,' Daphne answered, and followed the pressure of his arms.

*

'Now, Liam, dearest,' Daphne said, straightening her hat, when they had finished making love as satisfactorily, and even more, than the night before. 'About Divya.'

'What about Divya?' Liam murmured, on the edge of sleep.

'That's what we were talking about, before we got sidetracked with the travelling business. That's all settled now, isn't it, my treasure?'

'Perfectly settled, my dear.'

'So I think we should have a chat about Divya. I'm worried about her. She's unhappy.'

'I'm not surprised,' Liam said, trying to get back to sensible consciousness. 'Her life doesn't seem to be a model of stability. I wouldn't choose Sylvie to mother a cat. But it's none of our business.'

'I think we should take her with us, dear.'

'Take her with us, where?'

'Travelling.'

Liam sat up and stared down at Daphne's face on the pillow next to him.

'That's a good idea. Let's kidnap a seven-year-old child. If we're going to have an adventure, why not get Interpol in on the act, too?'

'I'm serious, Liam. It's not just that she's unhappy, I think something could happen . . . '

'Anything could happen, it does even in the best regulated of families, whatever they are. I should know. Daphne, you can't interfere in someone else's life just because you don't think it's going right.'

'Well, what should we do?'

'Nothing.'

'But what if something happened?'

'We can't do anything about it,' Liam insisted, partly from the position of a social scientist whose training was all about observing and keeping his distance from what he had observed, and partly in alarm at being faced with the idea of responsibility for anyone other than himself; and it had yet to be proven that he was capable of looking after himself. 'I've given Sylvie the flat, so she's got a base to look after the child. I haven't mentioned anything about the rent not having been paid since the week she moved in. Not that there'd be much point, anyway. She's got social workers watching out for her. That's as much as you can do for anyone.'

'I'm talking about the child, though.'

'So am I. You can't rescue someone from something that hasn't happened. Being unhappy doesn't count as something happening, not to the authorities – and not to me, either. How do you know what damage you would do to the child by taking her away from her mother, even if she is inadequate?'

'Don't be so silly, Liam. That's sentimental tosh. Being unhappy is *bad* for children; it makes them grow up all wrong. She's living in this house. How can we live with all that misery downstairs?'

'Well, according to you, we aren't going to live with it. We're moving on, and to tell you the truth, my dear, getting away from that lump of misery on the ground floor is one of the things that makes your plan so attractive.'

'Don't you care?'

'I'd rather not think about it clearly enough to care, Daphne. If I concentrated on that little girl's unhappiness and likely prospects, I'd have to think about all the unhappy little girls and boys in the world, and I haven't got the stamina for it. I don't have the heart. And what can you do, my dear? She's one of millions of victims of injustice of all sorts. Some people get strong surviving unhappiness and difficulty. All I can do is hope she's one of them. In the meantime, I just wish she'd keep out of my – I mean, our – bed.'

'But we *know* her. We don't know the others. We can do something.'

'No, we can't.' Liam was emphatic. 'Even if we had the right, how do you know what ought to be done?'

'Anything's better than what's going on down there.'

'No, it isn't.'

Daphne understood perfectly well what Liam was saying. She had had the same battle with herself over getting involved with Divya, but, having lost it, she found the idea of leaving the child to her fate unacceptable, even if there was a slim chance that all manner of benefits might flow from her situation eventually. Divya's unhappy prospects had poured into the place in Daphne where her own youthful misery was stored and mingled with it, so that walking away from Divya was the same as walking away from herself. Which was to say, as she had lately come to understand, impossible.

She sighed and said no more about it for the time being, letting Liam suppose that the subject was dropped. But it was not dropped as far as Daphne was concerned. For all that Liam was right in principle, she still felt that something should be done in this individual, known, personal case; the one they lived upstairs from. Not to do anything was too fatalistic for Daphne's new mode of being. Why leave things alone when you could do something about them?

She had to admit she didn't know what, though. Liam was right enough about that. Kidnapping Divya probably was a bad idea, and she supposed the authorities would be little difficult about allowing a small child to go off with Liam and his 68-year-old lover to nowhere in particular in a motor home. It wasn't very likely that they would get an official blessing, even if, as Daphne suspected, Sylvie might be grateful to have a problem lifted off her shoulders.

She wasn't so worried about Liam's lack of enthusiasm for Divya's company; she was sure she could talk him round, although there was a bit of a problem about how to manage their forthcoming vigorous sex life in a motor home with a small third party also in residence.

For the time being, she decided, she'd let it lie. Something would come to her, she was certain. She was sorry, though, that God had abdicated His responsibility for the planet, because He might have come up with a solution acceptable to everyone. But she knew Him well enough, by now, not to bother to ask Him. It was funny, really, how just when Daphne had decided to accept her involvement in what went on around and in her, everyone else, including everyone's Maker, seemed to have come to just the opposite direction. She felt, sometimes, very out of step with the universe; or rather, that it was out of step with her. You'd expect, she thought, life to reinforce the commitment she had made. Oh, well, timing was a very difficult business. It takes a lifetime to come to the right conclusion and then you get the timing wrong – or life does. Huh.

Liam had fallen asleep and was snoring gently, with the merest hint of a smile on his lips. Daphne hoped he was dreaming of her. She crept out of bed and dressed again. She was a little worried that she wasn't keeping to her fifty words a day schedule with *Happily Ever After*, but the organization had to be done. She would spend the rest of the day investigating the motor home situation. The sooner things were settled, the better. Later, when she got home, she would talk to Liam about what to do with the house over a supper of something delicious which she hadn't quite decided on. She was confident, though, that she would come up with just the right thing.

Sylvie looked balefully at Divya over the top of the duvet.

'Where have you been?' she demanded in a sullen voice. The rage had dissipated, now, there was no energy at all, just a large, pulsating tumour of resentment filling her up inside.

'Upstairs.'

Sylvie wasn't interested.

'Make me some tea. I've been waiting hours. Are you going to school today?'

'I suppose so,' Divya said, clearing enough room in the sink to fill the kettle. She longed, in truth, for Sylvie to tell her she had to go to school, because when she just asked, it gave Divya an awful, loose sort of feeling. She didn't particularly care for school; she was new there, and hadn't made any real friends, but she had a feeling of wrongness when Sylvie left it to her. It made everything begin to seem impossible, as if she were in a gigantic field, so big that she couldn't see the edges of it, and had no idea of which direction to go. It made her stuck in the middle of it, and fearful that there *were* no edges. At least in the home things were definite, meals at a certain time, school every day. Things here didn't feel right, even though being with your mother was supposed to be more right than living in a home.

'Do you want me to go to school today? Daphne says I should.'

'Who the hell's Daphne? Do as you please,' Sylvie said, refusing to make things right.

Daphne took the tube to Northolt, having found a place that sold motor homes in the Yellow Pages. The salesman explained how they convert second-hand vans into spacious and comfortable travelling accommodation, and showed Daphne the range. She was a little disappointed to find that none of them had electric windows, but the prices, ranging from £4,500 to £9,500, were well within the amount that she and George Maynard had discussed. She picked out the one that cost

£6,000 and said she would like to buy that. Delivery, she was told, would be eight weeks, which suited very well, because the contract for the book still had to be finalized and Liam would need that much time to sort out his affairs. Daphne had already sorted out hers, but there was still the matter of learning to drive to be attended to. She thought that eight weeks would be enough to get the hang of it. It couldn't be that difficult. Some of the most stupid people she had ever met were drivers. She would arrange on the way home to have lessons, and then, when the motor home was ready, so would everything else be. One example, at least, of nice timing.

She explained to the salesman that her publishers would be paying for the van, and gave him George Maynard's telephone number. He would send the cheque in time for her to pick the van up. The salesman readjusted his assumptions about Daphne. He had been as polite and helpful as possible, but he hadn't really believed she was a genuine customer. She wasn't their usual sort. Now that she had explained about being a writer, her bizarre appearance made more sense to him. He left Daphne alone in her chosen motor home while he went to his desk to do the paperwork.

Daphne sat on the foam-upholstered bench that converted, along with the bench opposite, into a double bed. She bounced up and down on it a few times, and then put her elbows on the fold-away table in front of her and looked around. There was, as the salesman had said, everything you could possibly need for living in the small space behind the two front seats: a fridge, cooker, sink, wardrobe, cutlery drawer, two small double beds – one she was sitting on, and another up by the elevating roof – and she had ordered a chemical lavatory that was an optional extra, though she didn't think it was all that optional – call her fussy if you like. Actually, she had not ordered just any old chemical lavatory. She had rather pushed the boat out in the toilet department. She was having a de luxe *cassette* loo. She was very taken with the notion, when the salesman had explained it to her, in the nicest possible way.

'It's top of the range. It means you don't come into contact with anything *unpleasant* when you empty it. The whole cassette automatically seals itself when it's full. All you have to do is take it away and dispose of the sealed contents. Hygienic, you see, very sanitary, and none of those *unwanted* odours left inside your motor home.'

Daphne said that she always tried to avoid unpleasantness whenever she could, and she would have one of those nice de luxe toilets, thank you very much, and damn the extra cost. She was sure her publisher would not want her to have to live with unpleasant odours.

There wasn't much room to swing a cat, what with all the handy built-in fitments, but they wouldn't have any pets, and it was all so homely that size didn't seem to matter. When they weren't making love or working — side by side it would have to be, since there was only one central table, although on nice days they would have picnic tables outside to work on — they could go for long, lovely walks in the beauty spots they would moor at, or park by, or whatever you did with mobile homes. She imagined the two of them lying in bed, waking to the smell of pine and the sound of birds nesting. They would come to slowly, at first unsure of their surroundings, but certain, even in their sleep, of whose arms they were lying in, and then they would make love as if there was all the time in the world. Which there was, because this would be their happily ever after.

Daphne had just got the sausages sizzling on the fold-away grill and the kettle on the boil, when the salesman came back with the sales agreement for her to sign.

'We're going to be very happy in this motor home,' she told him, with a smile, as she signed the document. 'Very happy indeed.'

'Are you planning to go anywhere special?' he asked amiably.

'Oh, everywhere, dear,' Daphne told him. 'We're going to go every-where and do anything and live happily ever after.'

The salesman decided to remember Daphne's name, because it sounded as though she wrote the type of books he liked to read; ones with happy endings. He couldn't see the point of reading about miserable people having rotten lives. The books he enjoyed were set in far-off, exotic places, and the people in them lived, as Ms Drummond said, happily ever after.

16

Domestic Bliss

There were several weeks of domestic bliss while Daphne and Liam
sorted things out. It had the charming, idiotic quality of newly-weds
playing house — a cocktail of cooking and sex. Daphne moved into
Liam's bedroom, making her attic a study where the Underwood,
useful at last, awaited her daily attention.

They lay in bed in the morning, after making love, but before Liam
got up to make Daphne a nice cup of tea, discussing their menu for
the day. Kidneys sautéd in sherry, perhaps. Or a leg of lamb braised
with coriander seeds. Sometimes, for a real treat, Liam would agree
with Daphne that fried egg and chips with brown sauce was to be the
high point of the day's eating.

And they loved to touch each other. Neither of them could walk
past the other without brushing a hand against a thigh, or the back of
the neck. Sometimes, Liam would get up from his armchair where he
sat reading, and walk across the room to kiss Daphne on the crown of
her hat, and she would look up from her copy of the Highway Code
and purse her lips, making the vertical lines around it that Liam had
come to love, and tempt him to bend lower and kiss them.

Liam, in the past, had been nothing if not fastidious — especially
about other people — but now he barely noticed the months of
accumulated grease and grime on the velvet hat which he now considered to be an organic part of his beloved, and therefore due as
much affectionate attention as any other part of her. He was quite
shocked the first time she took off the hat in his presence. Even
Daphne felt that it was inappropriate to keep it on while washing her
hair, which she had previously been in the habit of doing once a
month or so, if she remembered, but now did twice a week for the
new erotic activity it afforded. Liam watched her remove the hat

carefully with both hands, like a bishop might divest himself solemnly of his mitre when some more secular activity was at hand, and he marvelled at the wiry mass of crinkled grey hair that was revealed. She would sit nicely upright in the bath while Liam cherished, rather than washed, her hair, lathering, conditioning and combing it through, before gently rubbing it dry with his hands hidden in a towel.

Liam recalled that orthodox Jewish women kept their hair covered — with a wig, or a scarf — and understood about the sacrament of hair which was concealed from the world, only to be revealed to, only for the eyes of, the loved one. It was, he realized, a custom more sensual than holy; though, as Liam knew only too well, the holy and the sensual, if understood aright, were one and the same thing. He loved Daphne's hair which was only for him, and he loved Daphne's hat for hiding it, and therefore promising what was his alone.

In addition to culinary treats and devoted hair-washing, Liam liked to devise other pleasures for Daphne and himself. In the evenings he would read to her: they got through the Song of Solomon, the works of Gerard Manley Hopkins and *The Magic Mountain*, after each of which Daphne would smile happily at Liam and say, 'That was nice, dear.'

And they would go out: to art galleries, to look especially at Rembrandts, Turners and Van Goghs; and for walks to places neither of them had visited for years, to stare at the river from Waterloo Bridge, to feed the ducks at St James's Park, to discuss pruning techniques at the Rose Garden in Regent's Park. And always Daphne was pleased, her arm curled inside Liam's, smiling like a child on an outing, saying, 'This is very nice, dear. Thank you for bringing me.'

She especially loved Waterloo Bridge, because it reminded her of a film with Vivien Leigh, poor thing, that Daphne had seen as a girl (although she wasn't sure it might not have been *Westminster* Bridge in the film). And she was particularly partial to Rembrandt, because she thought the people he painted were probably a very interesting bunch, and wondered what they talked about during all the hours it took to make a painting.

'Money, probably,' Liam said.

In return, Daphne took Liam to old films at the National Film

Theatre and the Everyman, or just kept a watchful eye on the TV pages to see if something old and wonderful was on. Liam had never paid much attention to the movies, feeling vaguely that they were not serious, no more than an escape from reality. Daphne scoffed at his reluctance, and called him a pompous old fool, then took him along to *Bringing Up Baby*, which had Katharine Hepburn, Cary Grant and a leopard starring in it. It only took a few moments of sitting next to Daphne beaming with pleasure, and giving the charm the benefit of the doubt for her sake, for Liam to discover a little well in himself that filled with warm delight at the nonsense that flickered in front of his cynical old eyes.

'I used to go to the flicks all the time when I was a drunk. When things were bad,' Daphne said, and told Liam about those low days of her life.

'To tell you the truth, I think the flicks kept me alive. Of course, the films were better then – heaven knows what keeps drunks alive these days. But then,' she would reminisce, 'there was a whole worldful of films and stars that made me think – even at my foggiest – that human beings might be all right after all, in a hopeless sort of way. Watching a film with Katie Hepburn and Spencer Tracy was like having a warm bath and clean sheets all on the same evening. It set me up, it really did, although it made me very sad to think that I couldn't be part of their world. But, at least there were people some-where who could write and act as if wit and a sort of goodness did happen somewhere, and that was something.'

Liam thought about it while watching the films she remembered with special warmth, and realized that she might be talking about the same thing that happened to him when he snuck into the back pews for a mass which in reality had nothing any longer to do with him. He and Daphne were connected by similar longings, even if their routes had been apparently different.

'I think God enjoyed the *Pat and Mike* films much more than *The Ten Commandments*.'

Liam went with Daphne to a season of *Pat and Mike* films at the NFT, but was sceptical.

'Well, no doubt, my dear. There's no question which is in better taste. But one can't be sure about God. How do you know He has good taste? After all, He created Cecil B. De Mille in His own image as well as Frank Capra. Look at the evidence. For every Capra, Rembrandt and Mann, there's a peacock, or a turkey, or one of those dreadfully gaudy birds of paradise. What are we to make of that?'

Daphne wasn't bothered by this. She held no brief for good taste.

'Nonsense,' she said. 'Good taste has nothing to do with it. It's a matter of knowing what's what. And it's about goodness.'

'Oh, goodness,' Liam groaned.

'Now, Liam, there's no point in pretending you don't believe in goodness. Goodness is the whole thing.'

'The whole thing?'

'Yes, dearest,' she said severely. 'The whole thing. I know it isn't very easy to find, or even to recognize when you do find it, but we both know it's there, in small doses at least, don't we?'

'Do we?' Liam asked grumpily.

'Yes, we do. And what about us?'

'Is goodness something to do with us, my dear?'

'It certainly is, Liam. That's why we were destined for each other. Not because we're good. Obviously.'

Liam blinked a vigorous assent.

'But because we both believe in it, really. It's like being Adam and Eve, in reverse. Or Bonnie and Clyde. We're looking for the tree of knowledge of good and evil so that we can take a good hard look at the fruit. We might even take a bite. But this time, we won't let God or anyone else bamboozle us. Not with what I know about Him.'

'You're not suggesting that we're going to redeem the world, my dear, are you? Are we going to reverse original sin?'

'Oh, no, dear. That would be a bit arrogant, wouldn't it? I thought just a little investigation. We might find something more original than sin.'

'Such as . . . ?'

'Oh, I don't know,' Daphne said airily. 'What about original goodness, my darling?'

'Your theology is beyond me, as yet, my dear. Perhaps it will come clearer as we get to know each other better,' Liam said, blinking benignly at Daphne and the future.

*

When he wasn't devoting himself to Daphne, Liam set his house in order. He went to see his lawyer and made arrangements about the house, which, apart from the ground floor, was to be let, and any proceeds not needed for the running of the house and his children sent to him at addresses he would send from time to time.

He also tidied his desk. He wrote letters to the editors of the journals for whom he had failed to meet deadlines, apologizing, and explaining that he had been under severe stress, just in case he might need to work for them again. He judged that, if they lived modestly, with Daphne's monthly income from the advance for her book, the money from the house and an occasional article, they could manage well enough for the time being. And what other time was there?

During his visit to the lawyer, Liam instructed her to agree with Grace on a divorce. Alimony wouldn't be a problem, he thought, since she was going to marry Herman Marryville, who had a great deal more income than Liam.

In his spare time, he read three books with Daphne's name on the spine, which she brought down for him from her little bookshelf in the attic. He found them dreadfully depressing, but they enlarged his love for Daphne because he was able to fall in love with the distraught girl and young woman she had been, through the pages of her texts. He felt a rage about her miserable childhood – in this very house, he was even more pleased to be leaving it – and a terrible anger against the Bohemian set – most of whom were now dead – who had used her and thrown her away. He was moved by who she had been, and touched even more about who she had become. Her modest search for a little goodness made more sense to Liam, having read the whole story. She had nearly lost everything, and then become a seeker after ordinary happiness. Most extraordinary. It was, Liam told himself, a feat well beyond his own, bitter capacity. He loved and admired her all the more.

He was also better able to understand Daphne's anxiety about Divya. If he were her, he would want to rescue the child, too. But Liam was still his own person. If the pull on his emotions was greater for seeing it through Daphne's eyes, his head remained firmly of the opinion that it was neither possible nor desirable to interfere in another's life. It was all very well to take risks on one's own behalf – he was putting himself in Daphne's hands in full knowledge that the outcome would be disastrous – but it was out of the question to take an unknown path for someone else. Divya would have to stay where she was, and take her chances. And wasn't Daphne herself proof that it was possible to survive the worst of beginnings? He chose not to think of the argument he knew Daphne would make: how long it had taken to get herself straight; how easily she might not have survived; how dreadfully unhappy she had had to be for so many years.

Anyway, the truth was that he didn't want a complicated kid along on their love adventure. The trouble with seeing someone else's point of view in an argument is that you're obliged to face the fact that reason holds little sway compared with the desire to do, or not to do, what one wants, or doesn't. He felt sorry about Divya's situation, but he didn't want her coming along and messing things up. There it was.

Liam was perfectly well aware that Daphne was a witch and that he had been put under a spell. However, he had been under spells before, and he couldn't see what he had to lose. Well, everything, as a matter of fact, but the more he thought about it, the more everything didn't seem to amount to much.

Will-lessness was very much to his taste. It began with parents and then continued with God. Free will, he knew, was a pitiful attempt by the human race to pretend things were otherwise. Ancient and primitive (he mutely apologized to his ex-colleagues – he meant, of course, simple) societies knew perfectly well how things stood. Gods for this, gods for that; all of them arbitrary, unfair, given to high-handed favouritism. All you could do was send up the smoke signals of animal sacrifice, or gaze at the entrails of chickens, and hope some god somewhere would take a fancy to you.

It took courage to recognize one's cosmic helplessness. The doctrine of free will was for the weak-minded, who used the accidental acquisition of abstract thought to think that thinking could alter the blindingly obvious truth of our essential helplessness. Like small children, who spend far more time working out the rules of the games they play than actually playing them, civilized humanity invented a game where people were junior partners with God Almighty, being groomed for promotion, cared about, trained, so that when the time came, they could take over the running of the business of fate. God was the senior executive who planned to go into semi-retirement once His children were experienced enough.

Of course, the more sophisticated exchanged *God* for *Nature*, but the shallowness of that sophistication was evident in their incapacity to find intention-free language for its workings. Even if Nature wasn't a 'she', it was generally an 'it', an entity that had to be described in terms of strategy and goals. The most fastidious of scientists talked about 'genes replicating themselves', which made them sound like ant colonies, or workers in the rag trade, and not the thought-incapable enzymes 'they' are. How one spoke about things mattered, because however clear minded you might be, language put images into your head, and there was no getting away from them, once there.

So Liam would have no truck with word games that did no more than hide an ancient and understandable desire for a controlling mechanism in the form of something different and better (from the result's point of view) than accident. As a trained anthropologist he knew better than to imagine he could be outside the mental mould of his fellow members of the planet. Best to settle for God, call a spade a fucking spade and tremble and twitch with the knowledge that God does indeed play dice, in fact, does nothing else but play dice, even if you don't believe in Him.

Liam had an inordinate respect for discontent. He thought it was the best condition that anyone could attain. Not in the absolute sense – sainthood was the absolute best, of course – but in the sense of an ordinary response to the complexity of things. He had been a discontented academic, and it had suited him well. It enabled him to be grumpy and disgruntled, while still allowing him to feel there was something better to be, even if only the foolish and the holy could manage it. It was his bad fortune to be born hungry for what he could never be. But also his good fortune, because the mode suited him admirably. The break in his perfectly happy, discontented existence which had occurred with the advent of Grace had not been part of a plan. He had intended to continue comfortably bad-tempered, with an understanding and humorous wife, until, with relief, he drew his last breath. What had happened had been in spite of his desire for uncomfortable conformity. He was sorry, but once he was faced with a choice, he had no real choice. Black disaster, having offered itself unbidden, as it were, was irresistible.

And what of the Daphne's development? Was this another turn for the worse which he was unable to reject? Oddly, it felt different. It felt like salvation, though of a roundabout kind. He knew it would not take him back to where he was before. He knew now it could never be, and nor was it to be desired. But Daphne was offering him a path, a road, down which it was impossible to see, because it was all so unlikely. With Grace, he had been aware of embarking on a course that could only end in disintegration — it was a teleological move, the end was known. With Daphne, anything could happen. It was not disaster he would be walking towards, but it might be. And then again, it might not be. And wasn't that a rather good description of the way most people lived their lives? And wasn't the living of most people's lives something that he feared more than anything else? Catastrophe, cirrhosis, degradation and destitution were not just definite, but essentially desirable. Now, Liam had a large dollop of real life on his hands, however improbable it might look to anyone else. And he had decided, yes, he had chosen, to put himself in the highly realistic hands of Daphne.

'Sophie? I have to come and see you. I'm going away.'

He knew what she was thinking: another escapade, another tiresome drama, but now, thank goodness, it was none of her concern. He could only disconcert her once.

'I see,' Sophie said amiably. She meant, 'So what?'

'I want to make arrangements about the children. And the house.'

'Grace has decided she's had enough of London, then?'

'No, my dear, she's decided she's had enough of me. She's left me.'

'I see,' Sophie said again. She meant, 'I don't care.'

'I'm going away with Daphne Drummond for a while.'

There was a long silence while Sophie remembered who Daphne Drummond was — she would have seen her on the stairs while delivering or picking up the children — and then the silence became more like speechlessness. After a moment or two, she said, 'Well, Liam, you still have the capacity to surprise.' But her tone said that she refused to be.

'Sophie,' Liam said carefully, 'I want to say how sorry I am for everything.'

'Why do you need to see me?' She was anxious not to get involved in another of Liam's absurdities.

'I want you to have power of attorney, or whatever it's called, while I'm away. Do you mind?'

And now it crossed his mind to wonder whether he had ever done anything that he hadn't really *wanted* to do. His mood darkened a shade. It was a question that related to that other one he had found himself asking recently: the one about whether he had, in even the most trivial way, ever made a single real decision in his life.

Perhaps they were the same question, he brooded. In the technical middle of his life, he was close to discovering that he had been master of nothing, least of all himself. Certainly, he had developed a conceit about his essential will-lessness in the face of mysterious forces, but this thought had been nothing more than grandiose compared to the present, simple, humiliating assessment of his own personal inadequacy. It made him the very worm he had professed to be, though without really believing it, and not the secret existential hero of his own mythology.

His frame of mind darkened still further.

Daphne was wrong: he did *not* believe in goodness. In all likelihood he didn't believe in any of the things that would have made his losses large and dramatic instead of trivial and weightless. Did he even believe in love, he wondered. Until recently, it was the one thing he was certain he believed in, but now, he wasn't sure. Since Daphne had been in his life, since she had made him love her, he had been content to be happy and let her define that as love for both of them, but there was a cold-eyed, reptilian thing lurking inside him, which in truth was not new, though previously he had refused to face its existence. This staring, snake-like creature scorned the warm bath of heady emotions Liam had manufactured, and spat venom on it, not in envy, but in contempt for its dishonesty. There was nothing extraordinary about Liam's new thoughts on love; only his acknowledgement of the chilly truth was unusual — for him, anyway. It was easy enough to let the old loves go; let the snake hiss all it wanted, 'You didn't love Sophie, you didn't love Grace'; but to hear it whisper, 'You don't love Daphne', to deny the very present he was living, was something new and terrible. If he continued to listen, what would remain of his humanity? Of his life? Of anything? He *had* to love Daphne. It was his only chance. It had to be love, and love — real now, if not before — had to exist beyond a paltry need for comfort and self-satisfaction.

He found himself, in the midst of domestic bliss with Daphne, foundering on the edges of a black despair, and only a jaunty pretence kept him from plunging into its depths. He stuffed his doubts away as if behind an old sofa, and played the contented lover, which in previous weeks he had simply lived. But the doubts continued to thrive inside him where the reptilian thing lived, taking on the physical form of heartburn. He worked at being happy with his love for all he was worth. Which was not much, said his heartburn. *Not very much at all.*

Daphne, when she wasn't enjoying the pleasures of Liam's company, was also keeping busy. She was taking three driving lessons a week, and enjoying them hugely, although the same could not be said for her instructor, who thought her a charming old lady, but not one of the world's natural drivers. He suggested that she might prefer, at her age, to take it easy and be driven, but she insisted that she had to drive because she was going off travelling in the motor home, and her new lover — she actually said 'my new lover' — was not himself a driver.

'Why doesn't your . . . uh . . . he learn to drive instead?' the instructor asked.

'Well, to tell you the truth, dear,' Daphne explained confidentially, 'he's not a very practical person, and I don't think he'd get the hang of it.'

'Oh,' the young driving instructor murmured, as Daphne started the car with a grand crashing of gears. He was quite relieved when he later learned that she thought they might be travelling abroad rather than around England, although she hadn't fully discussed this with her lover. The driving instructor had a horrible feeling that, with enough lessons, it was just possible Daphne would pass her test. Her problem was absent-mindedness, and a disinclination to believe anyone else was using the road; but he thought she might be able to concentrate for just long enough not to fail the test, assuming nothing untoward happened. He considered very briefly the possibility of providing an untoward incident himself, but he took a pride in his work and wanted everyone he taught — even Daphne in a tiny part of his mind — to pass their test. After which, the world had better keep a sharp eye out, he reckoned, because Miss Drummond, nice old duck though she was, certainly wouldn't.

In addition to driving lessons, Daphne continued to write her novel at the steady rate of fifty words a day. By the time the motor home was delivered, eight weeks later, she had a total of 2,520 words, which was seven and a half pages. She felt it was going along quite nicely.

It began with a description of the main characters and how they arrived in the house in which they all lived, although, so far, she had done no more than to describe the state of affairs which had brought the hero to live in the same place as the heroine. Each character, she planned, would be introduced in this way: what had brought them together, what was their present condition. And then, when that was done, she would write about the heroine's belated commitment to happiness and her new-found love for the hero, who resisted, but was won over in the end. Then she would finish the book with a description of their travels and how happy they were together, at last, and forever.

It couldn't have been a simpler structure. She had no desire to do anything fancy or modern, only to write a novel about a love that ends in happiness. Of course, there would be darkness; there always was, but it would be no more than a contrast for the happiness the characters were to achieve against all likelihood. It took her a good two hours a day to complete her fifty words, because she liked to spend a lot of time reliving the moments she was writing about. Daydreaming, some would say. But so what, if she ended up with fifty new words on the page, who cared what it was called?

Daphne did not trouble herself to wonder what it was, if anything, that Liam felt for her. She called it *love*, and just as what some would probably call daydreaming produced fifty words a day, so love, which some would probably call something else, had produced happiness. She had no fear, and no thought about the future; a blissful state achieved only by those who are prepared to leave definitions lie.

A small miracle had occurred in Daphne: her long unhappiness and fear had, against all the odds, uncoupled themselves from the moving engine of her life and been left behind on the tracks. The rails ran on, all right, into the unseeable distance, but the old tainted carriages were left in the sidings. Their nature had not changed; they were what they were — unhappiness and fear — but it was no longer necessary to travel inside them. It was not the way things usually worked out, but there it was. Daphne was able to move through her days into the future without the burden of terror from the past. If there was trouble up ahead, it would be new trouble, not simple repetition of the old. There was, therefore, nothing to be frightened of. She trundled along, allowing everything to be as nice as it could be. And whatever happened, it couldn't fail to be less than interesting.

Only thoughts of Divya produced flashbacks to the old way of fear and nameless dread, but she tried to ignore them as best she could and, quite often, she was nearly successful.

17

Divya

Divya had decided on *Jane* for her new name. She thought it was the most proper name she could choose. All her dolls had been called Jane and, secretly, she had even called a small radio the home had given her one Christmas, Jane, although she knew radios weren't supposed to have names at all.

Now, when her mother or class teacher called her Divya, she would pretend they were talking to her, but she knew herself as Jane. She told Daphne about it since it was her idea, but no one else, because it was private. Daphne thought it was a nice, sensible name for the time being.

Divya spent a lot of time with Daphne now, although she didn't get into bed with her and the man any more, because Daphne had said she mustn't or the man would get cross and it might make it difficult to be friends. It wasn't that he wasn't nice, just a bit of a bad-tempered thing, Daphne said. Divya had decided to like Daphne, so she waited until it was morning, but early enough to ensure the man would still be asleep, before she put her head round the door. Daphne would be lying there with her old hat on, always awake, and give Divya a big smile when she pushed the door open. She'd put her finger to her lips and creep out of bed, put her big tartan dressing gown on, and they'd go downstairs and get breakfast ready together.

Divya was very interested in Daphne's body when she saw it for those few seconds before it was enveloped in the woollen dressing gown. She had never seen its like, all floppy and drooping; not like bodies she saw in pictures and on TV. She asked Daphne about her hanging breasts, although she had to point at them because she was too embarrassed to say their name.

'My titties, dear? No, they weren't always like this. They get this way as you get older. Well, mine did. Some don't. It depends. They were big firm titties once,' she smiled, without any apparent regret.

'Like you see in photos at the newsagent?' Divya asked.

'Well, not as big as you see in *some* photos, but they were big enough,' Daphne said, with just a hint of pride. 'Nicely pointed, too. Although in those days we wore bras that made them *very* pointy, so they stuck out under our tight sweaters like a pair of hunting dogs' noses on the scent of something. Men liked my big titties very much. But it's a funny, thing Div ... Jane, it's the very ones they like best that tend to get the saggiest, which they don't usually like at all.'

'Does that man like them saggy?'

'I'm happy to say he does,' Daphne told her with satisfaction. 'You see, dear, what a person likes often has a lot to do with what they think they should like. And sometimes people just find themselves liking things they didn't know they liked at all. Which, if they're not jolly careful, can make them very cross.'

'But they must feel nice with all that soft, squidgy skin and the little nibbles at the end.'

Daphne beamed at Divya.

'Exactly, dear.'

Divya was moved to a confidence.

'When I touch my nibbles it makes me feel thirsty.'

She felt a little funny telling Daphne about touching herself, but she did it every night before she went to sleep, and she wondered about the strange, thirsty feeling it gave her. She wanted to know what Daphne thought about it.

'That's nice. It's just the same with me,' was all she said.

Divya also asked Daphne to tell her about her mother and how she locked her in the cupboard under the stairs. It was like a story in a book, and Daphne always settled down to tell it, wriggling her bottom comfortably into the chair and beginning, 'Well ...' Divya was very impressed that Daphne should have actually *lived* something that was so much like a story in a book. Often, she had thought her own life was more like a thing you have read to you than how real people's lives were. It troubled her because she thought the whole point of stories was that they had never really happened. But it never occurred to her to wonder where she had got the idea of what a normal life was like.

Some of it was from school, where many of the other children lived at home with a mother, and often a father as well. But her detailed knowledge came from the very places she had decided only told about what wasn't usual. From books and films and television. So it was funny she should have concluded her life and Daphne's were storybook things, and everybody else's real and proper.

'Are you sad?' she asked Daphne once, at the end of the telling.

'About what, dear?'

'About being so unhappy when you were a little girl.'

'Well, I was sad. And I still am, in a way – for the little girl.'

'What little girl?'

'Me. The little girl I was then. Now, I'm happy. So I'm sad for her then, but happy for me now. That's all right, isn't it? I can't do anything about the way things were for her. Just feel sorry that they were like that.'

'I s'pose,' Divya said, but she wasn't sure about any of it. She wondered if she would one day look back on herself as she was now, and feel she was a completely different person. It was impossible to imagine.

Divya went to school almost every day now, because Daphne always said after breakfast, 'Well, I think you ought to go and get ready for school, dear.'

At first, Divya had said, 'My mum says I don't have to go if I don't want.'

But Daphne had shaken her head and told her it was important to go to school, not just to learn things, which was useful sometimes, but also because both she and her mum would get into trouble if she didn't. Divya understood, and Daphne was proved right because the next time Mr Daneford had come to visit – to snoop, her mother said – he congratulated her on her improved attendance, which meant he'd been checking up on her at school.

Life with Sylvie was still not what Divya thought of as a normal home life, but it was a more or less regular existence. Sylvie got up late and was always upset about something. It meant that Divya was generally anxious about her mother, but she had become used to that, and anyway, going to school, as she was now, meant she missed most of the anger. The worst thing was her mother crying on the sofa, or in bed. Divya would stand in the middle of the living room, or at the side of the bed, watching her mother sobbing, her shoulders heaving, her nose running, and it was hard to know what to do. But that, too, had almost become a routine. First, Divya would stand and watch, shifting from leg to leg. Then, as she knew somehow she must, she would go over to her mother and, a little awkwardly, put her skinny arms around her neck. There was nothing she could ever think of to say, partly because Sylvie's crying was hardly ever about anything in particular, only about everything in general. All Divya could think of was 'Please don't cry, Mum. Please don't.' But sometimes that would make Sylvie angry, as if her daughter were making impossible demands on her.

'Why shouldn't I cry? I'm unhappy. Why *shouldn't* I?'

'Sorry,' Divya would say, her arm frozen on her mother's shoulder.

Sometimes, Sylvie would scream and shout at Divya, as soon as she got home from school. She would have spent most of the afternoon working up to a fury, staring at the mess in the living room, and concluding that it was Divya's fault – the mess, all of it, everything. Then there would be more crying, a cup of tea made by Divya, two sleeping tablets, and Sylvie would take herself off to bed. Then Divya was free to visit Daphne if she was around.

But if things were miserable for Divya, she never said so to anyone. When Mr Daneford came round, or her mum's friend Sophie phoned to see how things were getting on, Divya never complained that she was unhappy or frightened. It wasn't that life was so much better than it was at the home, it was just that now she was at least where children were supposed to be, with her mother at home. This bald fact was a piece of flotsam in a sea of confusion which she felt she ought to hang on to. To complain, to tell people what it was like being with Sylvie, would only result in her being taken away, and somehow being *taken away* was, in itself, a terrible prospect, even if, as she knew might be the case, things might be nicer somewhere else.

Having Daphne in the house helped make things better, although, sometimes, Daphne would give her a funny, long stare, and eventually shake her head and sigh with an 'Oh, dear' whispered through the exhalation. But it wasn't as though Daphne was angry with her or anything, and when Divya asked, 'What?' she would just smile brightly and say, 'Nothing, dear, I was just thinking.'

Divya supposed that Daphne was thinking about the cupboard under the stairs at those moments, and she wondered if she would sigh like that when she was a grown-up. She thought she might.

The crying in the cupboard went on. Divya often woke in the night and heard the sobbing — a child's cry, not like her mother's, and distanced by two doors. It didn't frighten her so much now that she knew what it was, but she marvelled at the way unhappiness clung to the house. She would tell Daphne the following morning.

'You were crying in the cupboard again last night.'

Daphne would nod sadly and say, 'Well, never mind. Never mind.'

Divya did not realize how much she liked having Daphne there as her friend until the morning when, all wrapped in her tartan dressing gown, Daphne said, in a slightly funny voice, 'Jane, Liam and I are going away.'

It seemed to Divya as if the room jiggled as Daphne said it, or that the lights had suddenly flashed off and then on again very fast.

Divya was about to ask a question. It might have been, 'What do you mean?' or 'Where to?' or 'When are you coming back?' but somehow the answers popped into her mind before she could ask them: 'Leaving you. Going far away. For a very long time.' Her mind and the room filled up with a funny kind of fog, murky and almost damp, so she could hardly see Daphne, let alone ask questions. In the silence she had a picture in her head of being in the house alone with Sylvie, and the crying under the stairs, and there being nothing else. Things as they were, but without anything else. Bleak, and black and white was how it looked to Divya. Her mouth went stiff and she said nothing.

'Did you hear me, dear?' Daphne asked, alarmed by the look on the little girl's face.

'So what?' Divya said through tight-pressed lips.

'I wanted to take you with us, but Liam said we couldn't. What about your mother? And the authorities? I'm afraid he's right. They wouldn't let you come with us, and if we just took you they'd come and take you back, and your mother would be very sad to lose you ... I know she seems ... sometimes ... but ... she's ... she'd be very sad to lose you ... '

Divya just looked at Daphne, stony faced.

'We'll be leaving in a week or so. I *wish* we could take you ... '
The corners of Divya's mouth were set hard, and she pressed her lips even tighter together in an effort not to let the crying out.

'Don't want to go with you.'

The words came out, through the narrowest of gaps between her teeth and lips, as little explosions of air with sound attached.

After that, Divya didn't appear round the door in Liam's and Daphne's bedroom in the mornings. Daphne tried to catch her as she went to school, or in the afternoon, when she came home, by hanging around downstairs with her arms surrounding a wastepaper basket. But there was no sign of Divya. She was like a wisp of smoke that had disappeared. She seemed not to be going to school, and she never came out of the flat when she heard Daphne prowling around outside. Eventually, Daphne had to knock on the door, much as she didn't want to. There was no answer, so she opened it herself and found Sylvie sitting disconsolately on the sofa.

'I'm sorry to bother you, dear. I'm from upstairs, I'm looking for Divya.'

Sylvie looked vaguely around, as if Divya might be standing in a corner of the room, and shrugged.

'Not here. I don't know where she is. She's in and out, but never here when there are things to do. What do you want?' she asked morosely, noting that the silly old woman from upstairs hadn't wanted to see *her*.

'Just to have a chat with Divya.' After a moment she added, reluctantly, 'Are you all right?'

But as soon as she'd said it, Daphne decided that she didn't want to hear the answer. She retracted her head from the open doorway, muttering, 'Thanks, dear, must go ...' and closed the door behind her. It wasn't that she didn't feel sorry for the poor girl, who, Daphne was sure, couldn't help herself, but Daphne knew she just couldn't manage the great weight of misery, even from the distance of the door, and she wondered, with a shiver, how Divya must feel, living with it all the time. But the truth was she didn't have to wonder – she knew.

Daphne put Sylvie out of her mind. She had decided not to worry and fret about anything, but if she must, and it looked as if it were inescapable, then worrying about Divya was all she could manage. She went back upstairs heavy with sadness, and with a terrible, lurking sense of something awful about to happen.

She told herself it was the house, whose very air seemed to hold molecules of accumulated misery. Perhaps, also, the fact of leaving, much as she wanted to, created a natural anxiety, as any upheaval will. But for all the good reasons she might find, the dread inhabited her, and staying or going was irrelevant because she sensed that whatever the impending disaster might be, no one would be able to do anything about it.

She despaired of herself, feeling the old helplessness rise up in her. Still, it seemed, she remained at its mercy.

'Something *good* is about to happen. Something wonderful,' she insisted fiercely to herself. 'Everything *will* be all right. Yes, it bloody well will.'

She shoved the old, familiar nameless dread down as far as it would go, and stamped it into submission with her carpet-slippered feet as they fell heavily on each stair on her way up to the attic.

PART FOUR

18

Awaydays

As Daphne drove them down the street, away from the house, Liam thought that, very possibly, he was in paradise. He became increasingly convinced of this as the miles slipped by. The cloud of doubt in his own capacity to love or to choose freely, which settled over him during the final weeks in London, was gradually blown away by a gentle wind of happiness as he travelled further and further into the distance with Daphne. He was already half seduced away from the edge of the dark pit he had found himself staring into by the undeniable reality of his pleasure. Every time he and Daphne made love, he was astonished by the *fact* of his desire and his resulting satisfaction. The problem of whether he *really* loved Daphne – more or differently from any of his other 'loves' – was dissipated by Daphne's easy and convincing use of the word for what they were doing, and it was finally abolished by the sense of well-being that fell like manna over him from the moment they set off to pursue their roaming life.

If the reptilian thing that had told him he was cold and incapable of experiencing what he longed to experience was still inside him, it had gone dormant, defeated by a kind of joy which even it couldn't question. This was, indeed, and improbably, going to be the happily ever after that Daphne had promised. The very special and particular nature of Liam's love for Daphne had come clear to him on the motorway the morning of the first day of their trip.

It was for the possibility of Daphne passing her driving test that the idea of defensive driving had been invented. From the moment they turned the corner, away from the house, from Sylvie and Divya, from Grace, from the attic, from the cupboard under the stairs, it was evident their lives depended on the good sense and saintly forbearance of other users of the road.

Daphne drove as the mood took her. Sometimes she went fast, sometimes slow. Sometimes she decided to overtake, sometimes she was content to potter along. What she hardly ever did was signal her intentions. This, Liam understood, was because she did not know them until she was doing whatever it was she was doing. Driving along the motorway was noisy, since their progress was accompanied by the infuriated shrieks of car horns, howling protests in a more or less continuous Doppler effect. At first, Liam sweated, as his heart leapt and stopped at each near collision, but soon he found himself to be quite relaxed, and when he examined the reasons for this, he understood how very different things were with Daphne than they had ever been with anyone else.

He was unconcerned about her lethal driving because the worst that could happen was that they would be killed. Liam acknowledged this was a bad idea, because other people might be hurt, but for himself, he minded not at all if this was his last day. It was not, as he suspected for a moment, because he still carried with him his old suicidal streak, but because he would be perfectly happy to do *anything* in the company of Daphne – including die. He felt no terror at all. Yes, he wanted the future with Daphne, and yet it made just as much sense to him to die together on the road now, right at the beginning of their journey. He didn't mind; he was content. He had never felt like this before.

Miraculously, however, they were not killed, mostly because, as if by motorway telegraph, other cars kept their distance from Daphne. They continued their hell ride with a curious cocoon of space around them. Other people did not want to die, even if Liam and Daphne, at the moment of impact, would merely have turned and smiled their love at each other. Liam had given himself up to Daphne, entirely.

'Daphne,' Liam said, when they turned off their side street into the main road. 'Where are we going?'

No decision had been reached about this before they left. When Liam asked the question, all Daphne had said was 'Anywhere we want' with a happy wave of her hand, and somehow the conversation hadn't got any further.

Now, Daphne screeched round the corner in third gear, losing sight of the house.

'I don't know,' she said. 'Let's just go south, dear.'

Two hours later they passed a sign giving advanced warning of a turn-off for Dover and the southern edge of Britain.

'Why don't we go on going south?' Daphne suggested, changing lanes and causing the driver behind to thank God, and his wife, for having the car serviced and the brakes checked recently. 'Let's cross the water . . . Got your passport, dearest?'

'To Europe,' Liam said, nodding at the idea. 'Yes, Europe.'

'South,' Daphne repeated. 'We'll head south.'

So for three leisurely weeks they drove steadily south; down, down and down, through the centre of Europe, stopping for a few days wherever the fancy took them. The rich greens of vines and olives had gradually replaced the wheat and sunflower crops of northern France, and then the vines disappeared as Liam and Daphne trekked even further south and hit the stunning, breath-defying heat of the plain that led to and from Madrid. They travelled not as tourists, observing the interesting differences and remarking on strange customs of *abroad*, but as migrants moving through landscapes, looking for a particular and appropriate place to come to a halt.

In the meantime they entertained themselves with the changing backdrops and cuisines of Europe, unravelling before them like a ball of wool. They sampled local wines and produce with great excitement, discovering something new and delicious with every passing kilometre. But Liam was no longer drinking so heavily. He wanted the taste of pleasure in his mouth and the heady combined effects of fermented grape and languorous heat, rather than the deep unconsciousness he had sought in England. If neither of them knew exactly where they were heading, they were both aware that they were going towards *somewhere*, and enjoyed the everyday pleasure of scenery, food and climate as they went. Neither felt the need to stop and look at tourist attractions; they bypassed great cities, left famous art treasures to those who liked that kind of thing and positively avoided routes that led to areas of high population or famous natural beauty.

They were happy and they were passionate. At night, they lay in each other's arms, both snoring, both dreaming, both content. Every morning they woke up and were delighted to see each other and to know that it was the beginning of a new day that they would spend together. Where they had come from simply went from their minds. They gave London, England, no thought. It didn't cross either of their minds to buy an English newspaper, or to try and tune the radio to the World Service. There was nothing they wanted to know, beyond the fact they were with each other and happy. And that they knew, every minute of every day. They needed no other information. If Daphne had a moment or two of regret or concern about leaving Divya behind, she knew there was no use brooding. It was self-indulgence. She had made a decision; and Liam was right; she had to leave Divya, and probably everything would be all right.

A pattern of travel conversation developed.

'I wonder,' Daphne would invariably begin, 'what kind of tree that is.'

Liam would stare in the direction Daphne was indicating and answer, 'I don't know.'

'I wonder what caused the strange shaped rock over there.'

'Mmm. I don't know.'

'I wonder what people do in this village in the winter.'

'I can't imagine.'

'I wonder how they cure this ham.'

'I couldn't say, dear. Delicious, isn't it?'

'I wonder if those are rain-clouds.'

'They might be, my dear, but it's hard to tell.'

And so it would go on, with Daphne wondering about the whats and hows and ifs of things they passed, and Liam never spoiling her curiosity with answers.

Liam could allow hundreds of kilometres to pass him by without having a single thought. He experienced the sensation of movement and sat in a happy trance in the passenger seat, in a condition of utter peace, as relaxed and accepting as he had ever been in his life. From time to time, he would turn to look at Daphne, beaming his pleasure at what he saw until Daphne felt his eyes on her and turned her head towards him.

'Darling,' Liam would say. 'I'm so happy.'

'And so am I, dearest,' Daphne would smile back at him, before turning her attention, once again, to the road in front of her.

They were sleepy with heat, dizzy with travel, but they were contented. Daphne wasn't surprised at such contentment. Liam was astonished. But it did not fly away, as he had half suspected it might, with their continuing possession of each other. He had feared his — and perhaps her — passion was the result of novelty and excitement, and that an everyday togetherness — domestic, routine — would banish the thrill of the new and odd. And, in spite of their wandering existence, it *was* domestic and routine. There were cups of tea, and making beds, and putting things away in the very particular places they had to be put away in. There was cooking and washing up, and lying on opposite sides of the motor home in the evening reading books and listening to music on the local radio stations. There was washing and ironing, each of them taking turns, and shopping in markets and supermarkets, which they did together. The chemical toilet had to be emptied, and the water tanks filled, which Liam took care of.

And apart from chores, the close quarters meant that there was very little privacy when it came to dealing with their bodily wastes. There was a concertina door to the lavatory compartment, but it was more symbolic than genuinely private. There were no solid walls for them to hide behind. Daphne and Liam could not help but share an intimacy that terraced housing kept even the closest of couples from having to face. The compactness of their living space and the movable nature of their home required a more concentrated domesticity than static living, if things were not to get hopelessly out of hand. Yet both of them found it easy to do what had to be done to make their adventure comfortable; and to gather the inescapable biology of each other's body into their affection. It was not simply that they made the best of things in their tiny, mobile home; each of them found positive pleasure in performing the tasks and observing the private aspects of the other. The performance and the observation had come to seem more like small acts of love than tiresome or distasteful necessities.

So, for all the domesticity and routine (or even because of it), Liam's initial fears for their continued happiness were not realized; they were both still thrilled with each other; their sexual excitement was renewed nightly, and often at sudden moments during the day. Even when they were on the road Daphne would swerve into a lay-by without warning,

and Liam would blink with surprise, and at the inevitable row of car
horns passing them.

'What's the matter?' he'd ask, alarmed.

'Nothing, dearest. I want to fuck.'

'Now?'

'Now,' Daphne would insist.

'Only too delighted, my dear,' Liam would reply, getting up to
close the curtains on the road side of the motor home, and smiling to
himself at his incredible good fortune at having found paradise both so
near to, and so far from, home.

They had gone on going south, and, eventually, three weeks after leaving
London, found themselves on a snaking ribbon of a road with a sign that
announced: THE HIGHEST ROAD IN EUROPE. It took them into the heart
of a vast arid ocean of undulating mountains, one behind another, like
great waves, for as far as the eye could see. It was as if they had left the
planet, and found themselves in a moonscape which appeared to have no
end. The motor home climbed slowly and relentlessly upwards, while
Daphne carelessly negotiated hairpin bends on the narrow road that
curled round the mountainsides. They would drive for hour after hour
from one mountain to the next and discover that they had travelled no
more than twenty kilometres and seemed only to have arrived at exactly
the same bend whose tight angle they skidded around half a day before.

Liam was astonished by this landscape; by its deceptive distances,
its dangerous corners, its apparent sameness, and the fierce, dry, re-
morseless heat. The isolation excited and frightened him; the mountains
were as fearful and majestic as the sea. They had arrived, he thought,
at the very place where the two of them belonged, lost in a rocky
desert at the edge of Europe.

It was in precisely this kind of place that Liam wanted to live out
their passion; high up, in searing heat and drought, close to the sky,
with the world falling away beneath them. He wanted to view their
passion from a dizzy-making landscape of mountain tops disappearing
into the far distant horizon. He wanted to watch their love blossom in
the shrivelling temperatures and dried-up river beds. He wanted to put
the cauldron of their desire on the fire, and watch it bubble fiercely,
and concentrate into an essence.

Daphne didn't mind where they were, so long as they were heading due south, but she was pleased enough to find herself at the top of the world.

It had turned out they were right to suspect there was a destination. Liam recognized it not long after they had driven a mile or so up a track that led off the main mountain road, just to see where it went. In the middle of a barren, scrubby landscape they found a long abandoned, ruined stone house with a crumbling stone wall around it. Daphne braked hard when she saw it, and clambered into the back of the motor home. She came out with a blanket, and one of her plentiful supply of tubes of hormone cream.

'Liam, why don't we do it in the open air for once, dearest?' she said, spreading the blanket over the prickly scrub that covered the ground inside the walls of the roofless house.

Liam was always happy to consider any sexual suggestion from Daphne; since he had known her his sex life had been more joyfully varied than at any time before. But that applied to the *activity* of sex. It was his opinion that the *venue* needed only to be comfortable, and indoors, in bed, was hard to beat when it came to comfort. He had little interest in ringing the changes so far as *where* the act of love occurred. He was also somewhat worried by the prospect of snakes and scorpions, and suggested that it would be cooler and more private inside the motor home, but Daphne would have none of it.

'There's no one around, dear, and we'll be hidden by the walls. Come on, Liam, where's your sense of adventure?'

It was, frankly, not a great success. The blanket wasn't much protection against the sharp spines of the flattened scrub, and, although there were no snakes or scorpions in evidence, there was an abundance of flying, biting insects that took full advantage of the sudden feast of naked flesh. When Liam had come to a hurried climax, he lay for a moment with his head to one side on Daphne's shoulder, catching his breath, and found himself eyeball to eyeball with a lizard which had popped its head out of a crevice in the wall to see if the sudden excitement represented food or danger. It was during their mutual inspection that the idea came to Liam.

'Daphne,' he said slowly, keeping his eyes on the reptile, 'I've had a thought.'

'Yes, dear?' Daphne asked, a little breathlessly.

'What if we rebuilt this house? What if we rebuilt it, put a roof on it, and . . . live in it?'

'For good?' Daphne asked.

'Exactly, my dear. For good. Wasn't that one of the things we were after?'

Daphne was confused.

'What?'

'Good. Goodness. What about it, Daphne, my flower? Let's settle down in this sweltering paradise.'

'It's an interesting idea,' Daphne said, as she might to a child who had said something clever – for a child. 'But what would we do while we were living in it, dear?'

'You would write your novel, and we'd grow some olives and things, whatever people do round here to make a living, and I would . . .'

'Yes?' Daphne encouraged.

'I would . . . meditate.'

'But don't you meditate nicely while we're travelling, dearest?'

'Yes, it's true, but it's a different kind of meditation when you're in one place. On the move, you think in a direction because you're going in a direction; you think knowing that there's something ahead. But if one was in a quiet place, being still, with none of the distraction of travelling . . .'

'Like a monastery?'

'Well, yes, quite like a monastery, but with none of the inconvenience of celibacy, of course.'

'But I thought that celibacy was designed to help concentration.'

'I'm afraid it's not a design that functions very well, my dear. Celibacy would be a good idea if it weren't for the lack of sex. My idea is to lead a celibate, contemplative life with you.'

'No sex?' Daphne asked alarmed, sitting up and twisting her hat straight.

'Yes, sex. Absolutely, sex. But my concept is for a new kind of celibacy: *with* sex. So one wouldn't be distracted by unfulfilled desire.'

'That is an interesting concept. You're so clever, Liam. I wonder if the Pope has thought of that. Do you think you ought to write to him, dear?'

'No, let him work it out for himself. What do you think?'

'So you'd be making love with me, growing olives and thinking?'

'Not necessarily at the same time.'

'No, I see that. But we wouldn't be travelling any more? We'd settle down?'

'Yes, together. We'd make our home here.'

There was a pause while Daphne screwed the top on her tube of hormone cream and shook out the blanket.

'Have you ever built a house, dear?'

'Well, I've helped. When I was in Zambia. The foundations are here. I don't think it will be all that difficult.'

'Liam, what exactly is it that you want to meditate about? Is it enough to keep you occupied, do you think?'

'It's kept people occupied for thousands of years, my dear, and no one's come up with any definitive answers.'

'Yes.' Daphne nodded, climbing back into the motor home. 'But what if you do come up with an answer? What will you do then?'

'I'm confident I won't,' Liam said, settling into the passenger seat.

'That's a relief,' Daphne said. 'But what is it you won't be finding an answer to?'

'Everything, my dear. Purpose. Initially, the problem of the atheist who believes in God.'

'But what if God doesn't want to be believed in?'

'If that were true, I suppose, He and I could come to a perfect accommodation. But, unfortunately, God demands belief. He likes to be appreciated. In that respect, He's just like His creations.'

'Yes, dear. I see.' Daphne said.

Although Daphne knew that the problem between Liam and God could be sorted out just by explaining that she knew *for a fact* that God would be only too delighted not to be believed in, and that Liam could sit back and relax into contented atheism, she wisely kept her counsel. The fact was Liam had her, and his philosophical problem, and at the moment he needed both to be just the way they were. He had not begun to write his book on the nature of love, or anything else. It was clear that those ambitions had fallen away with the passing miles. He had no *work*, except for his passion and his problem. And Daphne knew, as well as anyone could, that everybody had to have work of some kind, or they were in mortal danger of getting hopelessly lost in the senseless passage of time that was, at base, the truth of everyone's existence. It would not do to tell Liam that he had no problem, Daphne concluded. Liam without a problem was like a woman without a fish . . . or a man without a bicycle . . . or . . .

Daphne gave her head a little shake, as if it might jiggle the slight confusion of the last thought into something closer to the sense she felt it ought to make. It didn't work, so she decided to let it go. She turned on the engine of their mobile home.

'So what shall we do now, dear?'

Liam felt remarkably decisive. For the first time since he was a young man he had something very like a plan. It was very exciting to find himself capable of answering a question like 'What shall we do now?'

'We'll go back down the mountain to that village we passed,' he said, astonished by the authority of his voice. 'We'll have some lunch and find out who owns the house.'

'Right-oh!' Daphne said, kicking up a storm of dust as she turned a sharp circle and screeched off down the track to the mountain road that led to the village they had passed, three hundred metres below.

Daphne and Liam lunched at one of the dozen or so formica-topped tables in the large dark room of the bar that served also as the village petrol station, local honey supplier and, in a desultory sort of way, entertainment facility. The cavernous interior was surprising considering that the entire village seemed to consist of no more than half a dozen houses built on either side of the road. No one sat at the other tables, but there were three men sitting, well away from each other, on the plastic bar stools, drinking beer in a sullen silence that may have been partly attributable to Daphne's and Liam's presence, but was more likely the customary mood of those who patronized the establishment.

A couple of old bullfighting posters and a dusty doll in flamenco costume on the top shelf behind the bar were all that signified the flamboyant, Latin passions for which Spain was famous. Otherwise the place was as gloomy and dour as its customers. There was a lot of noise, but that came from the shrieking electronic yelps and sudden

208

bursts of jingles from a fruit machine chattering dementedly away to itself in one corner, presumably trying to make itself heard over the full volume of the television that hung over the bar, which no one was watching.

Although Liam spoke fluent Arabic and French, he had no Spanish at all when they began their journey, but he had picked up quite a lot by the time they found themselves in the mountains of the far south. Daphne had decided long ago that it was quite difficult enough making oneself understood in English, and during their journey had settled for saying *please* and *thank you*, *yes* and *no*, and smiling broadly, which turned out, on occasion, to allow for surprisingly long and, she sometimes suspected, quite intimate conversations.

They drank icy-cold *cerveza* and stuck their forks into a heaped plate of grilled *calamares* that were more delicious than either of them felt they had a right to hope for in such a minimal and unwelcoming place.

'It's the garlic,' Daphne said.

'I beg your pardon?' Liam asked.

'The garlic, dear. If you use this much garlic,' Daphne pondered, 'lunch is bound to be delicious, so I suppose there's less incentive to bother with other ingredients like being pleasant.'

'Well, it's a theory, my dear. But if you ask me, what we're dealing with here are the well-known results of inbreeding. I dare say that the present company represents very nearly the entire population of this God-forsaken hole – everyone who hasn't the wit to get themselves out of here.'

'You can't be sure, Liam. They might be very warm human beings deep down. Perhaps they just don't like to show it in front of strangers.'

'Inbreeding,' Liam insisted, looking sidelong at the three large men with dull, dangerous eyes who glared at their own reflections in the mirror behind the bar, challenging themselves to put a foot wrong. Behind the bar, a husband and wife threw noisy abuse at each other, in a dreary, habituated sort of way, over the sounds of the television and fruit machine. It seemed, so far as Liam could follow it, that the señora was not washing up the glasses as quickly as the señor would have liked; while the señora was complaining to a spot on the ceiling about her husband's slovenly personal habits. No one took any notice of the

209

disagreement. Outside, a couple of small children played in the blinding sunlight, by the gasoline pumps, and occasionally one of then ran in, rustling through the plastic strips that hung in the doorway, and tugged at the arm of one of the men sitting at the bar, complaining about some misdeed of the other child. Each time, the man dragged himself away from his threatened and threatening reflection for long enough to deliver an impassioned speech to whichever child had not received the speech the last time. Then he'd return to his beer and the contemplation of his eternal stand-off.

Daphne asked Liam who he thought they should approach to ask about the ownership of the derelict house.

'One of the children, I should think,' he suggested. 'At least they move at something like normal speed — it might be indicative of a degree of intelligence. Not likely, though. Inbreeding will out.'

'Liam, dear, you're not going to get the best out of these people unless you make an effort to understand them.'

'Why? I'm not a social worker. Anyway, my dear, I don't begin to understand you, but I can't imagine anything better than you give me.'

'You must try to be nice. Try thinking anthropologically.'

'So the savages won't pop me in the soup pot? Don't you think I'd taste rather good with lots of garlic, my love? I could offer them a trade. Our semen-stained blanket for their information.'

'Liam.'

'Yes, my dear, you're right. I'll try and think nicely about them.'

Liam stood up and approached the bar. Three pairs of eyes swivelled and stared at him in the mirror. He smiled in the direction of the owner.

'Another beer, please, señor,' he asked, and when the glass was slammed down in from of him, without the bartender having once let up in his complaints to his wife, Liam continued in his slightly crooked Spanish. 'Could you tell me who owns the ruined house up the mountain?'

The man stared at him, along with the customers sitting at the bar.

'The house, the broken house, up the mountain?' he tried again, smiling all the harmlessness and amiability he could muster. He turned round to Daphne and hissed, 'It might be the soup pot after all, my dear.'

'Maria!' the owner bellowed over the noisy complaints his wife was continuing to make.

A young woman, in her late teens, emerged from the kitchen, wiping her hands on her apron.

'Sí, Papa?'

Liam heard him explain to his daughter that this foreigner – he jutted his jaw contemptuously at Liam – wanted something.

'I can help?' the girl asked, smiling.

She was a moonbeam in the twilight gloom of the bar. She had dark hair, tied back in classically Spanish fashion, and a pleasing though not excessively beautifully face. Her strange, grey eyes were striking. They looked with naked curiosity out on to the world, assessing what they saw and, without seeming wayward, clearly wanted more. She was slim, but had quite full, rounded hips and breasts which, along with her touching but speculating eyes, made her seem innocent and voluptuous all at once.

'The house up the mountain,' Liam said in slow English. 'I'd like to know who owns it. I'm interested in buying it, and a bit of land.'

Maria turned to her father and explained in Spanish what Liam wanted. Suddenly, the angry bar owner broke into a smile and his wife fell silent.

'It belongs to my father,' Maria said, with a broad grin. 'I think he would be interesting to sell it.'

19

Jock Makes Things Better

There was no reason for anyone to suppose that Jock was not doing his job in the way he had been doing it for the past twenty-five years. Which is to say, sensibly and conscientiously. It was to be expected he might be suffering from care fatigue, and, perhaps, lack the original optimism and energy he had brought with him when he qualified as a young man. That, in itself, was no bad thing. It helped create a certain balance when the sometimes over-enthusiastic younger members of the profession raised their committed voices. A little weary wisdom from the more senior workers did no harm, though there was a fine line sometimes between outright cynicism — a kind of deadness of spirit — and a more sophisticated knowledge of how things work in the real world.

Jock's senior, Michael Dibden, knew Jock to be tired, but did not think he was tired out. Jock had enough tenacity and belief in the usefulness of social work to have refused promotions which might have taken him out of the field and into the bureaucratic reaches of the profession. He had settled for less pay in order to keep in touch with what the job had been about for him in the first place. There was also no evidence of Jock cutting corners, or letting things slide. So Dibden was concerned, but not alarmed, at Jock's manner during the case conference on Divya Johnson.

His report had been clearly written; the situation was described well enough to show that her circumstances were not as good as they might be. There was cause for anxiety, the report said and Jock reiterated during the conference, but on balance, he felt it would be worse to take the child back into care: separation from the mother, he told them, would do more damage than staying with her. Divya Johnson had expressed the wish to remain with her mother and, providing there was adequate supervision, Jock's view was that Divya should not be returned to residential care.

There was nothing remarkable about this report. It was another borderline case. Sometimes they decided for one side, sometimes another. The decision usually hung on details. In this case, Divya making her mother a cup of tea and the presence of an elderly woman in the house, who appeared to have befriended her, made the difference between a care order or continuing supervision in the home. All such decisions were risks, but social workers were used to taking informed risks. Sometimes they were proved tragically wrong, but not very often, considering the workload. The conference decided to accept Jock's assessment, with the proviso that Jock visited the family at least once a week.

What bothered Dibden slightly about Jock was something indefinable which had to do with the set of his shoulders and the tone of his voice as he had made his recommendation. He spoke in a somewhat dull monotone that was not serious enough to give alarm, but was unusual for Jock, who, although no longer a firebrand, managed as a rule to put his case with energy. Dibden put it down to tiredness, and the case being so marginal. He decided to check when Jock's holidays were due when he got back to his office. But once the conference had broken up, he found a crisis waiting for him concerning one of the less efficiently run children's homes in his section, and Jock's holiday arrangements went out of Dibden's mind.

So Divya stayed with Sylvie, and Jock made regular, unannounced visits, and kept in touch with the school to make sure Divya was attending.

Jock's weariness, however, was more like metal fatigue in an airliner than a simple worn-down kind of tiredness. Too many and too great stresses had been placed on the same pressured seams for far too long. Jock knew it, his wife knew it and his two children knew it.

Life in the Daneford household had become strangely silent of late. The children skirted around their father when he was at home, and lowered their voices to whispers when they were in the same room as him. Carole Daneford behaved in much the same way; smiling hesitantly as he came in the door, putting food on the dining table very carefully so that it made no noise, getting into bed, where he already lay with his eyes open, his arms behind his head, so delicately that the mattress hardly moved. None of them spoke about it. Jock was not especially bad-tempered – it was more that he wasn't tempered at all. He was permanently abstracted: a presence which sometimes came to and said, 'Thank you' for his dinner, and 'Good morning' to the children at breakfast, as if he were a distant relative staying in their house. Underneath the polite absence was something that scared the people who lived with him, although they couldn't say what it was that frightened them.

Jock went to work every day, and dealt with his case load just as he had always done. His colleagues also noticed his distance, and felt he was a little vague, but assumed, like Dibden, he was just going through a tired patch. And who didn't in their line of work?

Divya was by no means the most distressing of his cases. He had several children who had been taken into care, bruised and beaten, and it was not unusual for him to have a mother come to him for help with the marks of a vicious attack by her boyfriend or husband. Hardly a week passed when he was not attacked himself, usually verbally but not always, by some overwrought parent who felt he was not giving them the help they needed, or that he was interfering in their private domestic arrangements. Most of the adults in the families he worked with were in some kind of trouble, and all the children he saw were at risk, many of them at far greater risk than Divya.

But Divya's situation bore down on him more than any of the others. Or rather, not her situation, which was not so very different from many others he encountered; it was the fact of her existence that bore down on him, sitting like a small but ever-growing tumour in the centre of his brain. And yet her existence – childhood unhappiness, insecurity, mess, a poor prognosis for a fulfilled adulthood – was also not so very unusual in Jock's experience. Perhaps Divya was simply the one too many that people postulate, but hardly ever really believe in. If you can cope with fifty, they think of their own capacity, as well as others', why not fifty-one?

And, why not. Because, presumably, some finely calibrated balance is tipped. But there is often no warning. You can feel that one more – of anything – will be impossible to take, and yet you take it, and later realize that you've taken a dozen more after that and still managed. So you come to assume, as Jock had, that you can always take one more, because you only *feel* it's too much for you, whereas life has proved it not to be the case on many occasions.

But life could still take a 48-year-old man by surprise. All the uncertainties he thought he had lived through and converted to known processes could re-emerge and turn everything upside down with hardly more warning that what appeared to others to be fatigue.

Jock's niggling sense that the achievements of social work were no more than sticking plasters on a grotesque festering wound of unhappiness was something he thought he could live with. He had done for many years. He had assumed others – not everyone, but some – had the same discomforting doubts. Like them, he had assuaged them with a notion of praxis; do what can be done. Something is better than nothing. There is no perfect solution, but that is no reason for doing nothing.

The doubts were an underground spring in his life, belonging to his darker, less guarded moments. Nothing wrong with that. Nothing dangerous. The great thing is to get on with doing what one can. But Divya was like a deepening crack in the surface of the earth, too close to the spring. When he thought of her, a bleakness came over him, body and soul, so he could not see properly through the murkiness; and he could not stop thinking about her. She preyed on his mind constantly; there was no time either at work or at home when he was free of his concern about her, as all social workers must be sometimes in order to maintain their balance.

He was depressed, he concluded, and sensibly went to his doctor, who confirmed his self-diagnosis and gave him a prescription for a course of antidepressants which would not interfere too much with his everyday activities. Carole explained about depression to the children, offering them a medical model so they could see their strangely behaving father as unwell, rather than something vaguer and more alarming. Jock spoke to Michael Dibden, who was relieved of his anxiety now there was a diagnosis, and suggested leave of absence. But Jock felt he would be better off carrying on, rather than sitting at home, and Dibden accepted his assessment, especially as Jock was under the care of his doctor. What about offloading some of his more difficult cases, just for the time being? But Jock said he couldn't, his sense of responsibility wouldn't allow him to drop cases he was involved with. It was agreed, finally, to let someone more junior deal with as much of Jock's paperwork as possible. And he was to keep Dibden informed about his condition. There would be no problem about leave if Jock, or his doctor, felt things were getting on top of him.

It had all been handled in a most reasonable manner, and everyone felt it was possible now for things to get better. But Jock had not mentioned to his doctor, nor to his family, and certainly not to Dibden that there were more alarming symptoms than just depression. For example, the feeling he had of something boring into his head, through the top of his cranium, like a drill. It was not just a feeling, though, it was no mere metaphor for stress: he actually felt it physically, the vibration, and the small hole spiralling down deeper and deeper into the centre of his brain. Nor did he mention the moments of absolute conviction, which came over him without warning, that behind all the doors of all the houses and blocks of flats in this city, and in every place all over the world, ran blood. He saw it, seeping through the internal doors, along corridors, down stairs; blood trickled and then flowed as it gained momentum; a stream running into a river, until it was dammed and forced to join the monstrously congealed mountains of blood within the closed front doors. It was not merely conviction; he could see them, the mountains of dark, dried blood, all of them at once, and he heard the howls and dismal moans of misery of those who were trapped and suffocating behind them. He had a terror now, which he fought down with increasing difficulty, of making domestic visits. He sat in his parked car, sometimes for an hour or more, shaking from head to foot with the horror of what waited for him behind the door he was about to knock on. Part of him knew there was nothing real about this, there was no blood awaiting him, not actually; but the partial knowledge was not enough to stop the spasms of terror coming over him.

He was, even so, more or less in control. He was able to function, if not in too social a way. And he was able to keep his hallucinations to himself. As a result, he concluded that he was not mad, but only under attack. He felt that his irrational fears would pass, with his determination and the help of the medication.

*

Very early one morning, six weeks after the day Daphne and Liam left on their journey, Jock woke with a splitting headache. Splitting in the precise sense that he knew the drill had reached down far enough to crack his brain in two. He felt the two halves open up, and the tearing pain of the parting of his mind. Carole was still asleep.

Jock got quietly out of bed and staggered downstairs to the kitchen. He was almost blinded with pain, and with the tears that welled up in his eyes and poured down his cheeks. In the chasm left by the separated halves of Jock's brain lay a piece of information, like a nugget of gold found at the bottom of a crater after an explosion. It lay there, glinting at him, like a bright eye, in the centre of his brain, telling him the truth of things, and of the necessity which followed from the truth.

Jock sat, doubled over, on a kitchen chair, with his head in his lap and his hands clutching his skull as if they would hold it together — when, suddenly, the pain left him. He sat up. The pain had disappeared, but it had taken all warmth with it. Jock shivered with cold. He was chilled, cold-blooded within, his bones icy, his very marrow frozen. He tried external sources of heat — he made coffee, had a bath, pulled on layers of wool, but nothing could reach him. He would not be warm again.

The information which lay in the ruins of Jock's cracked head — small, hard, perfectly spherical, and twinkling with light — began to pulsate inside the opened cavity of his brain. Like a newly activated electronic bug, the pulses sent wave-like signals through him, and he felt the information they carried radiate in every part of him. They did not warm him, but they exchanged the terrible cold for certain knowledge. The signalled information focused his attention and made him forget the cold that wouldn't end. He had a duty to perform. He was obligated as a social worker — not his job, but *what he was* — to act in the best interests of his clients. Now, he was in possession of the knowledge of what was best. Now he knew, and he was able — no, obliged — to act.

Divya's night wanderings had stopped since Daphne and the man had left, six weeks before. She had hidden in the cupboard under the stairs when Daphne called and called to her, wanting to say goodbye. She knew Daphne wouldn't look for her there. Divya wasn't frightened by the dark, nor by the crying, now she knew what it was.

After Daphne told her she was going away, Divya had shut herself in the cupboard for the first time, and she hid there whenever Daphne tried to find her. She had come to find the dark cupboard comforting, and the crying child – who only cried when no one was in there – something of a friendly presence. Divya went to sit in the cupboard quite regularly now, whenever there was anger or tears from her mother. She sat with her arms around her raised knees, enveloped by the darkness, and feeling a fellowship with the unhappy little girl who was for ever stuck in there. Both of them were being betrayed by Daphne going away to be happy. They were left behind, but, in a way, they had each other now. Divya would whisper things to the other child in something that wasn't quite language, but didn't have to be, and when she listened carefully, the darkness seemed to hum an answer in her ears which she almost understood.

Upstairs, now it was empty, held no interest for Divya. She kept to her territory on the ground floor. So, at eight o'clock on the morning of Jock's terrible headache and the nugget of information he found in its place, Divya was asleep in the living room, on the sofa that served as her bed. Sylvie was in the next room, still in the grip of the sleeping drugs which kept the day away for as long as possible.

The persistent ringing of the doorbell didn't wake Sylvie, but eventually Divya fought her way free from the confusing coils of her dreams and her duvet, and padded, barefoot and sleepy eyed, to open the front door.

Being half awake, Divya was not as armoured against the intruding world as she was usually, so when she saw Jock Daneford standing in the open doorway, her mouth didn't snap into a tight line, nor her eyes narrow. The truth was, without her daytime defences, she felt about Jock Daneford a little the way Daphne had felt about the anonymous man who had built the cupboard under the stairs. Jock had a crumpled but nice face, and his usual manner with Divya was friendly without being disrespectful. Deep down, Divya could have liked him, and without realizing it, she had an image of him at home, a proper home she had invented for herself from the story-books, with his wife and children. Somehow, in the secret picture inside her head, she managed to be one of the children, and he played with them – two of them, or sometimes there were three – in a tired but jolly way she could imagine from the expression on his face. This imagining was no more noticed by Divya than the picture one gets, when reading a story, of a person or a place you think has been described, but may, in fact, not have been.

Jock smiled at Divya with the same smile the man who built the cupboard had given Daphne when she summoned him up in her fright. It was a gentle, sympathetic smile, which said he liked her and was sorry for everything that was not right. It struck Divya in the same place as it had struck Daphne long ago. It made her want to cry and be comforted in his arms. It made her feel she could be safe and warm if this man took care of her. She stared at him, surprised and confused.

'Hello, Divya,' Jock said in his familiar voice. 'I thought we'd go out for the day. For a treat. No school. We'll just go off and have some fun. Don't wake your mother. I've arranged for someone at the office to ring her later when she's up and let her know you're with me. Would you like that?'

Divya continued to stare at him for a moment, not completely sure she wasn't dreaming still. Then a warm excitement grew in her stomach and put a brake on her residual suspicion of the man who made her mother so angry. She nodded without smiling, still holding something in reserve in case anything went wrong or it turned out to be some kind of trick.

'Good.' Jock nodded back at her with an affirmative smile. 'Well, you go and get your clothes on very quietly, and I'll wait here for you.'

'Why are we going out?' Divya asked in the car, still not sure about an outing for the fun of it.

'Because you deserve a treat. Now, where do you want to go?'

Divya couldn't think. Sometimes at the home, they had had outings – to the Natural History Museum, on a canal boat, to Thorpe Park – but that was for everybody. This treat was just for her. She didn't know where she wanted to go.

'I don't know,' she said, frightened that not knowing might disqualify her. And then, faced with the possibility that there might not be a day out after all, she reined her anticipation in. 'I don't know,' she said again, but this time tight-lipped and sullen.

'What about the zoo?' Jock suggested.

'All right,' Divya said, secretly excited at the idea of going on her own with an adult to the zoo, where she had once watched small families walking around at leisure, while she had been just one of a larger group which moved from cage to cage at the speed dictated by the residential worker in charge.

'Can we go into the children's zoo and touch the goats?'

When she had been before they hadn't been allowed inside the goat enclosure because there were too many of them to keep an eye on. She had watched other children squealing as the goats tried to nibble their jackets and nuzzled inside pockets to find something – anything – to eat, and the adults coming to the rescue, but laughing all the same.

'Of course, we'll go wherever you want.'

Jock was very clear in his mind about the way the day was to go. He would be focused minute by minute on giving the child pleasure, on both of them enjoying this day. It was the most important day of each of their lives.

The goats were a huge success. It was early in the day, and there was only Divya and Jock inside the enclosure. Divya was immediately surrounded by three large nanny-goats who pushed at her with their noses, like muggers on a raid. Jock watched her first moments of alarm and then growing delight as one of them got hold of the bottom of her woolly and began to eat it. She pushed it off and moved away, but the nanny-goat, liking the taste of the sweater, began to follow her. Divya and the goat played catch-me, as she wove patterns around the enclosure getting away from, but not too far away from, the goat who was intent on unravelling the delicious wool. Finally, squealing like the other children she had seen, she dodged behind Jock's legs for protection while he gave the greedy goat a good-natured telling-off. When Divya looked behind her, she found a kid staring up at her, a sweet-faced, delicate creature with two tiny bumps where its horns would be. It allowed her to wrap her arms around it and feel the warm, goat-smelling, pulsing life of it. Jock watched the two small creatures enjoying each other, until the goat's mother came along and the kid was diverted by the smell of milk.

'Want to see the rabbits?' he suggested.

Divya stood stroking a fat black rabbit.

'You like it?' Jock smiled.

'Yes,' Divya said, her fingers and her stomach tingling with the softness of the rabbit fur. 'Someone brought a rabbit in to school once. It was their pet. But we weren't allowed to touch it because there were too many of us and it would have been frightened.'

'Well, you seem to be making the rabbit very happy. It hasn't moved a muscle while you've been stroking it.'

'I wish I could have one of my own.'

'I'll talk to your mum about getting one, when we get back.'

Divya looked amazed at even the remote possibility of owning a rabbit.

'She wouldn't let me,' she said, shaking her head.

'Well, if you promised to look after it, I bet I could talk her into it.'

Divya was speechless at the prospect. Today was filled with magic.

They had lunch in the cafeteria. Jock just had a coffee, but Divya had sausages and chips and ice-cream, with a milk shake. Then they roamed around gazing at lions and tigers, peering squint-eyed at deadly spiders, reaching out to the investigating trunk of an elephant and laughing at the sea lions leaping for the fish that an entertainment-minded keeper flung always just out of their reach.

Divya enjoyed the macaques most of all. They were like wicked children. The young ones reminded her of her Divya dreams. Great games were played, teasing the adults and then leaping from strut to strut too fast to be caught. They fought and flung themselves about, just seeming to have a good time, while the bigger adults sat heavily on the struts grooming and being groomed. Jock watched Divya laugh all her sullenness away in front of the frolicking simians.

At four o'clock they returned to the cafeteria and ate sticky buns and drank tea, but Divya grew quiet.

'What's up?'

She shrugged.

'Tired?'

'No.'

She was, but that wasn't it.

'Would you like to see a film?'

'Don't we have to go home?' Divya asked, surprised.

'No, not for ages. I told the girl in the office to say you wouldn't be back until quite late.'

So the day wasn't over.

'Do you think she'll let me have a rabbit?'

'I'm certain of it. I know, let's celebrate the coming of the rabbit and go and see *Who Framed Roger Rabbit?*'

'Can we? Really?'

The dull feeling had gone. There was more to come.

'Absolutely. Finished?'

Divya loved the film, and only at the very end realized that it was time to go home. Just when the sadness hit her, in the pit of her stomach and the corners of her mouth, as the music faded away, Jock said, 'Fancy a hamburger before I take you back?'

And more. It was still not quite time to go back to real life, there was more exciting *ordinary* to come. She nodded, completely exhausted, but thrilled that it wasn't over yet. She wanted more and more of this. She didn't want it ever to end. It was the best day of her life.

Throughout the day Jock had behaved like a replacement fairy godmother for Daphne. Godfather, Divya corrected herself, wanting things to be straight and proper. He had made the day shining for Divya, making her every tentative suggestion actually happen, and even picking up on her unspoken reluctance to go home and throwing it, like an unwanted ball, as far from her as possible. The day had extended itself endlessly. Now, sitting in McDonald's, she was too full and too tired to feel much anxiety about going back to her mother and the house. But, just in case, Jock said, as she sucked up the last noisy drop of her milk shake, 'We can do this again. Very soon. I've had a wonderful time.'

'Thank you,' Divya said, for the first time in her life without prompting. Jock valued it as much as he would the final full stop in a difficult but beautiful book. It had been the day he had imagined. Now, it was night.

Divya yawned, and suddenly a great wave of sleepiness washed through her. The idea of the sofa and her duvet and blanket became very attractive. Jock watched her carefully with a look of extreme tenderness on his face. He took her hand and led her out of the restaurant. Her feet dragged and she leaned heavily against Jock's side, so he picked her up in his arms and carried her back to the car. He put her on the back seat and wrapped a blanket that lay on the floor around her. Divya blinked her eyes hard, trying to keep awake for every moment more that was left of this best day of her life.

'Let yourself go to sleep, Divya. You lay there and relax, and I'll drive you home. Everything will be all right, now. I promise you.'

He knelt in the open back door and stroked Divya's over-excited, over-tired forehead. Then he bent lower and kissed her gently on the lips, like a parent saying goodnight. Sleep drenched but smiling, Divya murmured, 'Thank you' and her eyelids fluttered shut. Jock closed the door gently and got into the driver's seat. He sat for a moment, looking out at the dark night through the windscreen, and took half a dozen long, deep breaths. Then he started the car.

Jock drove aimlessly around the West End streets for two hours or more, waiting for the theatre crowds to disperse, and to make sure that the sleeping pills had taken their full effect. He had judged that the contents of four capsules would be enough to put Divya into a deep sleep, but not to be noticeable in the thick, sweet milk shake into which he had slipped them while bringing the tray of burgers and drinks back to Divya, who had waited for him at the table.

At a red light in Trafalgar Square he turned and touched Divya, shaking her, at first gently and then harder, on the shoulder, and calling her name.

'Divya? Divya?'

Divya didn't stir. She slept on, breathing regularly through her mouth, which hung slightly open. Her hand fell limply back across her body when Jock picked it up and let it drop. It was warm and soft. Jock faced forward again, put the car into gear and, when the lights turned green, headed towards his intended destination.

It was past midnight. Most people had gone home. Jock drove south along Waterloo Bridge and parked halfway across. He got out

223

and walked to the side. It was a chilly night, but very clear. He stood against the railing at the edge of the bridge and looked around. There was nobody about. Across the road and further along on the Waterloo side of the bridge the coloured light sculpture on the top of the Hayward Gallery flickered and danced in the wind that controlled its movements. On the other side, along from where Jock was standing, the National Theatre's neon notice-board flashed its events, making the dark river twinkle in reflection. The chunky, concrete shapes of the South Bank loomed ominously, but the lights on the bridge and river banks reflected and shimmered in the water, and, like the good fairy arriving after the bad fairy has cast her cruel spell, ameliorated the hard ugliness, creating a charm of prettiness that one hardly had the right to expect. The river was dark and bright at the same time, moving slowly, more like a viscous fluid than running water. It was a serious river, solemn and black with depth, but it allowed the lights to play over its surface.

Jock, who had been calm all day, an understanding having been reached and a decision made, felt almost heavy with contentment. A profound peace came over him, as if he were in a state of sanctity. He knew the rightness of what he had to do, and knew that the rightness belonged, not to him as an individual, but to a great necessity. He was at peace with himself at last, and with the river and the lights, and the clear star-speckled sky. All would be well.

He went back to the car and, with great care, took Divya, wrapped in the blanket and still fast asleep, into his arms. He carried her like a small baby to the side of the bridge where he had been standing. He examined her face. She seemed to sleep contentedly, as if from the exhaustion of a full and lovely day rather than from the drugs he had given her. Her hand was to her mouth, her fingers curled, her thumb extended towards her lips in readiness to be sucked. She was a pretty, sleeping child who had had a wonderful day and would never have another bad one.

Jock pressed his lips to her forehead and held her close to his chest, letting himself feel Divya's smaller, quicker heart beating against his. He clutched her against him, letting his own breathing rise and fall with hers. He stayed like this, holding Divya, for several minutes. Then, unhurriedly, he straightened his elbows, extending his arms beyond the railing, out over the side of the bridge into the thin, clear air, and gently released Divya from his grip. Jock kept his eyes on her as she fell, until the tiny bundle splashed into the dark water below him, and made the reflected lights on the surface dance in the turbulence. She sank very quickly, with the saturated weight of the blanket around her, and, in seconds, the surface of the river was smooth, inky black and solemn once more.

When everything was still again, Jock returned to the car and drove home. He had done the best he could for Divya, as much as he could do for the young life which was his responsibility. He had made it better. He had let her out of a world where things very rarely came right, and help was misguided, or too late, or too little. She was released from all the pain and sadness with which children were afflicted. No occasional nice day out could compensate for all the other days that would not be nice. Jock had done his best for Divya; done for her what he wished for all the others, those he knew about and those he didn't, whose unhappiness now, and in the future, he knew he could do nothing about.

He let himself into his house and went to bed. Neither his wife nor his children woke. Jock lay in bed, still at peace with himself and the world. He had found the only certain way to do what his vocation required of him: he had, at last, truly helped someone. On his desk at the office was a letter he had written early that morning, before he drove to Divya's house, explaining what he was about to do, and why. Now, there was nothing more to be done but rest. He lay in the dark breathing steadily, listening to the sound pattern it made with his wife's regular breaths. Something would happen in the morning, when the day had started, but that was not in his hands. It was no concern of his. He was not anxious about sleeping; he had, finally, done what was in everybody's best interests, and he knew that from now on he would sleep easily.

20

A Castle in Spain

Liam stood in his pyjama bottoms at the doorway of the motor home, only just awake. His bearded lower jaw hung loose.

'Daphne, what *are* you doing?'

It was early morning. It was hot. It was not England.

Daphne sat a couple of feet from the motor home, at a plastic picnic table, in front of the big black Underwood. She smiled under the shady brim of her velvet hat at the sound of Liam's voice behind her.

'Working, dearest. Novel writing.'

'Daphne, you've got no clothes on.'

This was not true. Daphne did have clothes on. She wore a pair of baggy, knee-length shorts and her old camel-coloured carpet slippers. On her head was her inseparable black velvet hat. But it was true that, from the waist up, she was naked. Her long, loose breasts swung slightly as she hit the space bar and turned around to look up at Liam with a squint-eyed smile.

'Yes, I have, dear. I'm wearing your shorts.'

She stuck one brown, wrinkled leg from under the table and waggled it at Liam.

'But you've got nothing on your top. What are you doing, woman?'

'I'm writing my book. I told you, dear. It's so hot, I thought I wouldn't bother with a shirt. I am a novelist, after all. That Ernest Hemingway was always having his photo taken sitting at the typewriter with his shirt off, wasn't he? So why shouldn't I take my shirt off, too? I'm a writer.'

'That Ernest Hemingway didn't have tits, Daphne.'

'Well, I wouldn't say that. I seem to remember that he was really quite busty towards the end. You haven't got anything on the top half of you, either, dear – and you're not exactly Arnold Schwatshisname, are you? Not that I'm complaining, dearest. I like your breasts.'

She took a drink from a mug at her side, which unlike Hemingway's, did not contain an early morning slug of bourbon but a nice, reviving cup of tea.

Liam shook his head. Sometimes, first thing in the morning, it took a few minutes to adjust to his current normality.

'And I love yours, my dear, but . . . what if someone saw you?'

Daphne looked around. There was no one about in the empty, rugged landscape, and the only sounds to be heard were their own voices and the distant clinking of goat bells.

'The goats saw me when they passed by about an hour ago. They didn't take much notice. And the nice old gentleman looking after them gave me a very pleasant smile and said, "Hola."'

'And what did you do?'

'I waved and said, "Buenos días" back to him. And then he said, "Inglés?" with a lovely big smile on his face, and I said, "Sí, señor." And that was that. He went on after his goats and I wrote another sentence of my book. It's coming on very nicely, dear. I do hope you like it. You can read it just as soon as I've finished the first part. I'd like to know what you think.'

What Liam thought was how fortunate, how blessed he was, six weeks after leaving London, to be on their mountain top with his wonderful Daphne, discussing the sartorial habits of novelists.

The motor home had been parked for three weeks by the ruined house on the dirt track. They were two thousand metres above sea level, with the blazing blue sky above them and not a care in the world. And Liam was building them a house to live happily ever after in.

For the past three weeks, he had been getting up early (although not as early as Daphne, who liked to be up and writing with the sun) and setting about the business of making the ruined house habitable. It had not been difficult to get Señor Moreno's permission to start work before the papers were signed and the money handed over. It was no skin off his nose if the hairy Englishman wanted to improve his property. If the deal fell through, then, he thought, with more than just his Moorish chromosomes at work, so be it. He would have his useless house partially rebuilt at no cost. It was agreed. Liam could start work while he arranged to sell his house in London, which would provide him with the money to live on, and cashed in an insurance policy which would cover Señor Moreno's asking price.

It was, of course, from Liam's point of view, a bargain. Señor Moreno had demanded only a few thousand pounds, a fraction of what Liam would realize from the London house alone, even if it sold for well under its value with Sylvie and Divya as sitting tenants. He was amused by the symmetry, remembering that he had bought it cheaply because Daphne, who was now the source of all his joy, had been a sitting tenant. He toyed with the notion that the new buyer might find his heart's delight with sniffling Sylvie, though he doubted it. But perhaps the house, far from being the dark burden he had once thought it, was, after all, a conduit of happiness which bestowed improbable contentment on those who passed through it. He was happy, Daphne was happy, he supposed that Grace was happy; so why not its other occupants?

He winced at himself. He had been, he recognized, in the most belligerently benevolent mood ever since he had begun the rebuilding work. He recollected something he had read about physical exercise increasing the production of endorphins in the brain; home-made morphine. Perhaps his well-being was all biochemical. At least some of it was, he knew, since, while giving Daphne her due, the fact was he was getting the first exercise he had had for years, if you didn't count the work he had done on his knees in front of Grace, and lifting his whisky glass. Just the shock of having sweat on his brow (not caused by sexual terror) was probably enough to send him into a chemical high.

Daphne was pleased, too, of course, about the project, although as they left the bar, whose owner was by then beaming happily at them, the deal having been shaken on, she had halted Liam's bounding step for a moment with a restraining touch on his elbow.

'But if we live in the house, dear, when it's done up, what about the mobile home?' she asked quietly.

'It's just what we need while we're getting the house ready,' Liam had told her. 'Plenty of room for materials, and somewhere to sleep. But soon we'll have a real home, Daphne, my dear, to be together in. A permanent structure.'

'Yes, I see that, dearest,' Daphne said, tucking a damp lock of hair into her hat and walking on with him. 'But what about the mobile home?'

'When the house is finished, we can sell it and buy a little car. Something more suitable for mountain roads, so we can go into the village when we want to.'

'Yes, that does sound sensible,' Daphne said.

Since then, a comfortable routine had evolved. Daphne wrote early, before Liam got up; they had breakfast together, and then Juan arrived from the village below. He had experience as a builder and had offered his services, at a very reasonable wage.

Between the three of them, they had made remarkable progress. Daphne cleared and prepared the ground between the house and the encircling tumbledown wall to make a garden with a central path running all the way round, while Liam and Juan humped stones and set them in place, building up the walls of the house in readiness for the roof that would finally be put on with the help of a couple of men from the village.

Daphne worked with a will. She continued to wear the velvet hat, in spite of the heat and everyone suggesting she trade it in for a straw one. But she did buy a pair of plastic flip-flop sandals at the market in the town in the valley below the village, and wore them with Liam's shorts which were baggy and cool, and left her lower legs, veiny but now brown and strong looking, free and comfortable. On her top, as a concession to Juan's presence and Liam's sensibilities, she had an old cotton shirt, also Liam's, tied at the waist. She set about clearing the land of scrub and forking in donkey dung where she planned for things to grow. Water was a problem, but it snowed in the winter and streams ran in the spring. She supposed water melons and tomatoes and other hot weather crops would grow if they were carefully tended. There were to be two beds, one following the perimeter of the wall, the other against the curves of the house, surrounding it. At each outside edge of the planned beds she planted broken rocks and stones that were too small to use for building, making the contours of a path between the two beds that encompassed the house.

Every now and then, Juan and Liam, who talked very little when they worked, caught each other's eye and smiled about Daphne and her gardening. There was no doubt that she was working as hard as they were, both men gave her her due, but it was not, their eyes told each other, *men's* work. If Liam felt slightly treacherous about his unspoken manly pact with Juan, he told himself that it was only superficial camaraderie – and a useful way of cementing his relationship with his differently acculturated co-worker. He had no doubt, fundamentally, that everything that was happening was happening because of Daphne's insight and determination. He knew exactly how much he owed her, and he intended to repay her in every way he could – with his love, with his care, with his support for her work, with a home for them to be happy in. In the meantime, he made sure she didn't overdo it, or work in the full heat of the sun, and in the evening he insisted on cooking their meal if they didn't eat down in the village. His years of tending to Grace had not been in vain.

They never talked about London; about what they had left behind. For Liam, the great joy of their adventure was the casting off of *then*; the brand newness of his life. But Daphne often thought about Divya. When she was working, it would cross her mind that Divya would have enjoyed making a garden with her, and at dusk, when she sat with a glass of Rioja and watched the sun go down quietly while Liam read a book, she would remember the child and wonder how she was. Without saying anything to Liam, she had sent two postcards to her with pictures of their mountain and the simple message *Love from Daphne* on the other side. She wondered if, in a few years from now, when Divya was a young woman, she might visit them. She said nothing of this to Liam, but she thought that then it might be all right, not interfering, not damaging or anything. Just a holiday.

But there was something improbable to Daphne in this dream of hers. It was not the notion that Divya would want to come and visit a boring old couple in the middle of nowhere that caused her uneasiness, but something else that she couldn't quite work out. The fantasy was simply *improbable*, like a promise made by a grown-up that the child listening *knew* somehow or other wouldn't come about.

When she worked on the garden, she tried to imagine herself tending the growing plants, and then walking into the house and chatting to Liam about their progress. There was nothing actually fantastical about this picture; they were making everything ready for just such a life together. It was not a misty castle in Spain she was trying to imagine, but a real solid stone house, with real smelly donkey dung being forked into the ground at the very moment of her fantasy. So why did it, too, have such an unlikely quality about it? Daphne's mind itched uncomfortably, on the verge of knowing why, but never quite crossing the boundary into full awareness of the answer. The result was an ever-present anxiety; nothing unbearable, just a lurking discomfort which would not go away even when she was happily engaged in something else. She would catch herself being worried, and then not have the faintest idea why. As she tried to remember what it was that she was supposed to be worrying about, the reason, still across the borderline of her mind, would retreat backwards to somewhere irretrievable, and she would be left with nothing but the scratchy anxiety, like a washing line with nothing hanging on it.

Daphne was perplexed by this, because, after all, wasn't she living the outcome of her decision to be happy? Her dream had come true, and everything was exactly as she had wished it. She had done with her misery, and the subsequent years of terrible numbness. She had made things right. It was as if the cupboard under the stairs had travelled with her, and ignore it as she might, as she had tried to do when living in the house, it was always there, always a presence that didn't need her acknowledgement in order to radiate its influence. She wished away the weight, the disturbance, inside her with all her might. There had been a time, she knew, when she fed on her old unhappiness, like a bacterium that owed its existence to the agar on which it thrived. But it wasn't true any more, she was sure. She was not in love with unhappiness. She didn't want it; she *truly* didn't want it.

She was astonished to find herself thinking that she might be *unhappy*, because she wasn't. It was extraordinary that the word had even crossed her mind when it was in no way a description of her current mood. Oh, dear, she thought, oh, dear, and wondered if it wouldn't be better not to think about herself, her inner condition, at all. All the worrying about how she was feeling might be the very worry causing the anxiety. Snakes eating their tails; eggs giving birth to chickens; selfish genes demanding their current carriers do their will, and all that sort of thing. Best not to think, she thought. But she knew it was neither possible, nor true.

'Daphne, are you feeling all right?'

Liam had been watching Daphne for several minutes. She had been standing quite still, half bent over holding a shovelful of donkey manure she had been about to shake on to the ground. Daphne came to and let the manure fall.

'Oh, dear, I'm sorry, Liam. I was in a dream.'

'Not one about me, I hope,' he said, walking over to her and taking the shovel from her hand. 'You looked quite stricken.'

'No, dear, just a bit tired, I suppose.'

'You mustn't overdo it. I don't want you collapsing from heatstroke, my love. I think we deserve a couple of icy glasses of *cerveza* and a nice plate of garlic flavoured with calamares. At the very least. Let's call it a day and go down to the village.'

Things had improved, over the weeks, in the bar. Not that it had become a place of gaiety exactly; the three men on the stools, or their counterparts, still sat glowering at themselves in the mirror, and Señor and Señora Moreno continued their dissonant duet of mutual complaint. But Liam and Daphne had become accepted as an economic, if not social, part of the village. Their money was welcome, and they caused some gloomy entertainment as peculiar foreigners who planned to work unworkable land, and live in an unliveable house. There was also, of course, no end of discussion about their relationship; the *mother and son lovers* they were known as – behind their backs, of course. There was a curious mixture of hilarity and distaste in the tone in which they said it; if it stirred mysterious, long lost feelings in these taciturn, practical people, it showed only in that tone.

Maria was more aware of her own curiosity about the unlikely pair. She might have dismissed them as typically foreign, and therefore typically peculiar, and left it at that, but she couldn't help wondering about the two of them having sex together. She was no more able to understand it than Grace had been, and she found herself staring at Daphne trying to imagine her naked body – her breasts, her thighs, her bum. She filled with disgust at the vision, especially when she added Liam to the picture.

If Liam was not exactly her ideal man, he was different, a stranger in her world of familiar villagers. She was technically a virgin, though various experiments with her brother, who had now gone to work in Granada, and one of the boys at school made it a marginal virginity. She knew how much her taut flesh was appreciated; how attractive her rounded hips and thighs, and plump breasts, were to the eyes, hands and mouths of men. She knew it from her brother and her school friend, and from the furtive looks that the men in the bar gave her when her father was looking the other way. She knew it also from looking at herself naked in the mirror; she could quite understand that her body was desirable. She was unable, therefore, to imagine how anyone could feel desire for the used-up body of a scraggy woman in a peculiar hat, who was older even than her own mother. Did it mean that Liam could find nothing better, she wondered. Or was she very rich, in spite of her pitiful appearance? Liam was softer looking than the men Maria knew, rounder, older, but his disarrayed gingery hair and beard were rather endearing, and he had something in his eyes that looked interesting, though she couldn't say what it was.

There was no one, of course, that Maria could talk about her thoughts to. Most people of her age had left, and when they came back, they had very little concern about what went on in the village. They came back out of duty, and spent their time itching to get back to the city and its excitements. Maria knew their desperation. She had hoped to go away, too, but her parents would not consider it. They wanted her help in the bar. When she was married, they said, she could go with her husband to the city, which is where most of the men eventually went. But who was she going to marry, if she stayed here? She was an intelligent girl, clever, her teacher had said. She didn't want a man who was too stupid not to have found somewhere better to live than a dying village up a mountain.

But neither did she want a man who, like her brother, had gone to Granada in search of his fortune. She couldn't see what was so glamorous about going into the nearest big city to become a workman. It was no different really from staying where they were and being workmen. She despised the ones who returned, with their flashy cheap clothes and their kids on their hips. How much better off were they?

Maria wanted to be somewhere else and to be someone else, not to be the same thing but down the mountain. She had only a hazy idea of what she wanted, but it had to do with style. It was about women she read of in magazines, about places where they didn't even speak Spanish, about real restaurants with delicious, delicate food, about knowing things that she couldn't imagine, but *knew* existed. It was about finding a completely different destiny from the one everyone envisaged for her. Everyone except that one teacher who had seen and encouraged Maria's genuine curiosity. But, eventually, the teacher herself fell foul of Maria's critical eye. What was she doing teaching in a hole like this, if she had any real quality about her? Maria withdrew from their friendship. She wanted someone else. Someone who really knew, and who belonged out there in the big world.

Daphne saw Maria's hunger clearly. She saw it in her eyes, and in the way she moved, as if she was practising for something better. Daphne knew well enough about Maria's hunger. She remembered it. She watched the girl behind the bar with a sad but admiring smile.

'Feeling better?' Liam asked after their first long sip of cold beer.

'Yes, I feel splendid, dear. It was the heat, I expect. I had such an odd dream last night.'

'Not another chat with the Almighty?' Liam smiled.

'No, my chats with God aren't dreams. This was a proper dream, when I was asleep. I was ... well, it wasn't exactly me, I was watching ... but there was this old woman. It was by the seaside, and she was standing on the esplanade facing the sea, and she was wearing a white lace wedding dress – an old one, because it was rather Edwardian, with a long narrow skirt, and old, as well, because it was a bit grubby, as if she'd been wearing it for a very long time. She had my hat on her head, and her grey hair was sticking out underneath. So I suppose it had to be me, dear, didn't it? Anyway, she was trying to kill herself, although she didn't seem in the least upset; she was very calm. She kept climbing on to the railings and then jumping off into the sea – except that it was more like she was flying towards it. But every time she got near the water, a great swirling wind picked her up and threw her back on to the esplanade. And that's all there was, just her in her wedding dress jumping with great determination and being flung back again. But she always landed on her feet. So I suppose that was something.'

'Landing on your feet is always something, my dear. No easy trick. It's a very elegant dream, and there's nothing I admire more than a psyche with good taste. Perhaps you should put it in your book.'

'But someone might think it meant something.'

'That's true, they might.'

'Well, I don't want that. I don't want people reading meanings into my book, it's supposed to tell the truth.'

'I thought it was going to be a novel.'

'Exactly.'

'You're right, my dear, as usual. Better leave it out. You don't want to give people any extra opportunities for thinking. It does no one any good.'

The house was very nearly finished. After three months the walls were rebuilt, the roof was on and the ground ready. There remained only the carpentry, which both Liam and Juan were handy at, and buying furniture, which could be got, cheap and simple, in Granada; and the house would be habitable.

While Daphne planted some herbs, she watched Liam sawing a piece of wood that was to become the door lintel. She liked the way his body went with the movement of the saw, as if the rhythm of the task came from inside him. He had clearly done a lot of woodworking in his time, before Daphne knew him, before he had slumped into the armchair in his study to die of Grace. It pleased her to see his new energy. It seemed to make the air around him shimmer. If that was the outcome of her passion for him, then it was everything, and more, than she could possibly have hoped for. She had considered her own happiness when she set her cap at Liam, and she supposed that he, too, would find contentment, but she had never imagined the physical manifestation of it. A Liam up and moving about with purpose, who smiled quietly to himself, who could make the air zing. She was pleased and proud that she had taken him to this point.

And she, too, of course, had found energy enough to make her plans real; to get the advance, to buy the motor home, to begin her baglady existence. Well, she thought, as Liam measured up the next piece of timber, it was time to get going on that last bit of her plan.

She blinked, and brought the thought back into the centre of her head where she could have a jolly good look at it. It had just floated into her mind and taken off again, as passing thoughts will. But this was a thought that took her by surprise. She wanted to hold it steady for long enough to see what it was.

It was, of course, the hazy uneasiness that retreated from her awareness whenever she had tried to look at it, so she was never able to attach any explanation to it. But it was clear enough now. And as she held the thought still — *it was time to begin her baglady existence* — all the other thoughts that made up its context shuffled in from the back of her mind and gathered around, like a platoon of soldiers getting into formation.

She could not live in this house. It was Liam's house, built for his needs, to be his home. Daphne's home was the mobile home. It was not merely the vehicle that Liam supposed it to be, a conveyer that had got them to where he wanted to go. Certainly, that's what it was for him. And it was good Daphne had been able to get him here, to play out his monkish fantasies for as long as he needed to. But it was Daphne's *home*, her first home really, and the exact kind of home she wanted, one that moved with her, not one that stood still.

That was what had been the trouble; the discomfort she hadn't been able to find a reason for. Naturally, because leaving Liam would be a wrench. She hadn't wanted to see, because she loved Liam and she loved their passion. But Liam's happily ever after was not hers. She and Liam had had a wonderful love affair. She had enjoyed it enormously. What luck, at nearly seventy, to have found love, and refound sex. If it never happened again, she wouldn't mind. This had been perfect. But Liam needed to stay still, and she needed to move. Specifically, she need to move south, down and further down. And more specifically, she needed to cross the edge of the continent, just a few miles south of where they were, into another place. She wanted to leave Europe. She wanted to go to Africa; go through Africa. She had to go on and travel through the world, taking her home with her. She would be a transcontinental baglady that made the whole world her territory, and the mobile home her home.

Daphne took off her hat and examined it. It was wonderfully weathered. A filthy, astonishing object. After the domestic grease and damp she had applied to it in London, the building work and the dust of Spain had made it one of the finest examples of a baglady's hat she had ever seen.

Liam looked up and saw her grinning happily at her hat.

'It's coming on nicely, my love,' he called, approvingly.

'Yes, dear, it is, isn't it? I think it's as ready as it'll ever be.'

21

Aftermaths

Liam was not going to have to lose money on the sale of the house. It would go on the market with vacant possession. Sylvie did not need permanent accommodation any more. Circumstances had changed.

It may often be the case that once nameless dread has been transformed into actual disaster, the worst is over. Life had proved Sylvie right, and there was some satisfaction to be had in that.

Sudden death is always a terrible shock. People live in a world of maybes and mights for most of the time. When something real happens it feels, strangely, unreal; people feel incredulous, as if they never actually believed their terrors, but only titillated themselves with them, like interior versions of horror movies that make them shiver in the certain knowledge that they are safe and warm and cannot really be touched by the phantoms of the screen.

For a while Sylvie was stunned by Divya's death. She genuinely mourned the little girl, and felt from the child's powerful absence that she was missing Divya. But as friends, doctors and social workers rallied round, she began gradually to feel that the tragedy was *her* tragedy, and that she had been vindicated by events. Would any of this have happened if it hadn't been for *them*? For Sophie making her take the flat, for the shrinks and social workers not listening to her, to her needs, not actually helping her at all?

Everyone had said everything would be all right if she sorted herself out and settled down, and, as she had told them and told them, it wasn't all right at all.

They, of course, felt something of this; a degree of guilt, a remissness in their desire to get Sylvie off their hands. Even those who, quite rightly, rationalized that what happened was terrible but utterly unforeseeable were still subject to an underground guilt, feeling, obscurely, that, even so, if they had not pushed Sylvie, it *would not have happened.*

They could not, at any rate, say no when Sylvie turned up at their door. No, of course Sylvie couldn't stay in the flat. Yes, of course she needed time and support to recover and sort herself out.

Sylvie now had a genuine tragedy that no one could deny. It had happened to her. She had a peculiar feeling of triumph as she stood, bleak and alone, in the old doorways she used to stand in, bereft and bereaved, and a genuine victim. Let them, with their comfortable houses, their living children and their good fortune, turn her away now. And, of course, nobody did.

Sylvie returned to her old life, relieved of her unmanageable burden, left only with the burden of daily existence and the need to notice when it was time for her to move on; the burden she could just about manage. The tragedy of a lost child clung to her and gave her disorderly life a weight, an heroic quality, that previously had been missing. Her state of perpetual homelessness having been legitimized, Sylvie at last had the security she needed to get through the rest of her life.

Liam had acquired a hat. It was a straw hat he found in the market, with a round crown and flat wide brim, to keep the sun off the top of his head when he walked around the path that circled his house. He spent a good deal of his time treading the dusty path, slowly, listening to the natural sounds amid the silence of his isolated portion of the mountain.

The house was finished, but part of his day was spent weatherproofing it against the winter which would soon arrive. The rest of the time he walked, sometimes exploring the landscape surrounding him, but most often slap, slap, slapping around his path in his open leather sandals.

He was content. He had been astonished when Daphne announced one morning, apparently out of the blue, that she was moving on. He wept, begging her to explain what the matter was, telling her he would do anything, *anything*, to make things right so she would stay with him. But, holding him in her arms, and brushing his cheek with the brim of her hat, she had insisted nothing was the matter, except that she wanted to go on to Africa, to keep going.

'All right,' he had said. 'I'll come with you. We'll let the house, and carry on travelling together, if that's what you want.'

'No, dear,' she told him gently. 'That wouldn't be a good idea. You must live in this house. You made it. You've even got a sort of cloister to walk in when you meditate. You must stay and I must go. But we've had a wonderful time, haven't we?'

'I don't want to live the rest of my life without you,' he moaned. 'I don't want to live alone. I want you.'

'I know, dearest. Only, I've got to get on. And I'm sure you won't spend the rest of your life alone. You'll enjoy it for a while, and then, perhaps, something else will happen. That's life, my darling, that's what happens.'

'But I've found *you*, you're what happened,' Liam said, outraged. 'I don't want anything else.'

Even as he spoke, though, he found himself adjusting to the idea. He would never love anyone but Daphne, yet the house was so close to his dreams – if not a monastery, at least a place where peace of mind might be quietly sought – that the idea of leaving it was out of the question. He went on urging Daphne to stay, but it was clear that she had made up her mind.

They made love all that night in an epiphany of passion and friendship. Then, eventually, Liam and Daphne fell asleep in each other's arms and snored together gently until the sun rose.

When Liam woke, Daphne and the motor home had gone. Liam found a note on the table, that read: *I've left, dearest. I'm off on my way south. I'm so excited that my toes itch (unless it's athlete's foot, in which case I hope they've got something for it in Africa). Isn't it wonderful that the world is round? If I keep going, I'll be passing your way on my second go. So, perhaps I'll see you then. If not, I love you madly, my darling, and I'm taking all our memories, and all your fingerprints from last night with me. I think I may give up washing. Have a lovely life. Yours ever, your darling Daphne.*

He had found the peace he wanted – the silence of asking unanswerable questions – in the house he built on his bit of mountain. His mind became curiously quiet, and the dismal strivings of his past seemed to fall away. He didn't know any more about God or purpose than when he had started out on his journey with Daphne, but he had learned to create a silence, and a great peace had come with it.

He didn't spend his time entirely on his own. Two or three times a week he walked the mile and a half down the mountain, into the village. He would stock up on supplies and spend the evening sitting at the bar, enjoying a few glasses of beer and passing the time of day with whoever happened to be there. Maria was always there, of course, and she enjoyed practising her English on Liam. She came out of the kitchen, wiping her hands on her apron, and chatted with him. She was eager to know about England, and asked Liam about this or that famous place she had heard of, and if the Princess of Wales was as beautiful as she looked in the pictures. Liam often did not know the answers; he had not been to most of the places that Maria mentioned, and hadn't come across the Princess of Wales in the flesh. But he told her what he did know, describing the streets, and the markets, and theatres and art galleries. He told her about the long, grey winters, and the lovely slow autumns. She laughed when he said it was really a rather dull place, assuming that he was teasing her.

Liam enjoyed his conversations with Maria. He liked her curiosity and the way she listened to him. He noted, too, that in a special way, she was beautiful. Obviously her body was young and full and lovely, yet, for Liam, her beauty resided most in the way her eyes paid attention, and drank in what he had to tell her. Sometimes, he found himself irritated when he caught other men at the bar staring at her with frankly lustful eyes. It was true that occasionally, as he walked back up the mountain swinging his torch, he would have a momentary spasm of desire as the image of her body came to him suddenly out of the darkness. But Liam was not to be distracted from his monkish existence. He put the fantasies away, telling himself that it took time to learn to live a fully contemplative life. Look at Saint Augustine. Still, he was warmed by the thought that she would be waiting behind the bar next time he went into the village.

Señor and Señora Moreno were delighted with the money they received for the ruined house. They came to a temporary truce in the face of such good fortune and even planned a holiday together in Granada, visiting their son and his family, to celebrate. Maria would take care of the bar while they were away, and Señor Moreno's brother, who lived in the village, would keep an eye on her.

241

They understood Liam to be one of the eccentric Englishmen they had heard tell of, and supposed him to be rich, if not actually a nobleman. He was pleasant enough, and he and Maria seemed to get along well. It was good that she was learning some English from him. As to the future, they shrugged silently at each other. Who knew about the future, they would say, with the hint of a smile. Liam would not be staying for ever, and when he decided to go ... well, who knew?

The Morenos were certain that Liam wouldn't stay for very long because they doubted that he would want to rebuild the house a second time. It had tumbled down so long ago, that house on the tiny piece of land owned by Señor Moreno's grandfather, and no one had bothered to do anything about it. What was the point? The underground spring that ran below it was too near the surface. Nothing would stay standing for very long. Or so it was said. Nothing in this life was certain, that was for sure, Señor Moreno had told himself, and what would have been the point of mentioning such a disheartening rumour to the Englishman when he had been so set on building the old ruin up?

Daphne beamed through the exhaust fumes and other less analysable smells as she sat in the throbbing motor home, waiting for her turn to board the ferry that would take her from Algeciras in the southernmost tip of Europe, to Ceuta, and her first footstep on another continent. She didn't mind the wait. She was at the end of Europe, and at the age of sixty-nine, later this evening, she would drive her home off the boat and on to the dry, hot land of Africa; a new continent after all her years on that small island at the edge of Europe.

While she waited, she passed the time chatting with the Lord, who, it so happened, was ready for a break from brooding.

'An adventure, eh?' He said.

'Another adventure, Dear. They're coming thick and fast these days. But I do hope Liam will be all right.'

'Oh, I wouldn't worry about him,' God said, and then, in case He should be misunderstood, added, hurriedly, 'Not that I'm prophesying or anything, you understand.'

'Oh, no, Dear, this is just a little chat.'

'Well, I wouldn't be too anxious. I should think Liam will go on being Liam. A bit of meditation, a bit of excitement. After all, that's the point of life, isn't it? Although, I'll say this for him, he doesn't make a terrible noise about praying, like some people I could mention. I wouldn't know he was there, if you hadn't kept Me informed.'

'Is that the point of life?' Daphne asked.

'You're trying to catch Me out, aren't you? I've a good mind to turn My face from you. Don't you dare quote Me, Daphne Drummond. I'll deny everything. I said, that's the point, *isn't it?* See? A question. But if you ask Me — off the record, of course — it's as good a point as any, considering there isn't any point so far as I can see.'

Daphne thought that sometimes God was too legalistic to be a good conversationalist. And a bit childish, too. It's what comes of spending too much time on Your own, she decided. But probably He was right about Liam, and she was pleased.

'What about that book you're writing?' God asked, changing the subject.

'It's coming on, Dear, thank You. It doesn't seem terribly important now, but I enjoy doing my fifty words a day. I'm going to have my two lovers leaving the house and going off on their travels, and I think I'll just leave it there.'

'But what about telling the truth? What about the aftermath?'

'It's a novel, Dear,' Daphne explained. 'That will be enough truth, I think. Everyone is going to live happily ever after. I don't have to say what all the happily ever afters will be, do I? Readers have to do something for themselves, don't they?'

'So does everyone live happily ever after? What about the woman and child they leave in the house?'

'Yes, them too. I'll leave a hint that things will take a turn for the better for them. Why not? Those things happen sometimes, don't they.'

'Yes, sometimes, I suppose they do. So you're off to Africa?' God said, changing the subject.

'I'm off to everywhere, Dear. But Africa's a jolly good start. I must say, You did a wonderful job. There are so many places and so many things to see. You're really very good at making worlds.'

'Thank you,' God said, pleased by the compliment. 'Though in all fairness, I had a bit of help from physics.'

'Oh, did You study physics? I suppose You must have done biology, too.'

'Questions, questions. That's all I ever hear. Look, it's your turn to get on the ferry. I'll leave you to it. Have a lovely time. Daphne. Stay in touch.'

'Right-oh, here I go,' Daphne said, lurching up the ramp in second gear.

'Oh, and by the way,' God added, as Daphne gave a wave to her invisible Friend, 'make sure you don't lose your hat – it's a very nice hat, indeed!'

The house in the Edwardian terrace was empty. The estate agents would soon receive the keys and the instruction to sell from the vendor's solicitor. The purchaser was likely to be a developer; it was reasonably priced, and an attractive proposition for someone planning to convert it into three flats. There was a decent profit to be made out of it.

The house was empty. For the first time since it was built, no one lived in it. It took very few weeks for the smell and feel of disuse to develop. In a year or two, the walls would be bright white, partitions would segregate each floor into separate, self-contained accommodation, there would be modern kitchens and bathrooms with gleaming fittings, and an entryphone on the black front door with three name-plates. Three new homes would soon be available.

In the meantime, the house remained in its newly uninhabited state without feeling anything about its condition, or its emptiness, as any sensible, experimenting angel would tell you. The condition of the house was of no significance except to prospective buyers, nor did it matter to any being, human or angelic, who, if anyone, lived in it and called it home. Obviously.

Sometimes the floorboards creaked, as they expanded or shrank very slightly with the changing weather; twice a day the central heating, which had been left on to prevent damp, came to life, and the boiler hissed into action. Once or twice, in heavy rain, water came in through a tile on the roof that had become dislodged, and a pat, pat, pat of raindrops dripped on to the attic floor. But there was no one to hear the noises made by the deserted house and it might be said by some – experimenting angels, for example – that, not being heard, the sounds did not, in fact, exist.

And no one heard the other sound that echoed sometimes through the empty entrance hall and floated up the staircase. It was a sound like crying; a low tuneless sobbing in a single, unchanging note which went on and on in the darkness. It was hardly more than a gentle murmur. Anyone hearing it might mistake it for the wind whistling through a forgotten crack. But the house was empty. There was no one to listen, and so, no one heard anything at all.